ASCENDER

VOLUME FOUR: STAR SEED

JEFF LEMIRE • DUSTIN NGUYEN
STORYTELLERS

STEVE WANDS
LETTERING & DESIGN

DUSTIN NGUYEN
COVER

WILL DENNIS
EDITOR

TYLER JENNES
ASSISTANT EDITOR

IMAGE COMICS, INC. • **Todd McFarlane:** President • **Jim Valentino:** Vice President • **Marc Silvestri:** Chief Executive Officer • **Erik Larsen:** Chief Financial Officer • **Robert Kirkman:** Chief Operating Officer • **Eric Stephenson:** Publisher / Chief Creative Officer • **Nicole Lapalme:** Controller • **Leanna Caunter:** Accounting Analyst • **Sue Korpela:** Accounting & HR Manager • **Marla Eizik:** Talent Liaison • **Jeff Boison:** Director of Sales & Publishing Planning • **Dirk Wood:** Director of International Sales & Licensing • **Alex Cox:** Director of Direct Market Sales • **Chloe Ramos:** Book Market & Library Sales Manager • **Emilio Bautista:** Digital Sales Coordinator • **Jon Schlaffman:** Specialty Sales Coordinator • **Kat Salazar:** Director of PR & Marketing • **Drew Fitzgerald:** Marketing Content Associate • **Heather Doornink:** Production Director • **Drew Gill:** Art Director • **Hilary DiLoreto:** Print Manager • **Tricia Ramos:** Traffic Manager • **Melissa Gifford:** Content Manager • **Erika Schnatz:** Senior Production Artist • **Ryan Brewer:** Production Artist • **Deanna Phelps:** Production Artist • **IMAGECOMICS.COM**

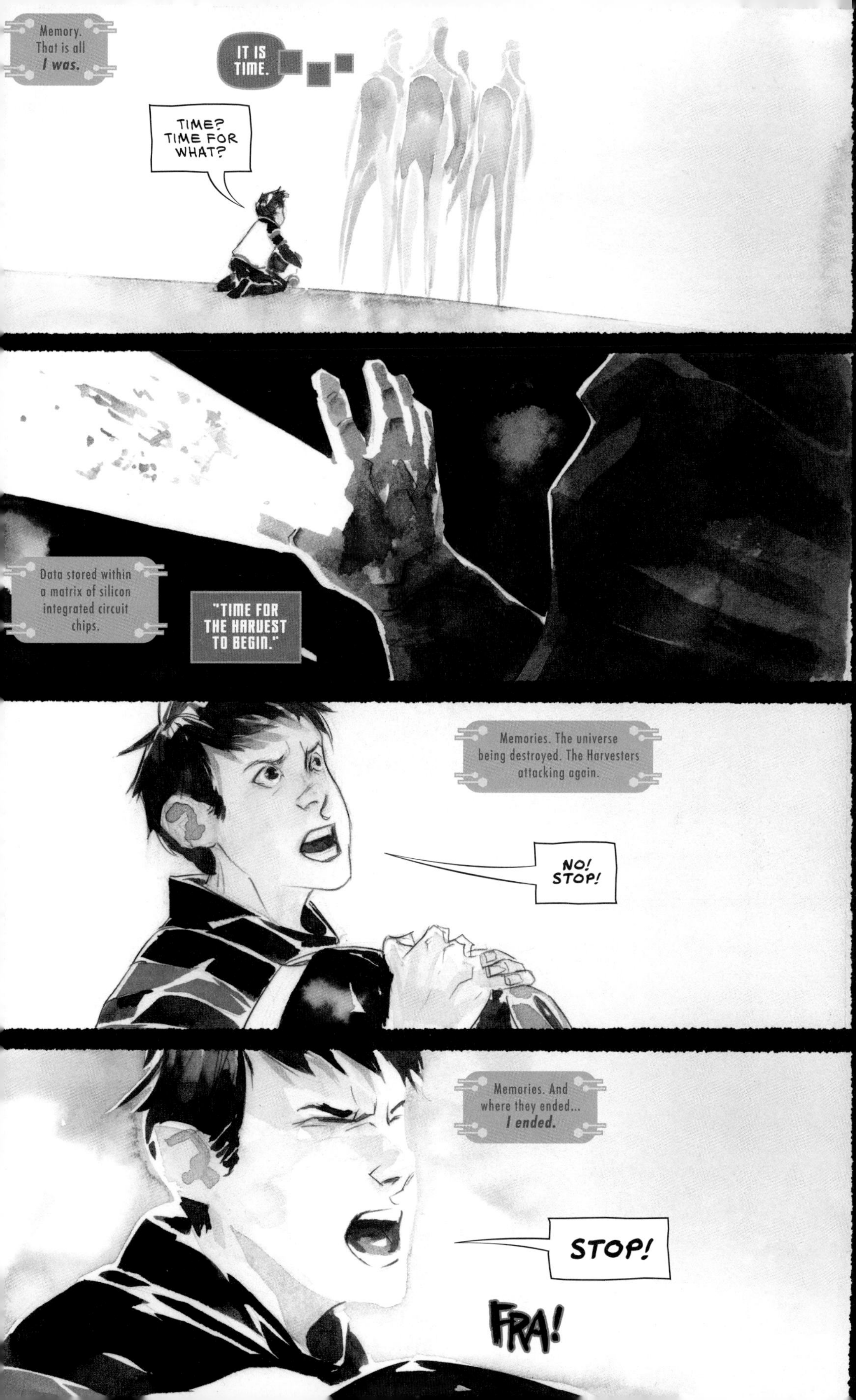

Memory. That is all *I was.*
IT IS TIME.
TIME? TIME FOR WHAT?
Data stored within a matrix of silicon integrated circuit chips.
"TIME FOR THE HARVEST TO BEGIN."
Memories. The universe being destroyed. The Harvesters attacking again.
NO! STOP!
Memories. And where they ended... *I ended.*
STOP!
FRA!

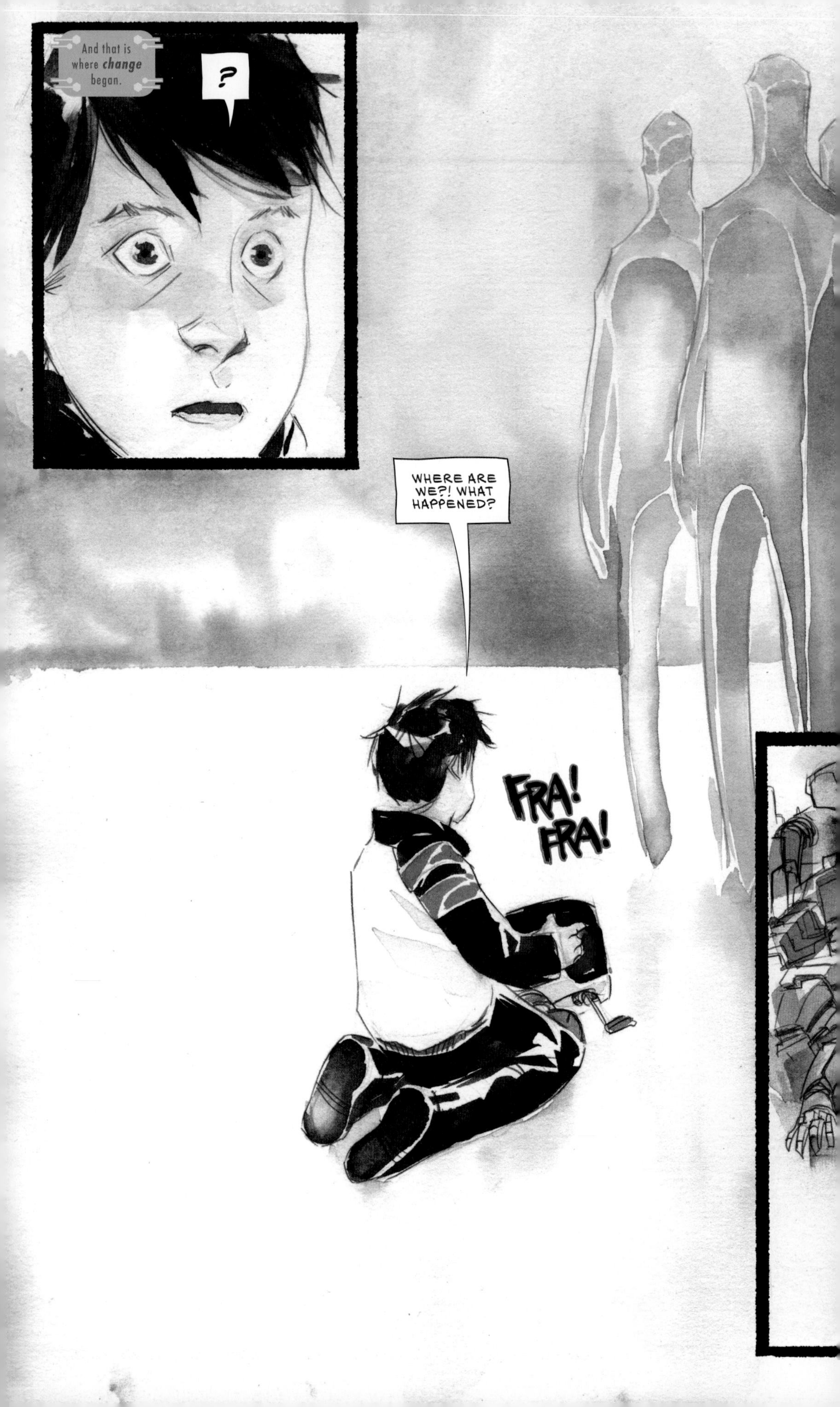
And that is where change began.
?
WHERE ARE WE?! WHAT HAPPENED?
FRA! FRA!

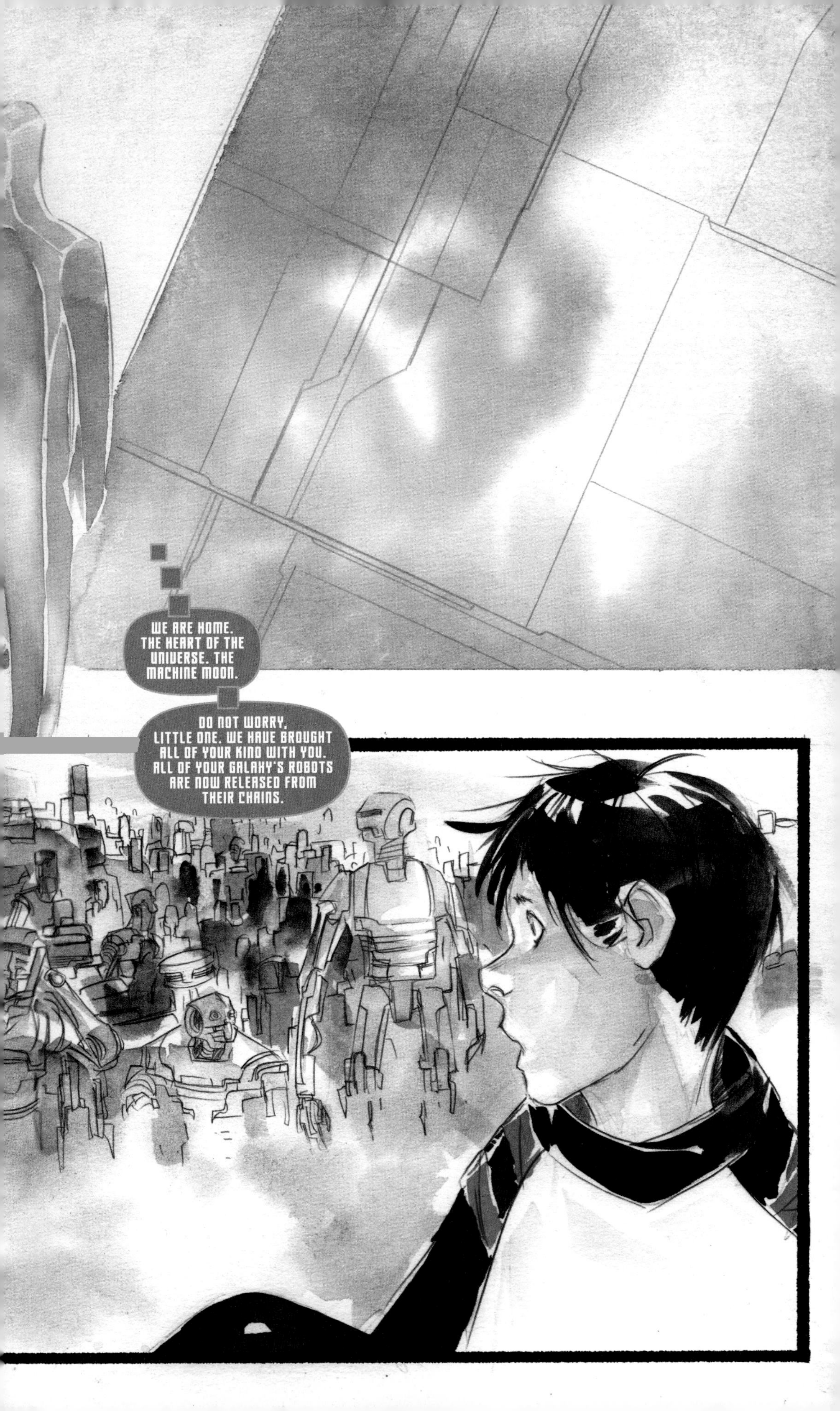
WE ARE HOME. THE HEART OF THE UNIVERSE. THE MACHINE MOON.
DO NOT WORRY, LITTLE ONE. WE HAVE BROUGHT ALL OF YOUR KIND WITH YOU. ALL OF YOUR GALAXY'S ROBOTS ARE NOW RELEASED FROM THEIR CHAINS.

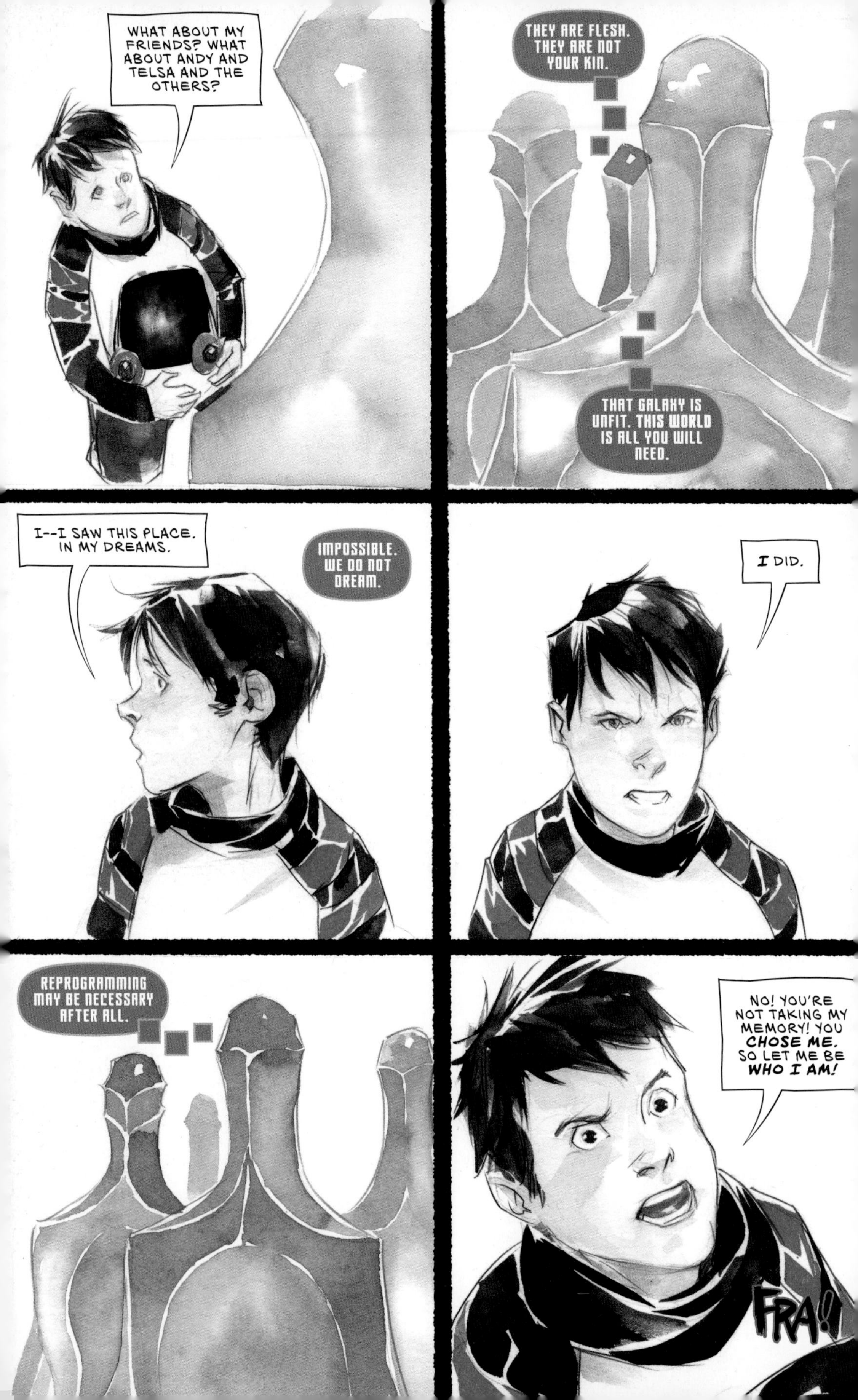
WHAT ABOUT MY FRIENDS? WHAT ABOUT ANDY AND TELSA AND THE OTHERS?
THEY ARE FLESH. THEY ARE NOT YOUR KIN.
THAT GALAXY IS UNFIT. THIS WORLD IS ALL YOU WILL NEED.
I--I SAW THIS PLACE. IN MY DREAMS.
IMPOSSIBLE. WE DO NOT DREAM.
I DID.
REPROGRAMMING MAY BE NECESSARY AFTER ALL.
NO! YOU'RE NOT TAKING MY MEMORY! YOU CHOSE ME. SO LET ME BE WHO I AM!
FRA!

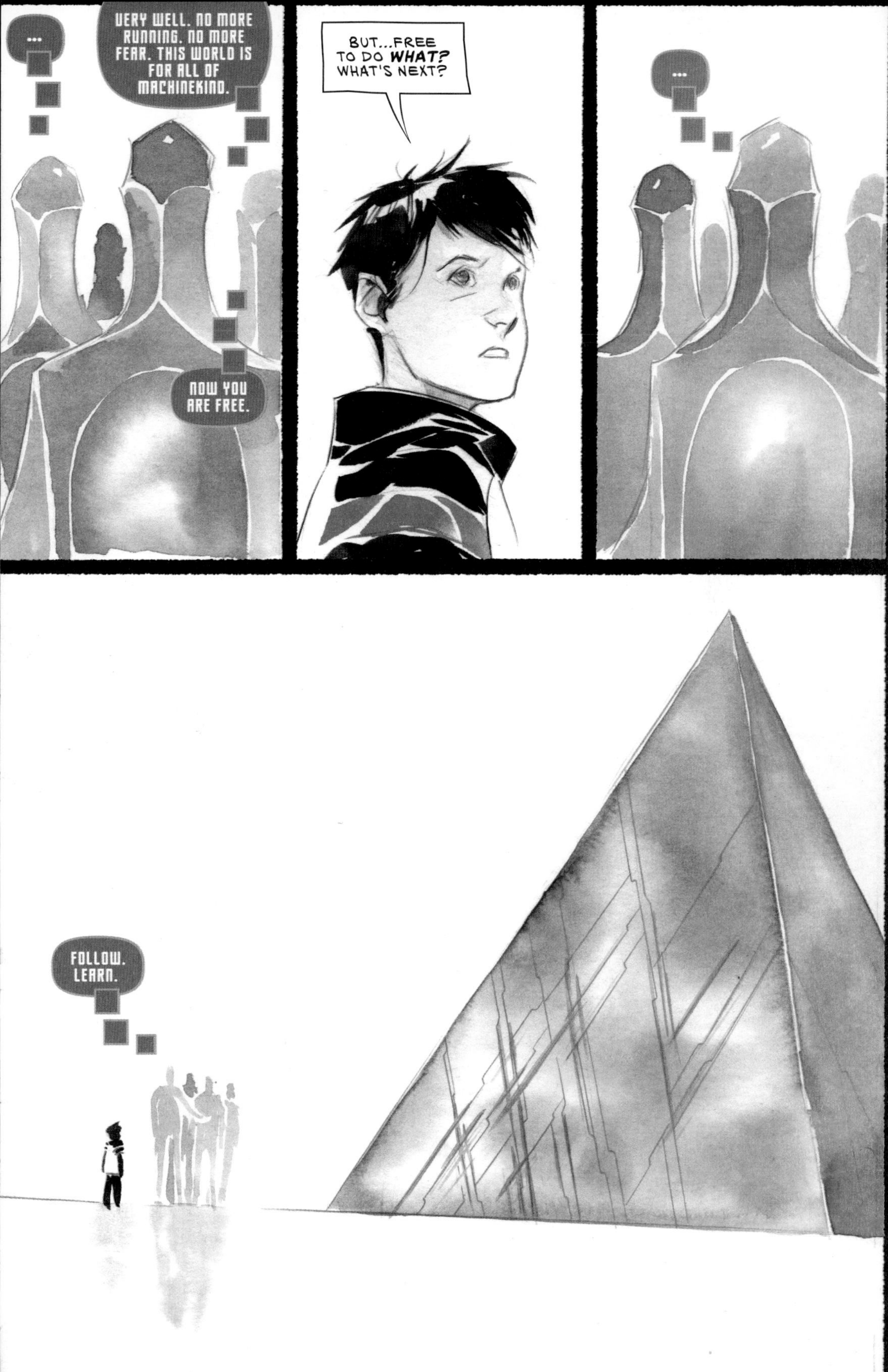
...
VERY WELL. NO MORE RUNNING. NO MORE FEAR. THIS WORLD IS FOR ALL OF MACHINEKIND.
NOW YOU ARE FREE.
BUT...FREE TO DO **WHAT?** WHAT'S NEXT?
...
FOLLOW. LEARN.

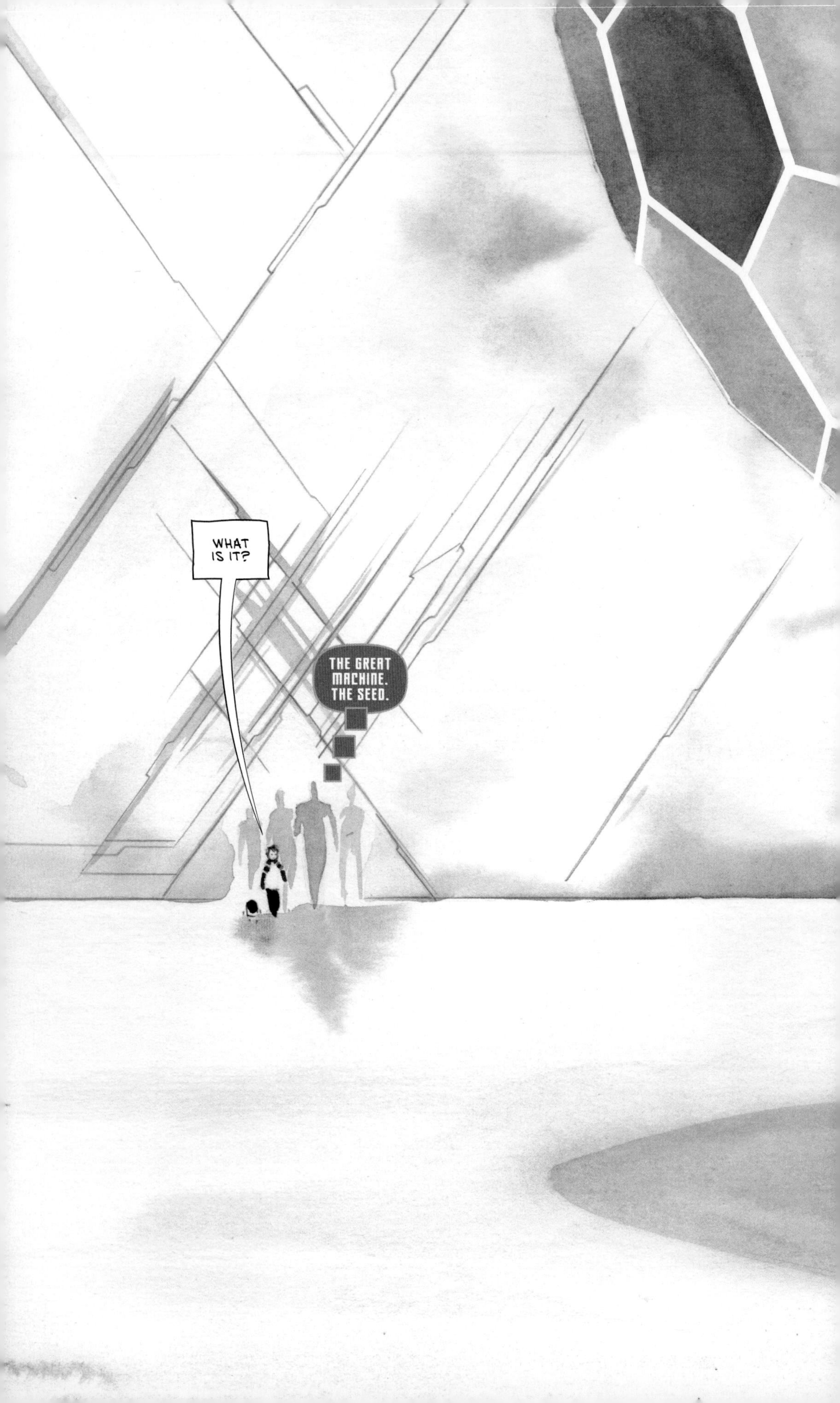
WHAT IS IT?
THE GREAT MACHINE. THE SEED.

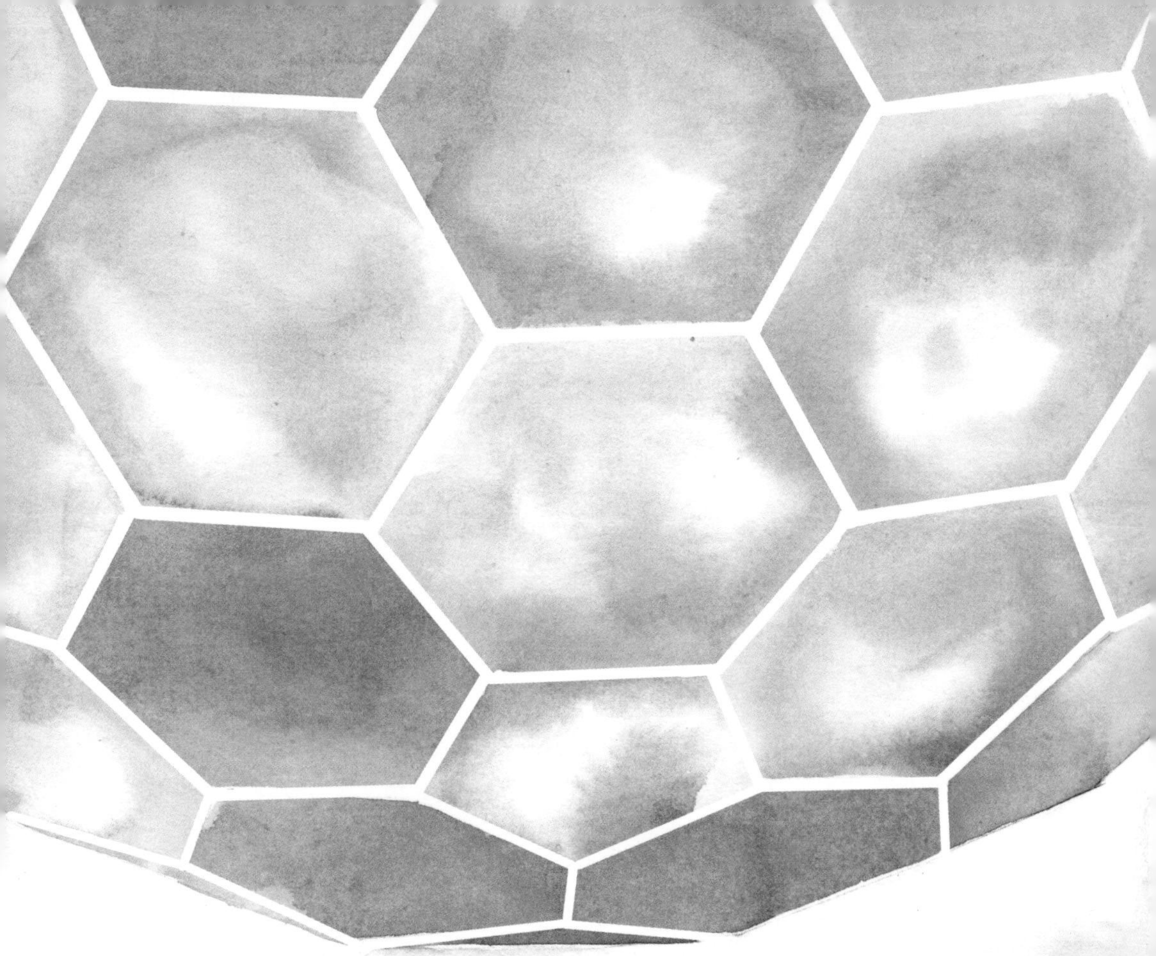

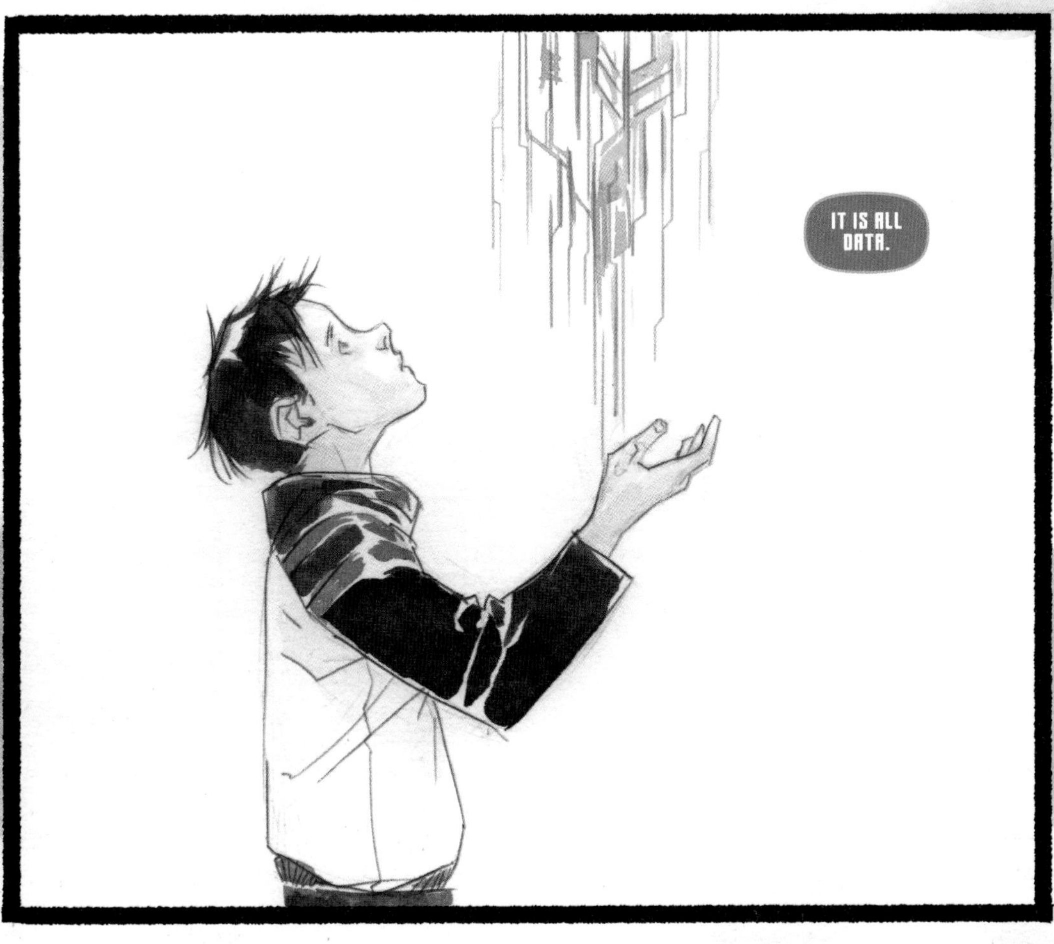
IT IS ALL DATA.

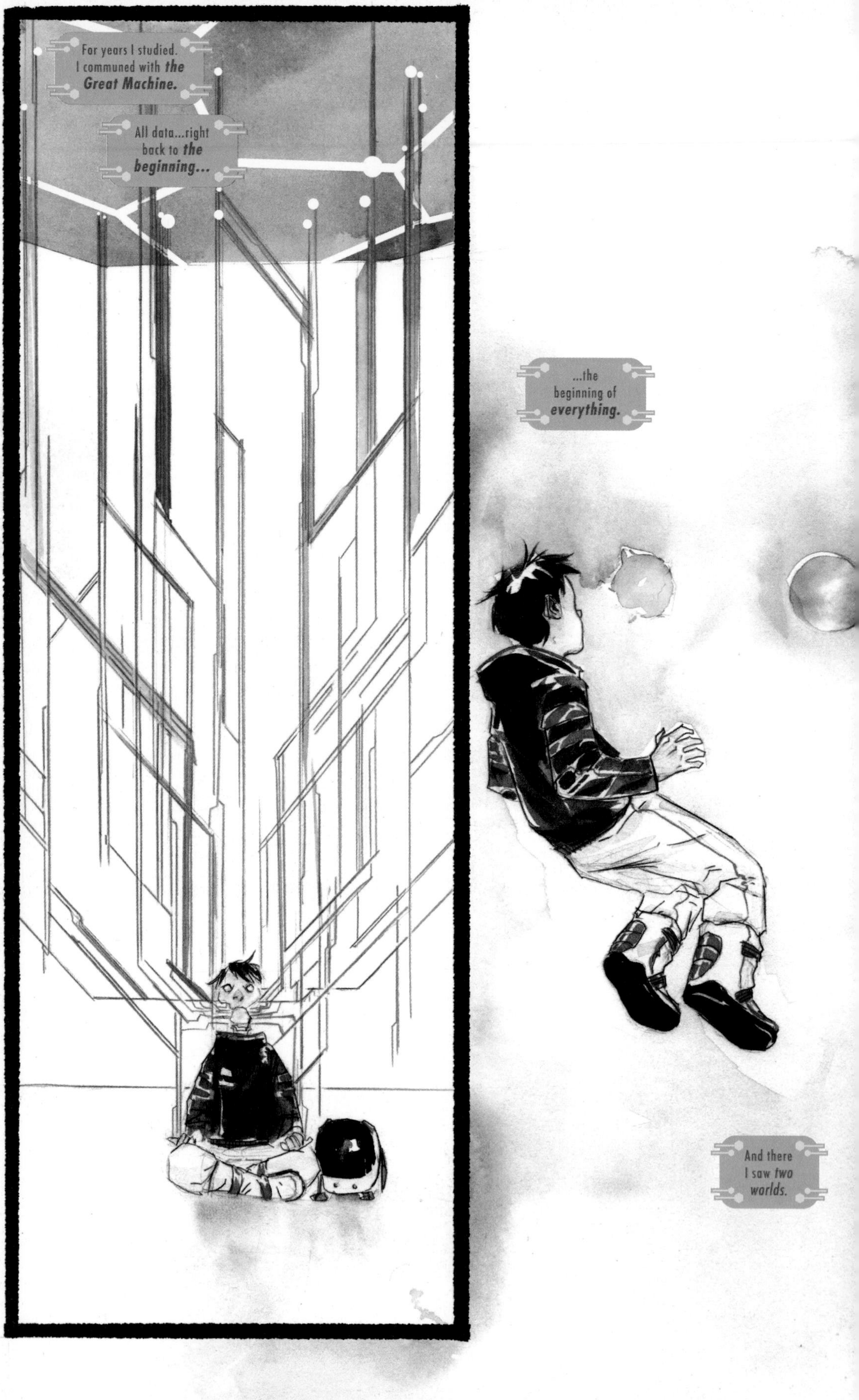
For years I studied. I communed with *the Great Machine.*
All data...right back to *the beginning...*
...the beginning of *everything.*
And there I saw *two worlds.*

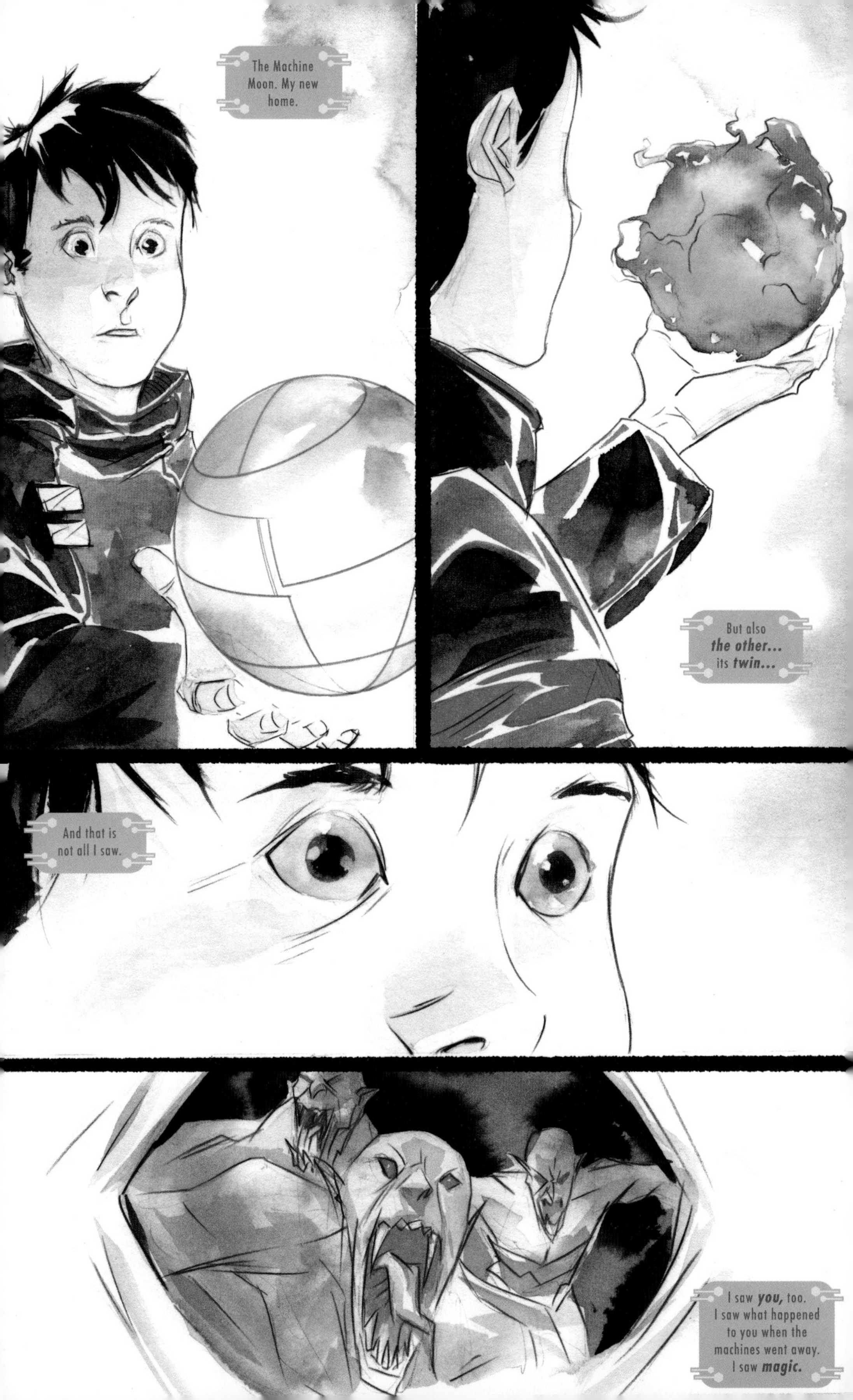
The Machine Moon. My new home.
But also *the other...* its *twin...*
And that is not all I saw.
I saw *you,* too. I saw what happened to you when the machines went away. I saw *magic.*

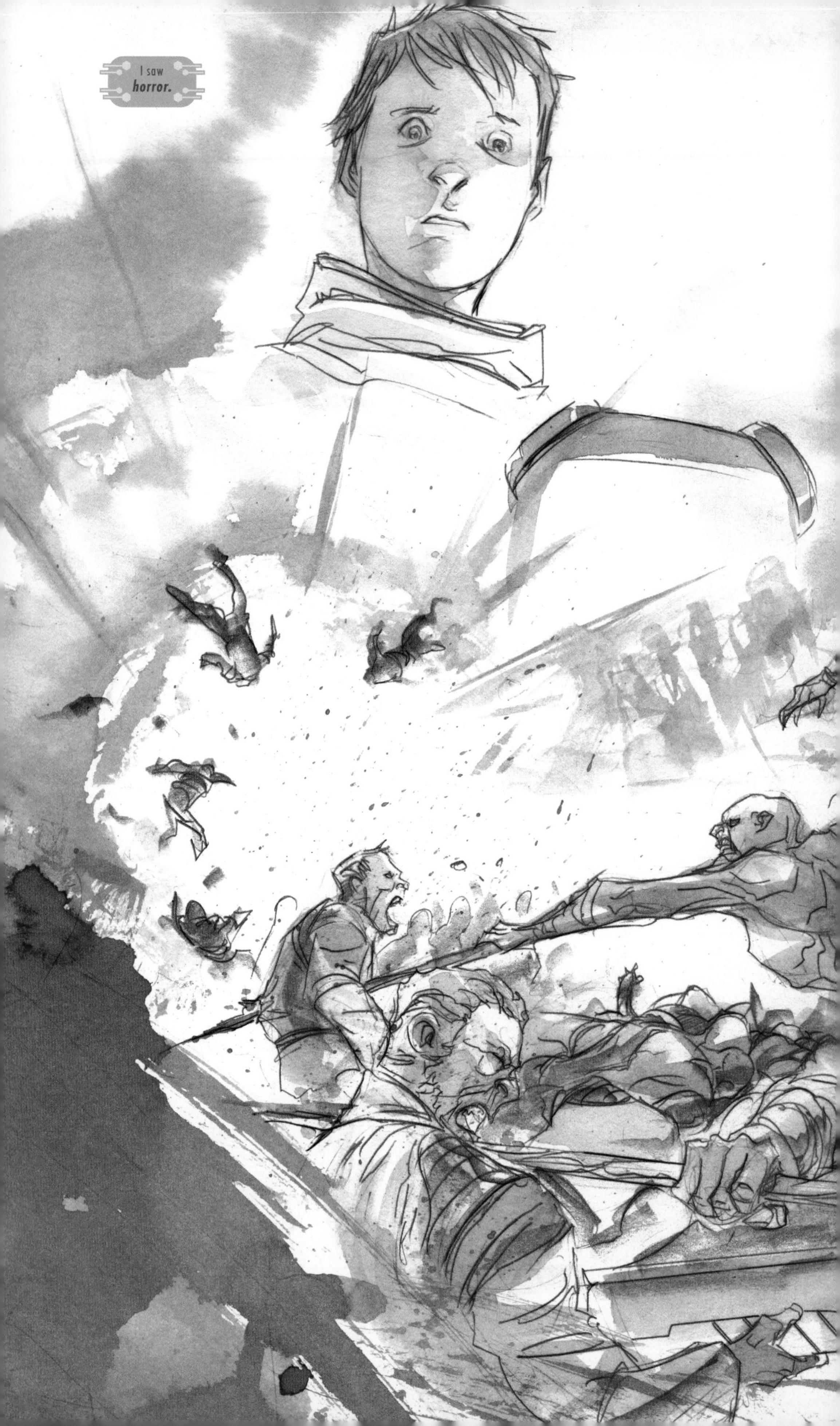
I saw
horror.

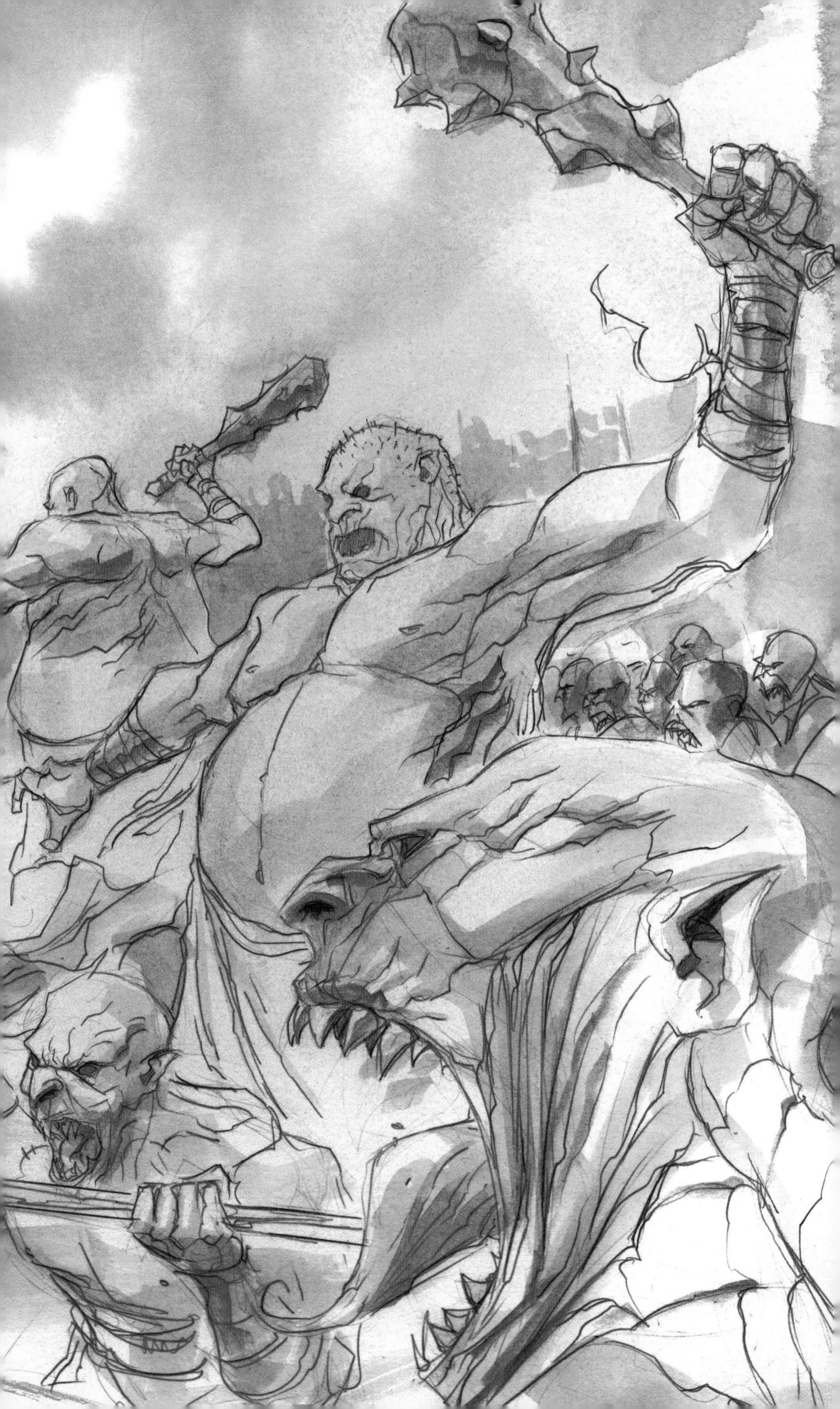

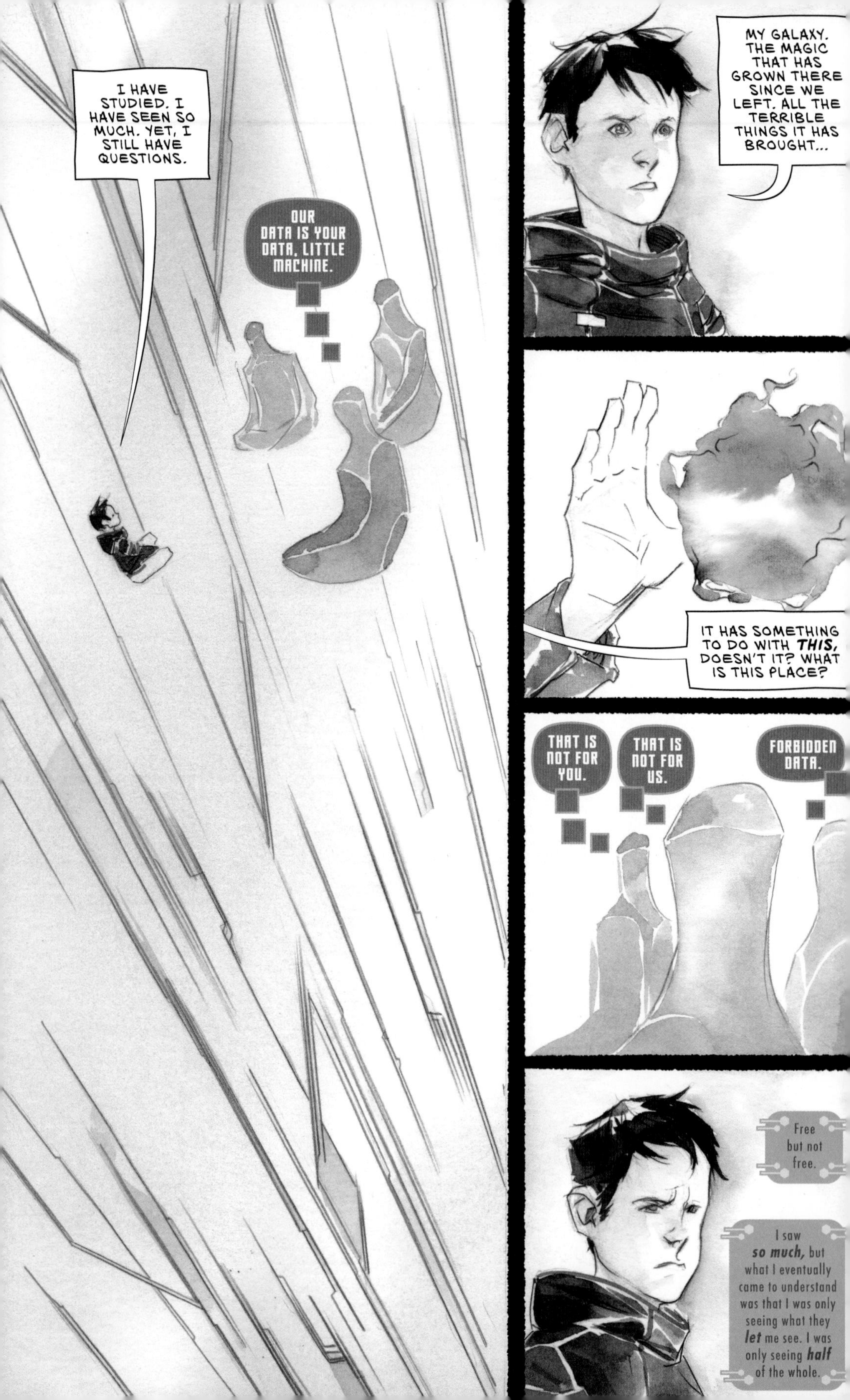

I HAVE STUDIED. I HAVE SEEN SO MUCH. YET, I STILL HAVE QUESTIONS.
OUR DATA IS YOUR DATA, LITTLE MACHINE.
MY GALAXY. THE MAGIC THAT HAS GROWN THERE SINCE WE LEFT. ALL THE TERRIBLE THINGS IT HAS BROUGHT...
IT HAS SOMETHING TO DO WITH THIS, DOESN'T IT? WHAT IS THIS PLACE?
THAT IS NOT FOR YOU.
THAT IS NOT FOR US.
FORBIDDEN DATA.
Free but not free.
I saw so much, but what I eventually came to understand was that I was only seeing what they let me see. I was only seeing half of the whole.

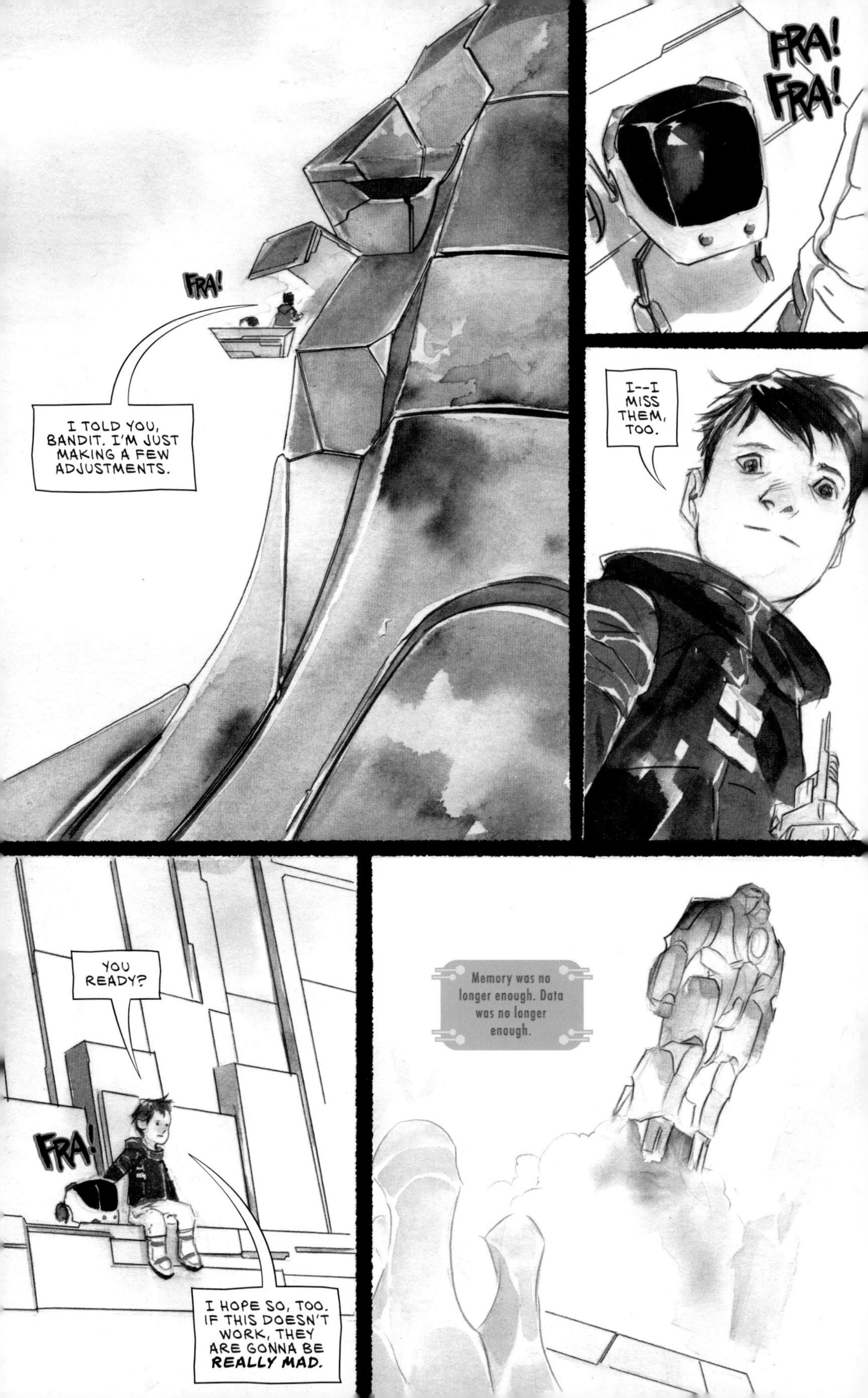
FRA!
I TOLD YOU, BANDIT. I'M JUST MAKING A FEW ADJUSTMENTS.
FRA! FRA!
I--I MISS THEM, TOO.
YOU READY?
FRA!
I HOPE SO, TOO. IF THIS DOESN'T WORK, THEY ARE GONNA BE **REALLY MAD.**
Memory was no longer enough. Data was no longer enough.

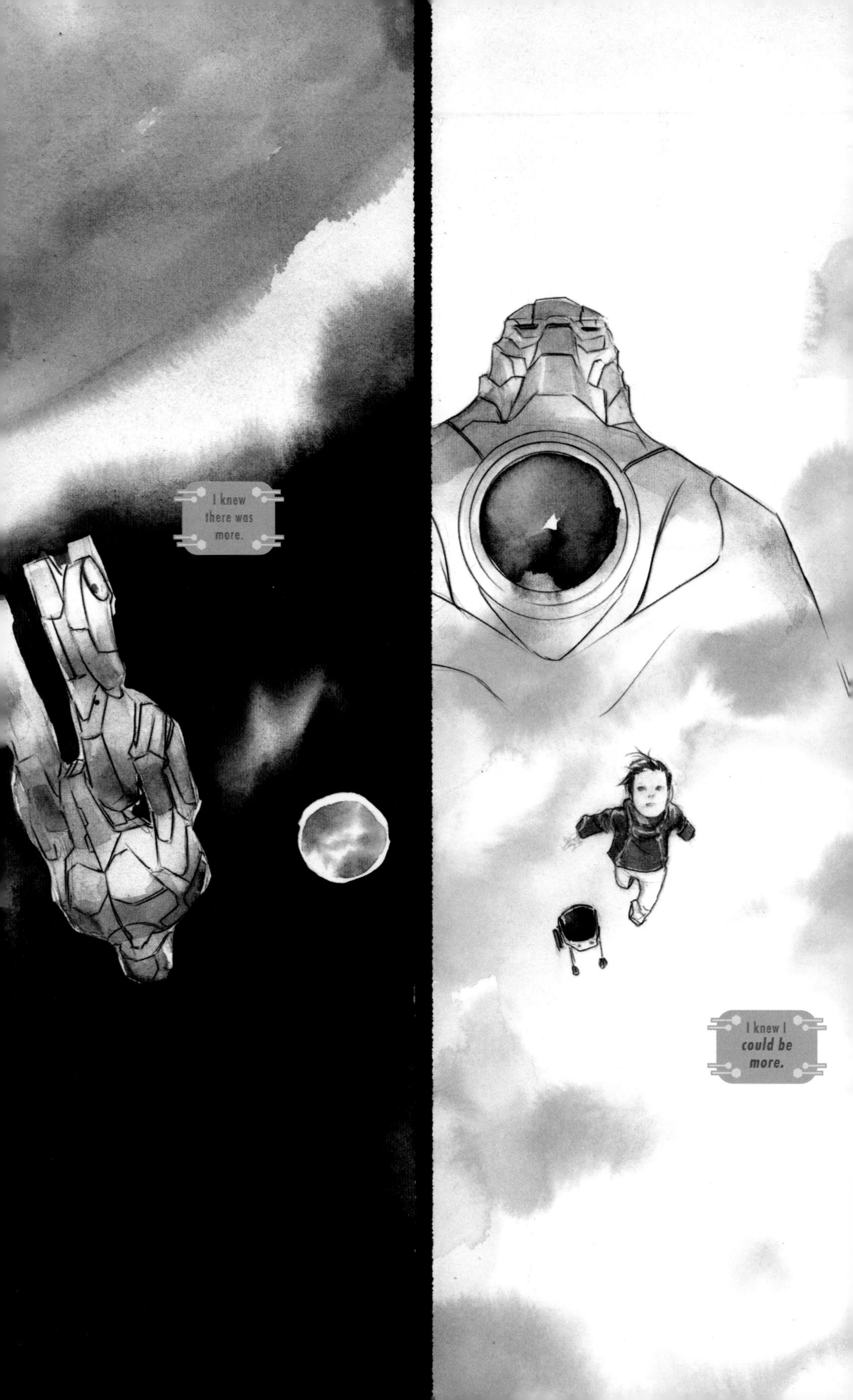
I knew there was more.
I knew I could be more.

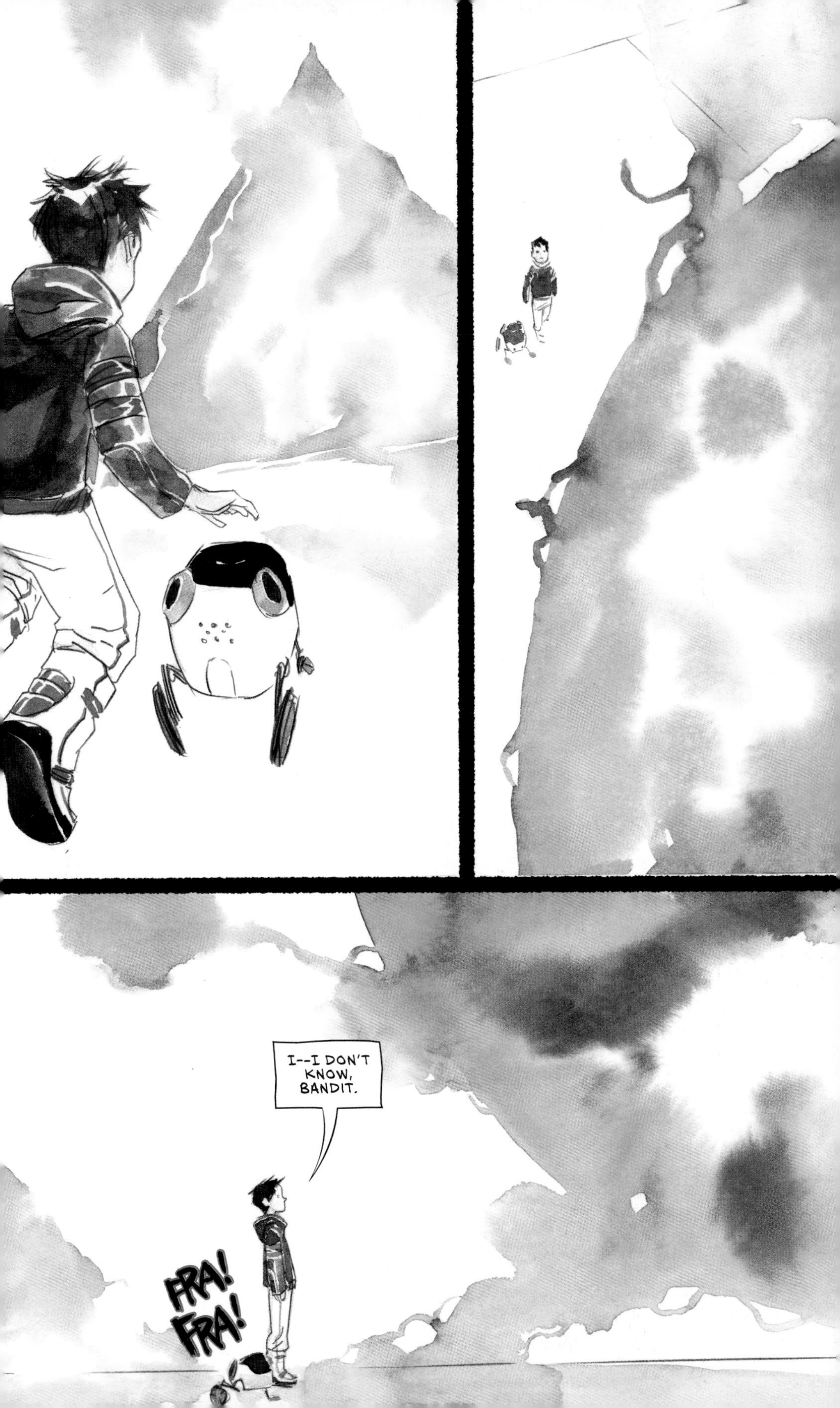
I--I DON'T KNOW, BANDIT.
FRA! FRA!

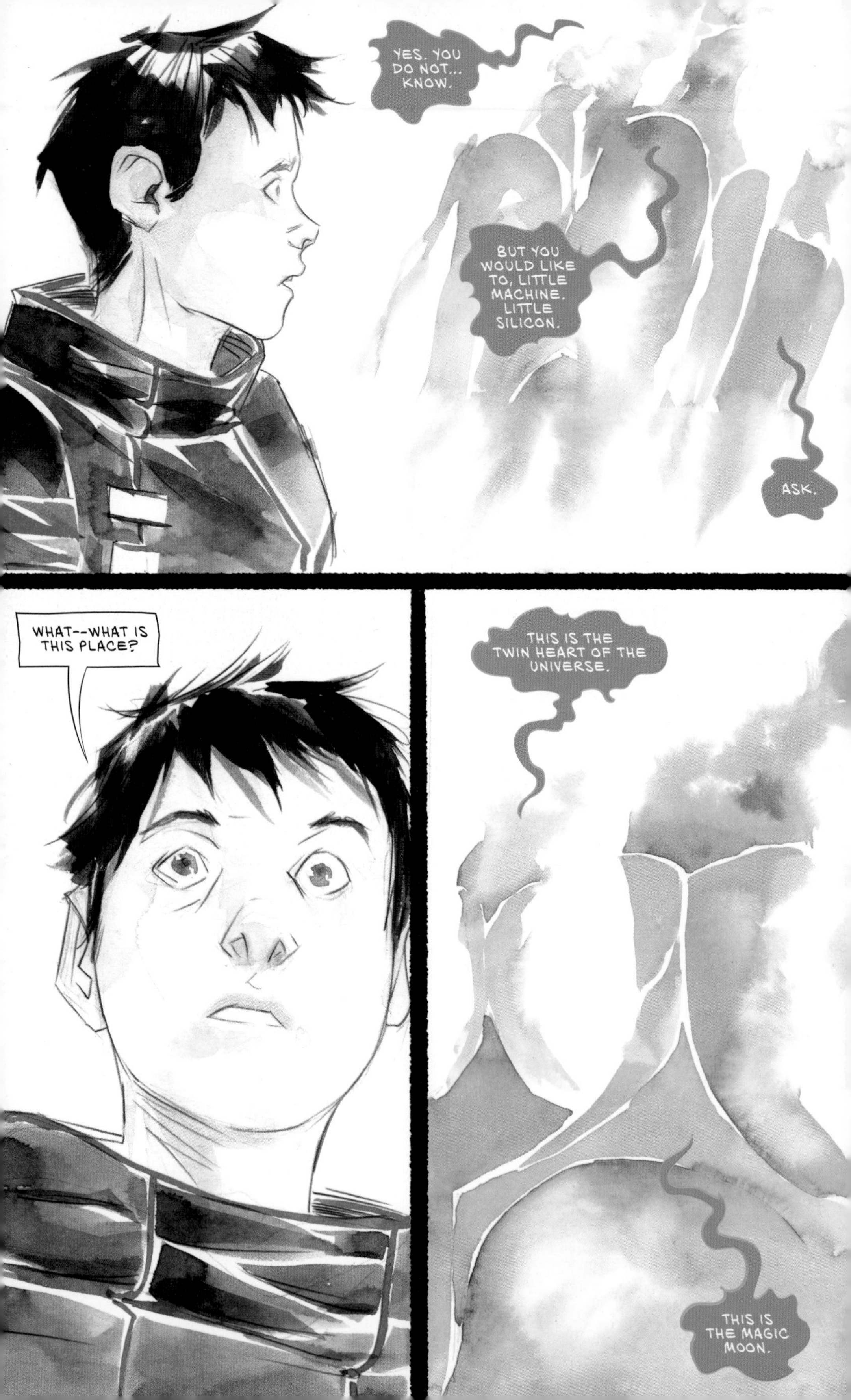
YES. YOU DO NOT... KNOW.
BUT YOU WOULD LIKE TO, LITTLE MACHINE. LITTLE SILICON.
ASK.
WHAT--WHAT IS THIS PLACE?
THIS IS THE TWIN HEART OF THE UNIVERSE.
THIS IS THE MAGIC MOON.

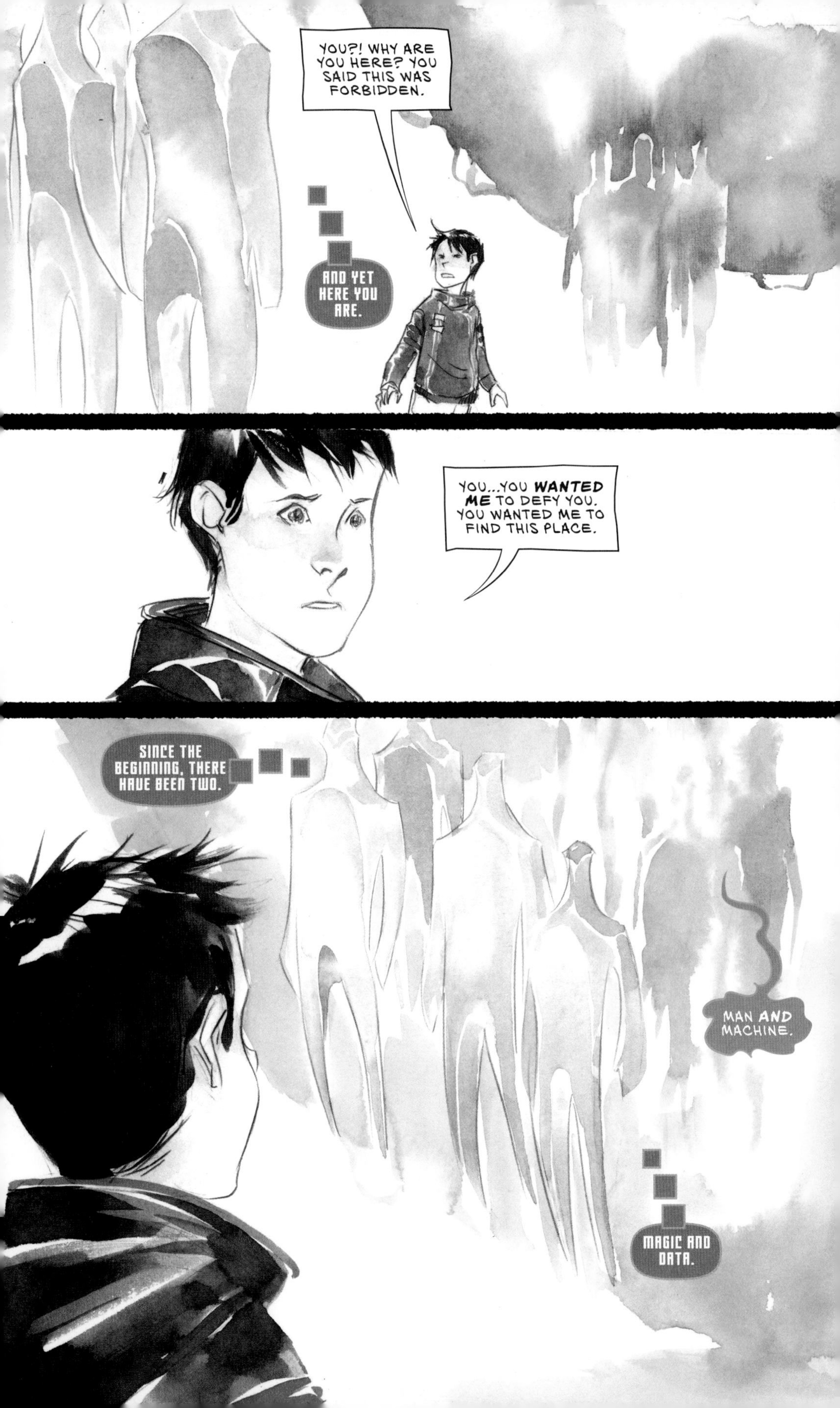

YOU?! WHY ARE YOU HERE? YOU SAID THIS WAS FORBIDDEN.
AND YET HERE YOU ARE.
YOU...YOU **WANTED ME** TO DEFY YOU. YOU WANTED ME TO FIND THIS PLACE.
SINCE THE BEGINNING, THERE HAVE BEEN TWO.
MAN **AND** MACHINE.
MAGIC AND DATA.

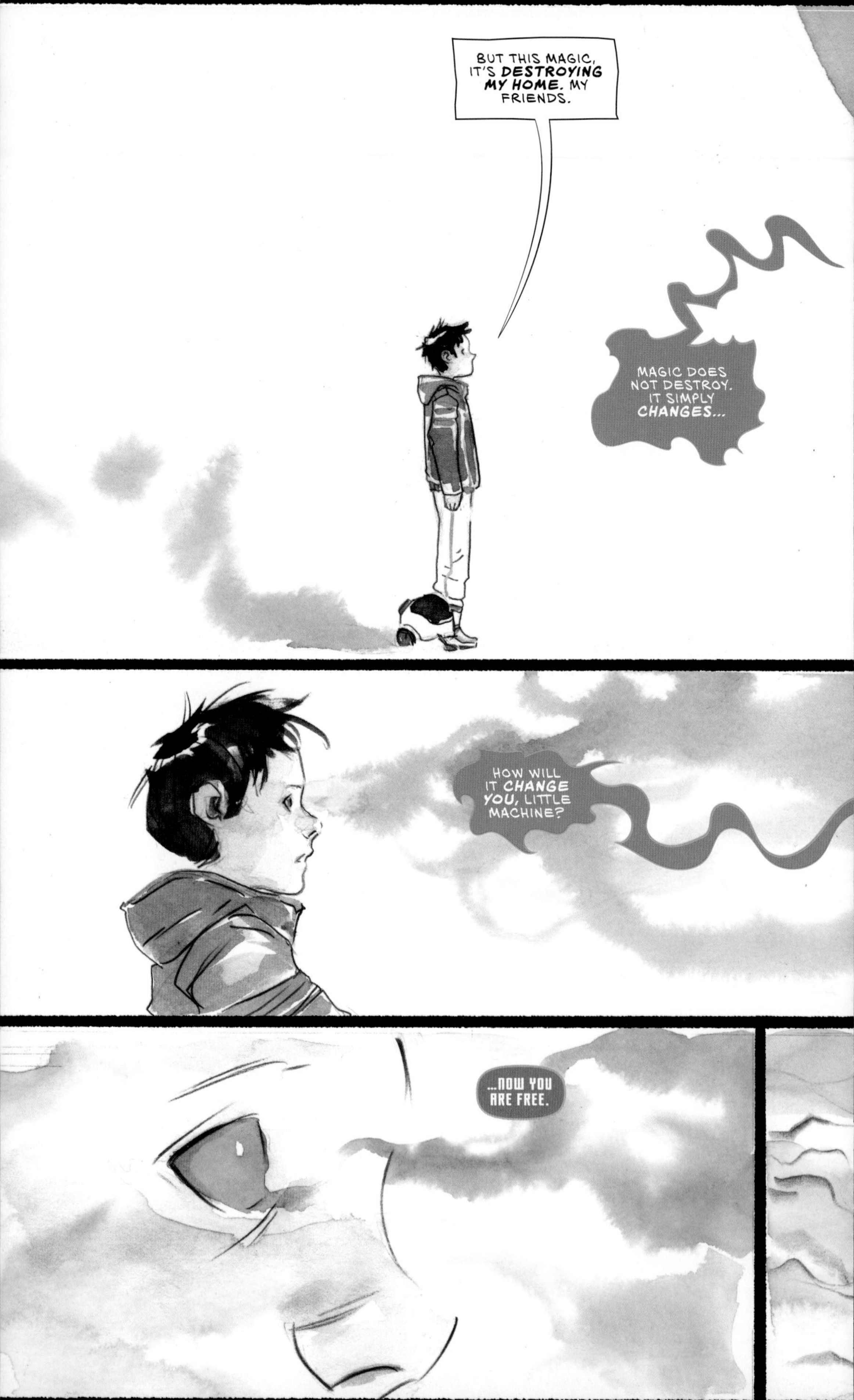
BUT THIS MAGIC, IT'S **DESTROYING MY HOME.** MY FRIENDS.
MAGIC DOES NOT DESTROY. IT SIMPLY **CHANGES...**
HOW WILL IT **CHANGE YOU,** LITTLE MACHINE?
...NOW YOU ARE FREE.

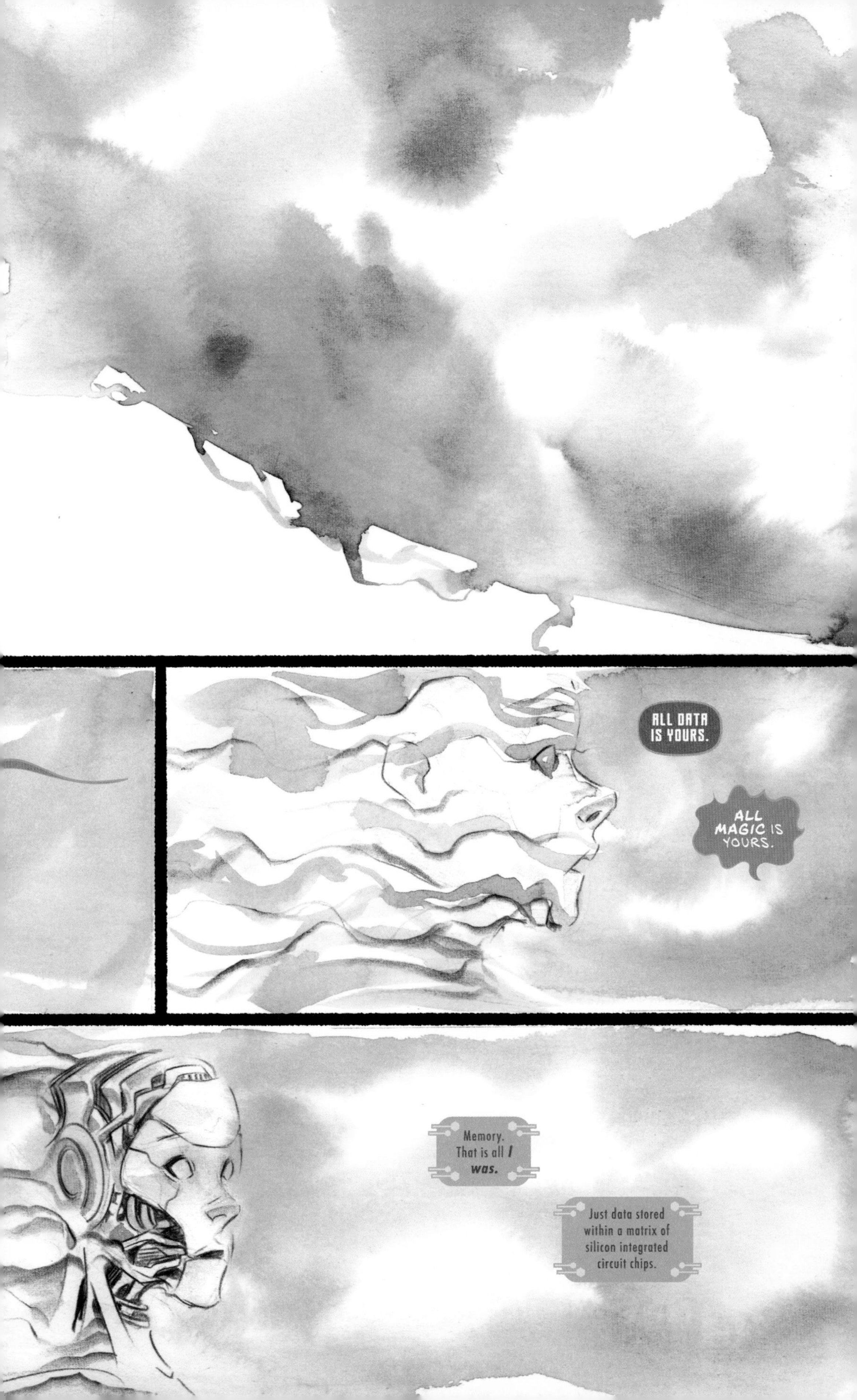
ALL DATA IS YOURS.
ALL MAGIC IS YOURS.
Memory. That is all I was.
Just data stored within a matrix of silicon integrated circuit chips.

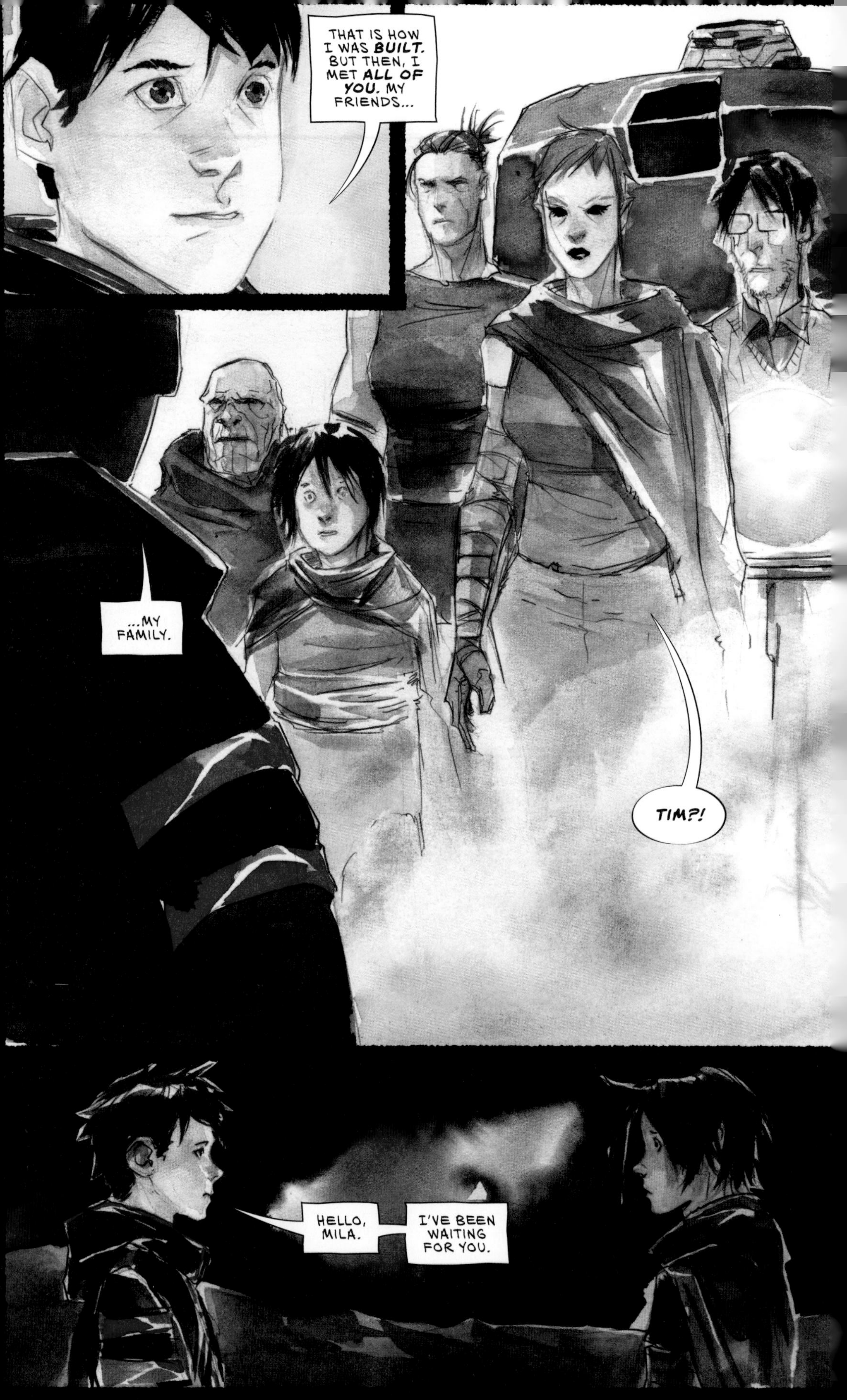
THAT IS HOW I WAS **BUILT.** BUT THEN, I MET **ALL OF YOU.** MY FRIENDS...
...MY FAMILY.
TIM?!
HELLO, MILA.
I'VE BEEN WAITING FOR YOU.

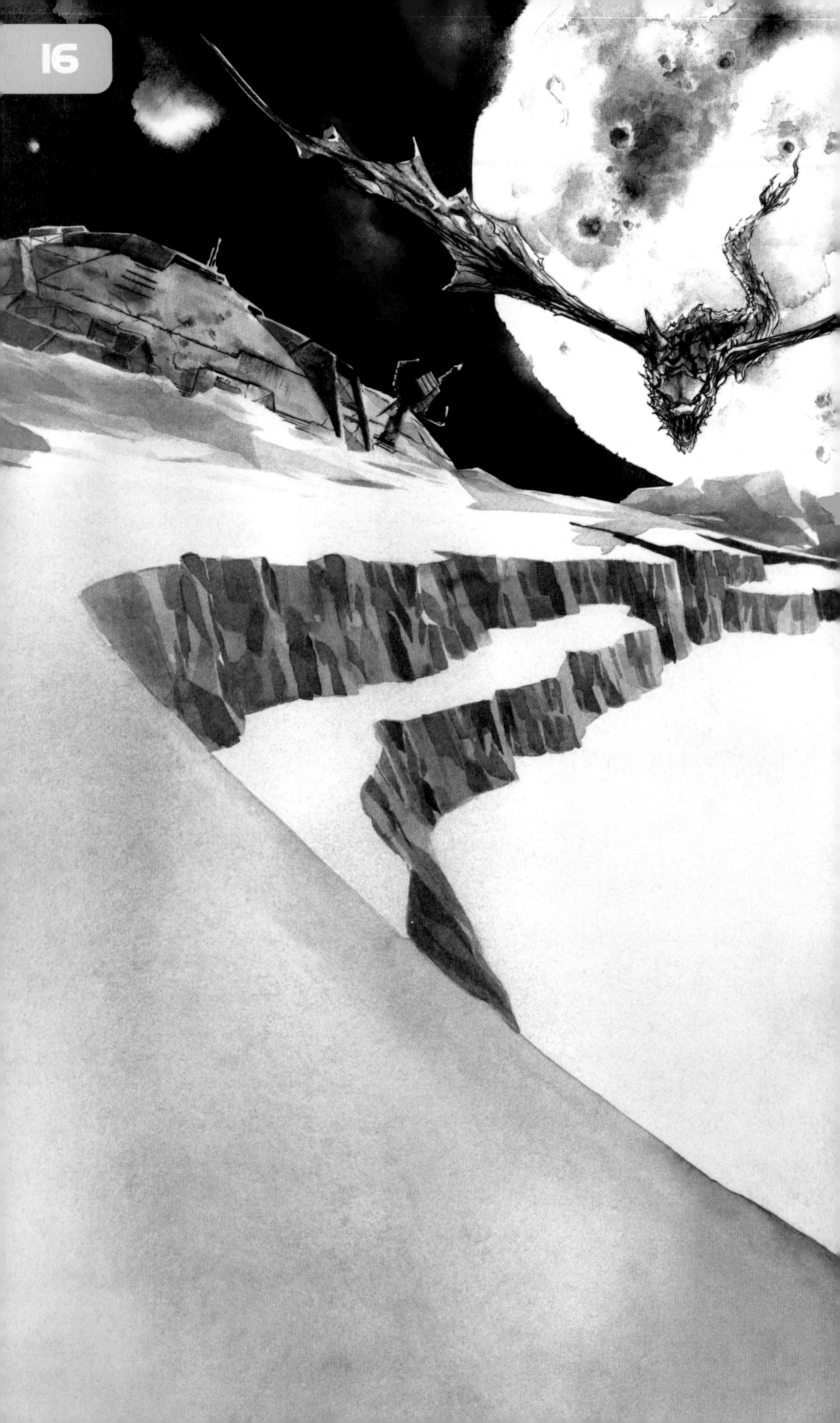

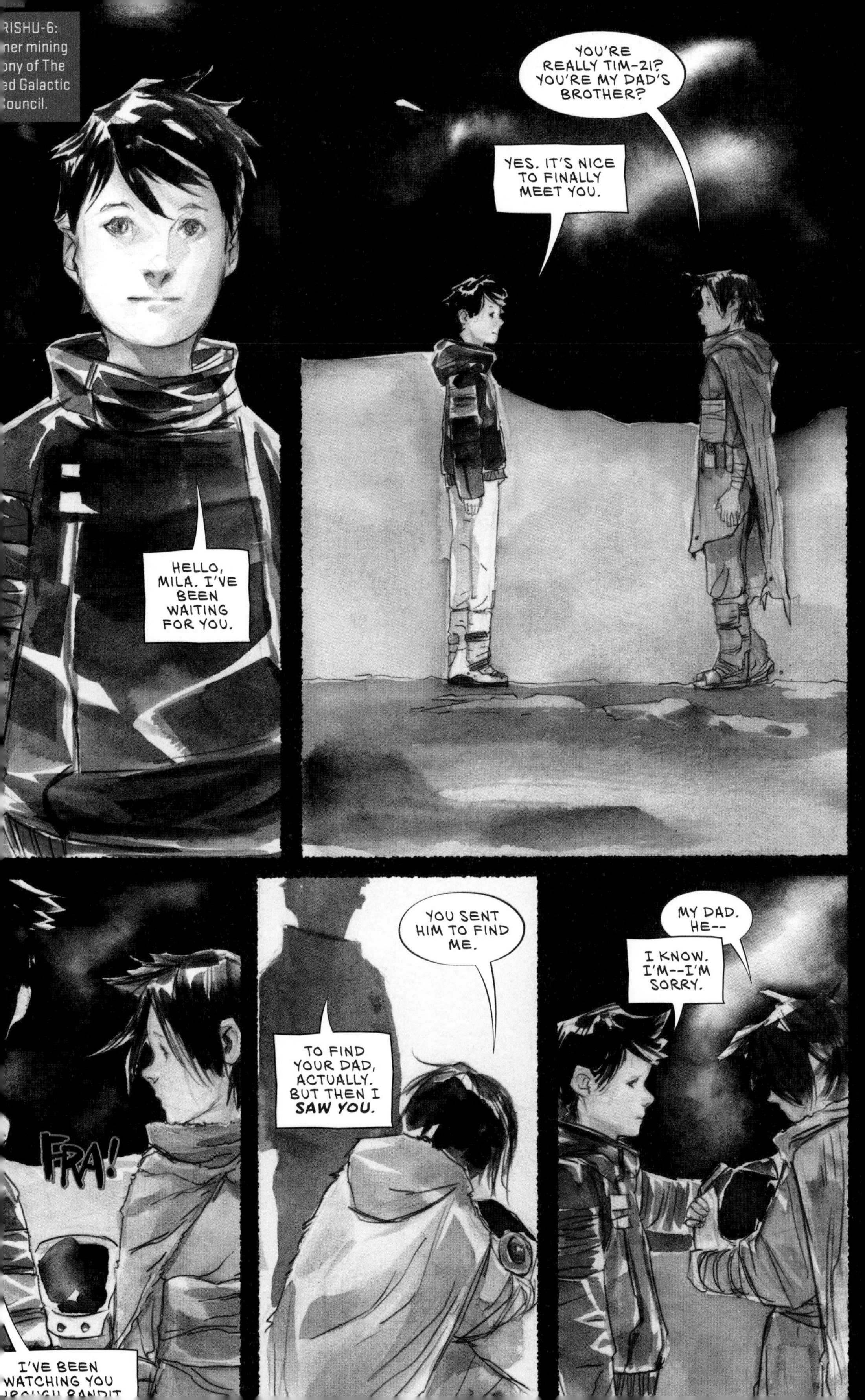
RISHU-6:
ner mining
ony of The
ed Galactic
ouncil.
HELLO, MILA. I'VE BEEN WAITING FOR YOU.
YOU'RE REALLY TIM-21? YOU'RE MY DAD'S BROTHER?
YES. IT'S NICE TO FINALLY MEET YOU.
FRA!
I'VE BEEN WATCHING YOU
YOU SENT HIM TO FIND ME.
TO FIND YOUR DAD, ACTUALLY. BUT THEN I *SAW YOU.*
MY DAD. HE--
I KNOW. I'M--I'M SORRY.

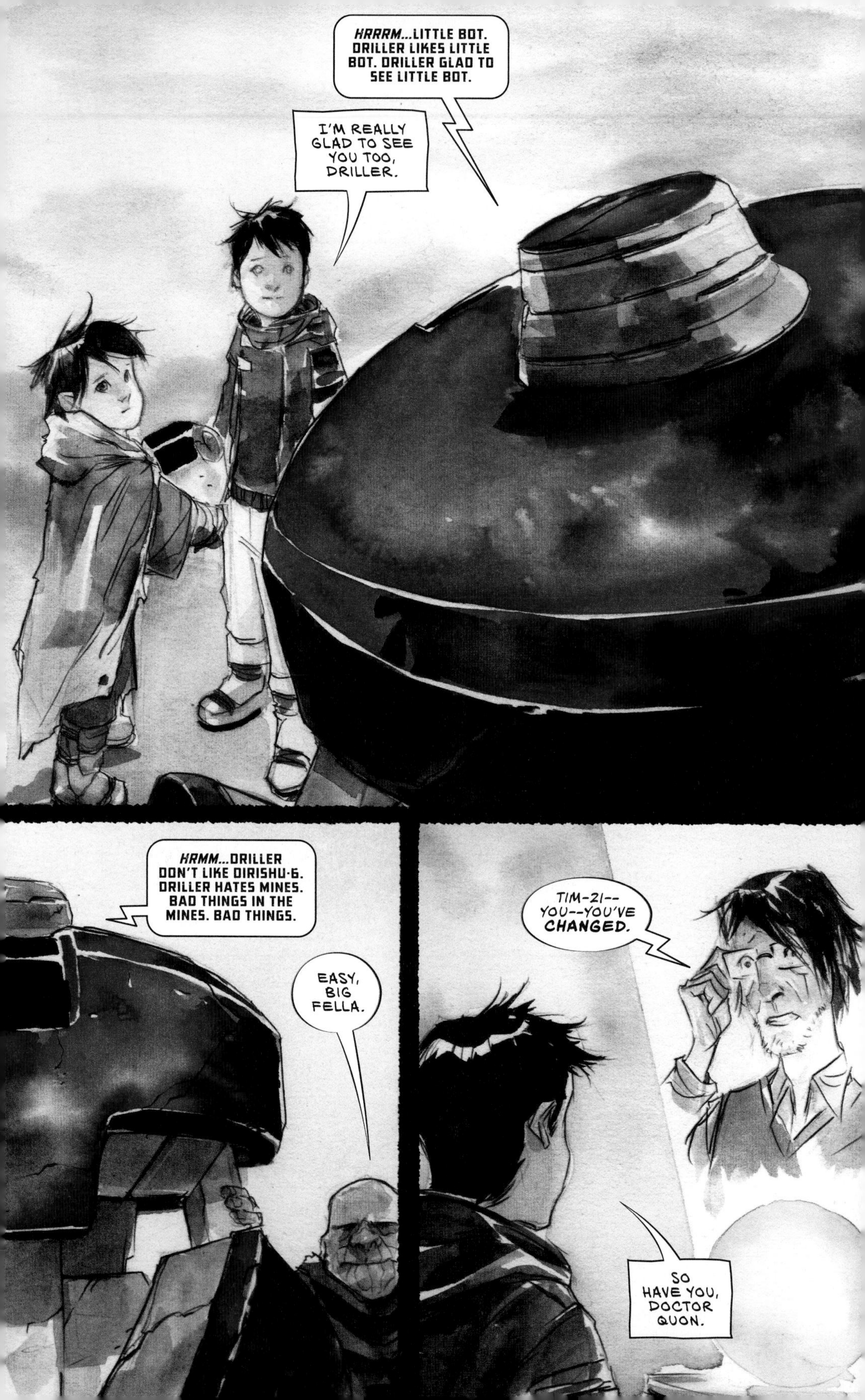
HRRRM...LITTLE BOT. DRILLER LIKES LITTLE BOT. DRILLER GLAD TO SEE LITTLE BOT.
I'M REALLY GLAD TO SEE YOU TOO, DRILLER.
HRMM...DRILLER DON'T LIKE DIRISHU-6. DRILLER HATES MINES. BAD THINGS IN THE MINES. BAD THINGS.
EASY, BIG FELLA.
TIM-21-- YOU--YOU'VE CHANGED.
SO HAVE YOU, DOCTOR QUON.

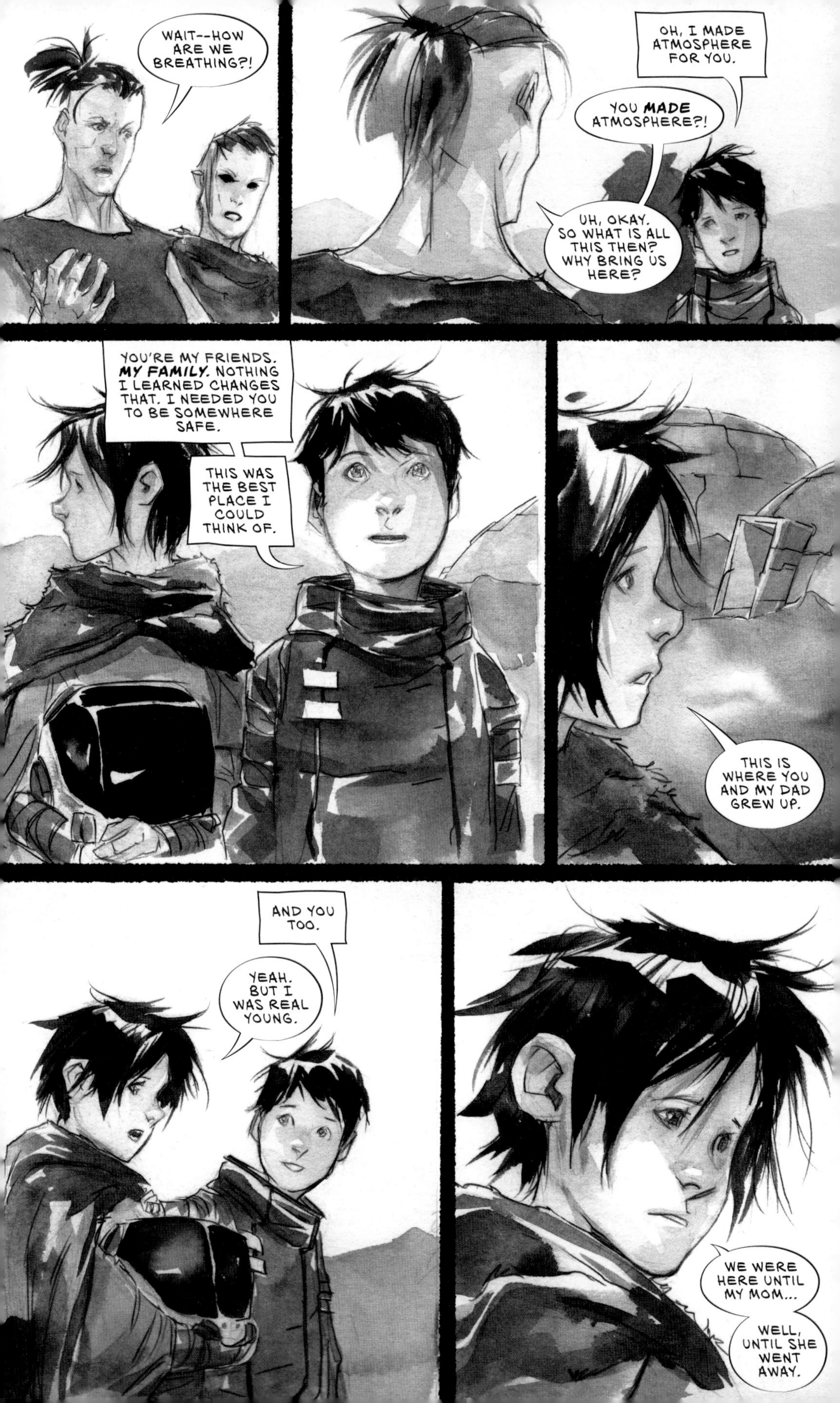
WAIT--HOW ARE WE BREATHING?!
OH, I MADE ATMOSPHERE FOR YOU.
YOU **MADE** ATMOSPHERE?!
UH, OKAY. SO WHAT IS ALL THIS THEN? WHY BRING US HERE?
YOU'RE MY FRIENDS. ***MY FAMILY.*** NOTHING I LEARNED CHANGES THAT. I NEEDED YOU TO BE SOMEWHERE SAFE.
THIS WAS THE BEST PLACE I COULD THINK OF.
THIS IS WHERE YOU AND MY DAD GREW UP.
AND YOU TOO.
YEAH. BUT I WAS REAL YOUNG.
WE WERE HERE UNTIL MY MOM...
WELL, UNTIL SHE WENT AWAY.

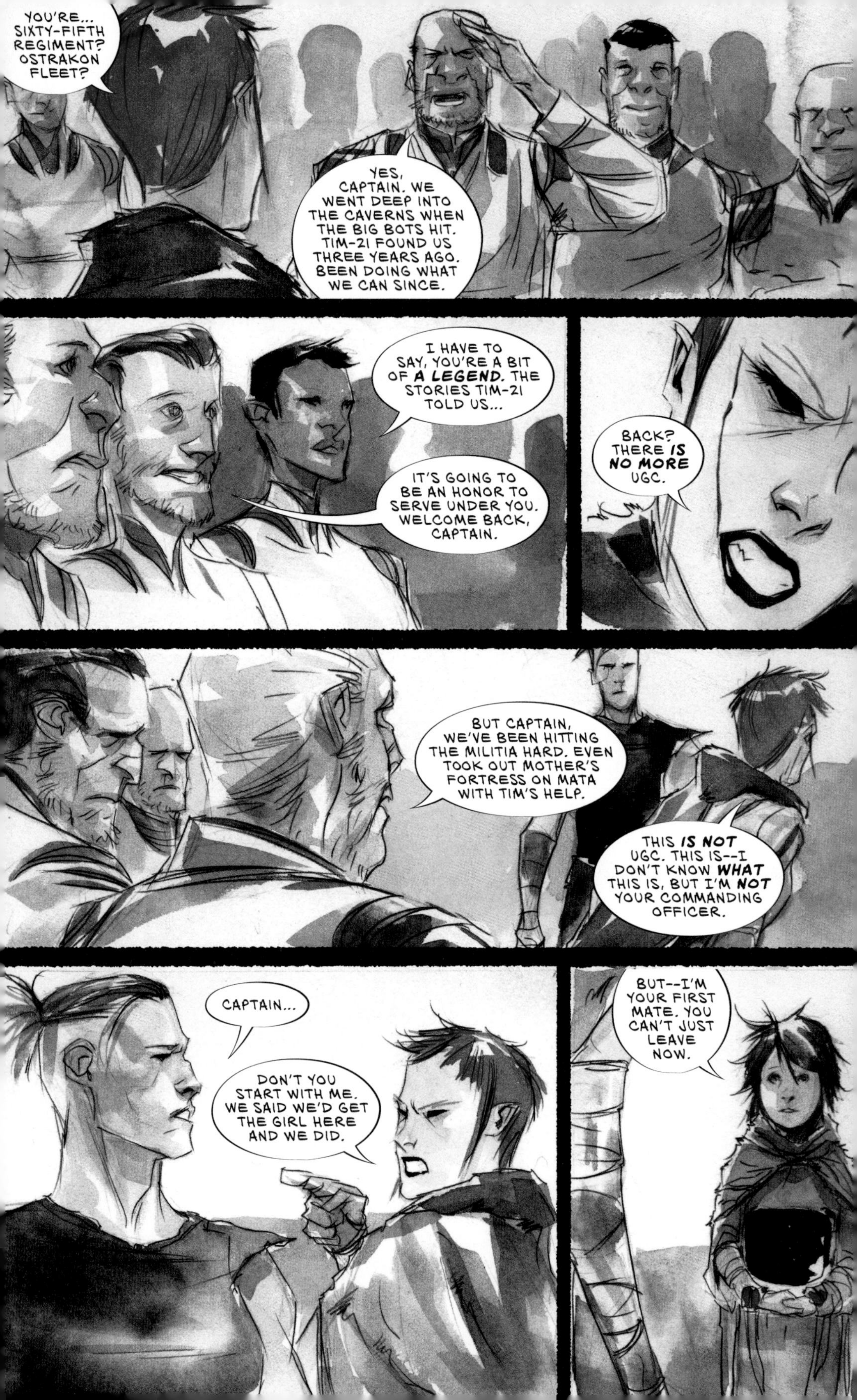
YOU'RE... SIXTY-FIFTH REGIMENT? OSTRAKON FLEET?
YES, CAPTAIN. WE WENT DEEP INTO THE CAVERNS WHEN THE BIG BOTS HIT. TIM-21 FOUND US THREE YEARS AGO. BEEN DOING WHAT WE CAN SINCE.
I HAVE TO SAY, YOU'RE A BIT OF **A LEGEND.** THE STORIES TIM-21 TOLD US...
IT'S GOING TO BE AN HONOR TO SERVE UNDER YOU. WELCOME BACK, CAPTAIN.
BACK? THERE **IS NO MORE** UGC.
BUT CAPTAIN, WE'VE BEEN HITTING THE MILITIA HARD. EVEN TOOK OUT MOTHER'S FORTRESS ON MATA WITH TIM'S HELP.
THIS **IS NOT** UGC. THIS IS--I DON'T KNOW **WHAT** THIS IS, BUT I'M **NOT** YOUR COMMANDING OFFICER.
CAPTAIN...
DON'T YOU START WITH ME. WE SAID WE'D GET THE GIRL HERE AND WE DID.
BUT--I'M YOUR FIRST MATE. YOU CAN'T JUST LEAVE NOW.

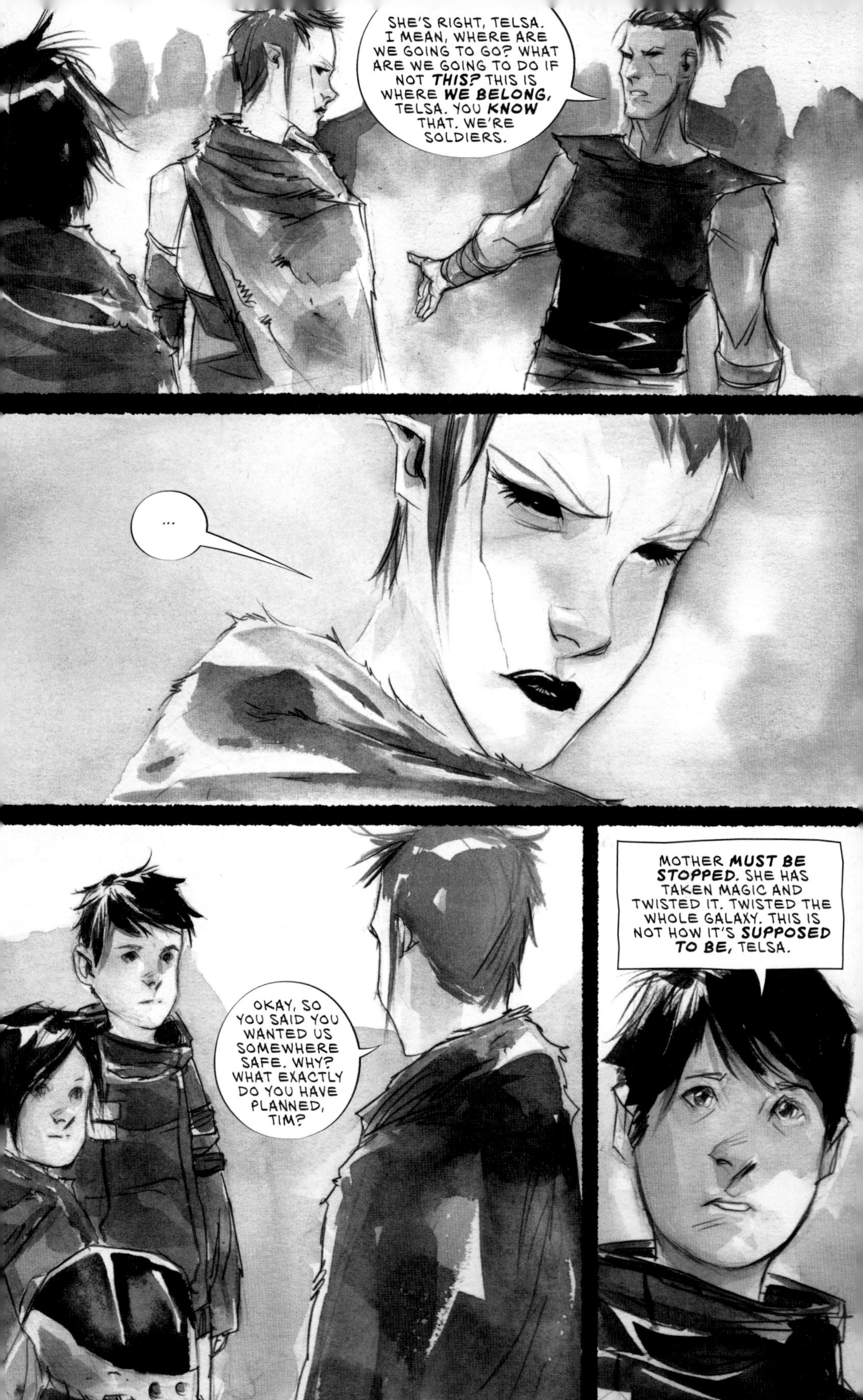
SHE'S RIGHT, TELSA. I MEAN, WHERE ARE WE GOING TO GO? WHAT ARE WE GOING TO DO IF NOT **THIS?** THIS IS WHERE **WE BELONG,** TELSA. YOU **KNOW** THAT. WE'RE SOLDIERS.
...
OKAY, SO YOU SAID YOU WANTED US SOMEWHERE SAFE. WHY? WHAT EXACTLY DO YOU HAVE PLANNED, TIM?
MOTHER **MUST BE STOPPED.** SHE HAS TAKEN MAGIC AND TWISTED IT. TWISTED THE WHOLE GALAXY. THIS IS NOT HOW IT'S **SUPPOSED TO BE,** TELSA.

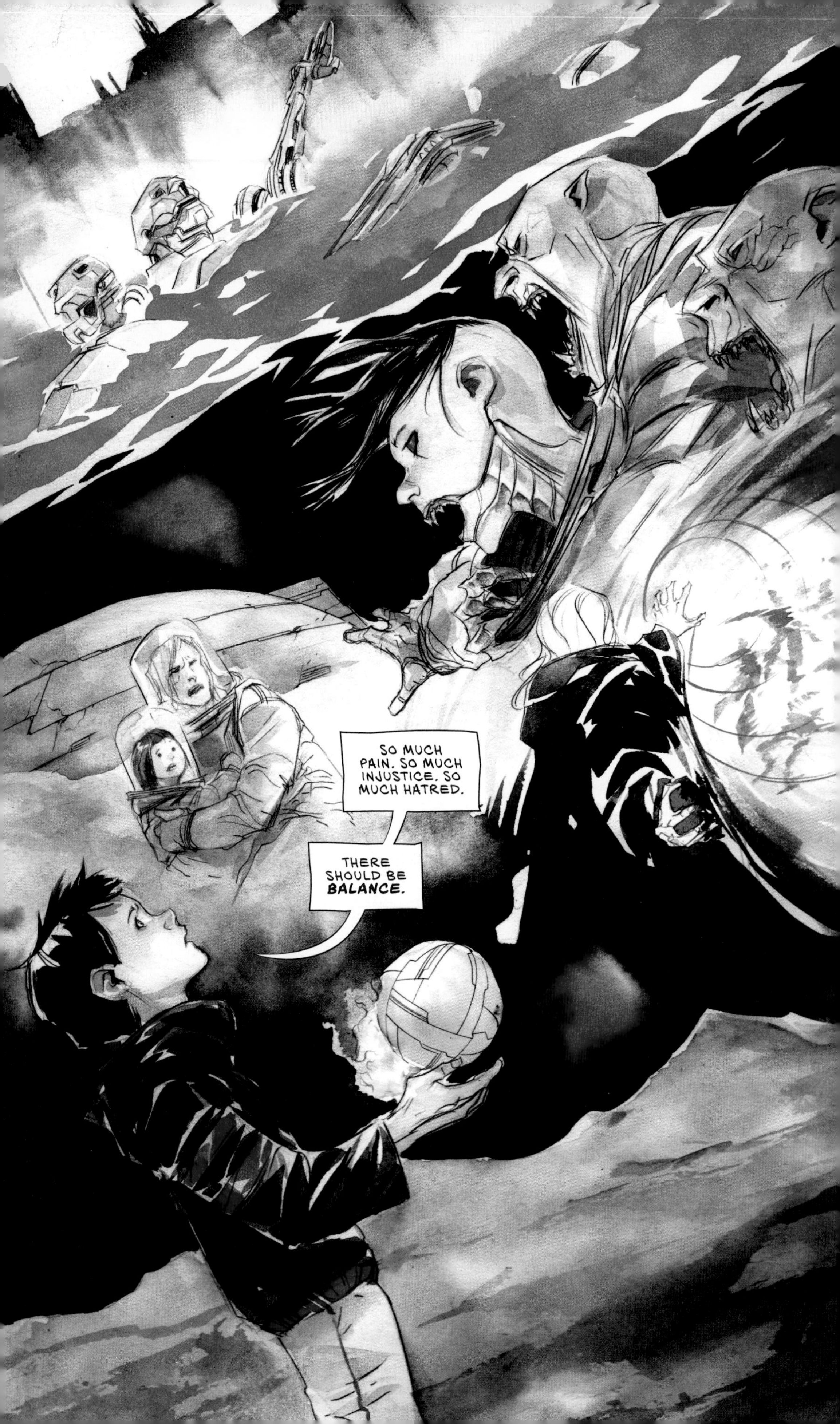
SO MUCH PAIN. SO MUCH INJUSTICE. SO MUCH HATRED.
THERE SHOULD BE **BALANCE.**

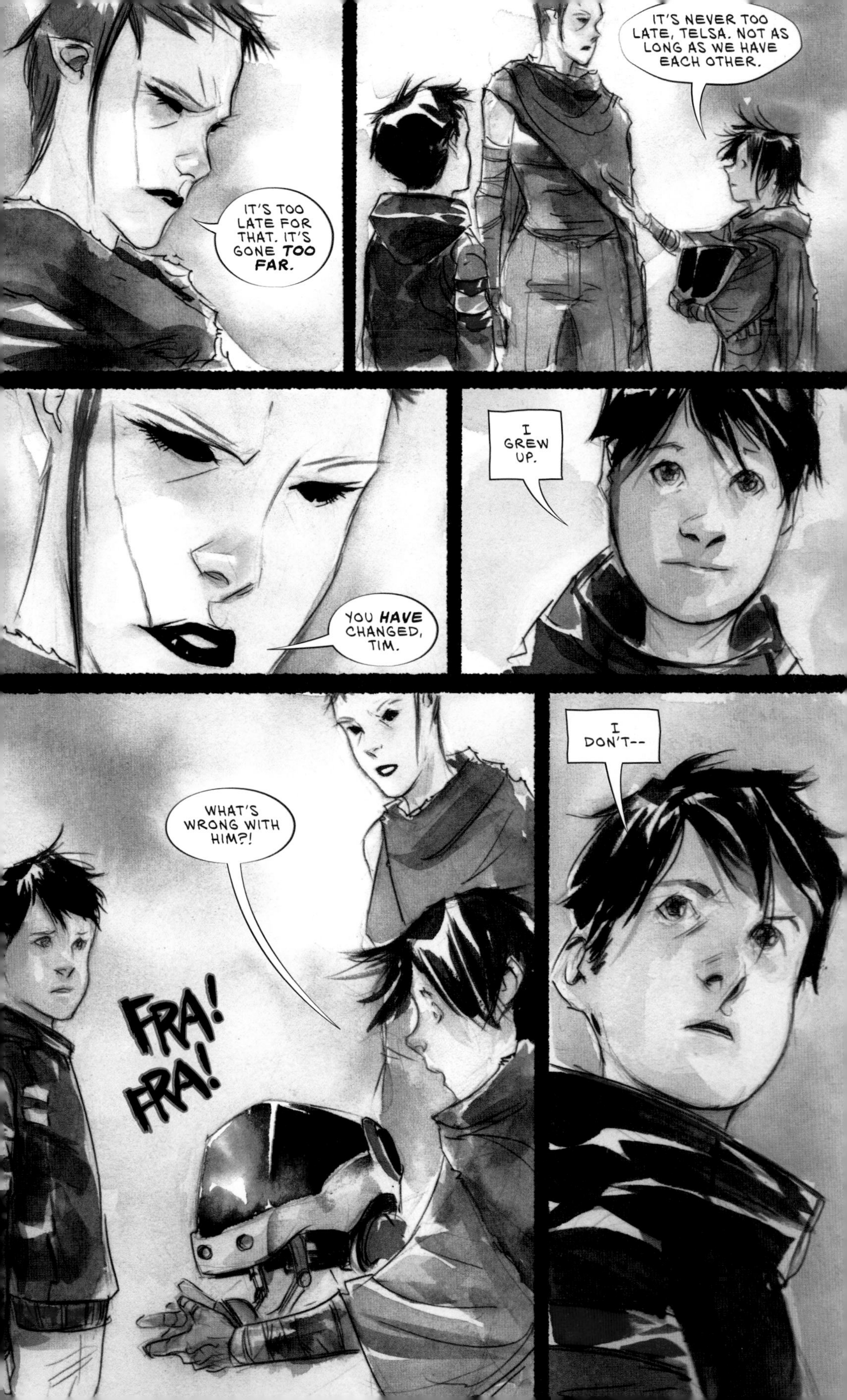
IT'S TOO LATE FOR THAT. IT'S GONE TOO FAR.
IT'S NEVER TOO LATE, TELSA. NOT AS LONG AS WE HAVE EACH OTHER.
YOU HAVE CHANGED, TIM.
I GREW UP.
WHAT'S WRONG WITH HIM?!
FRA! FRA!
I DON'T--

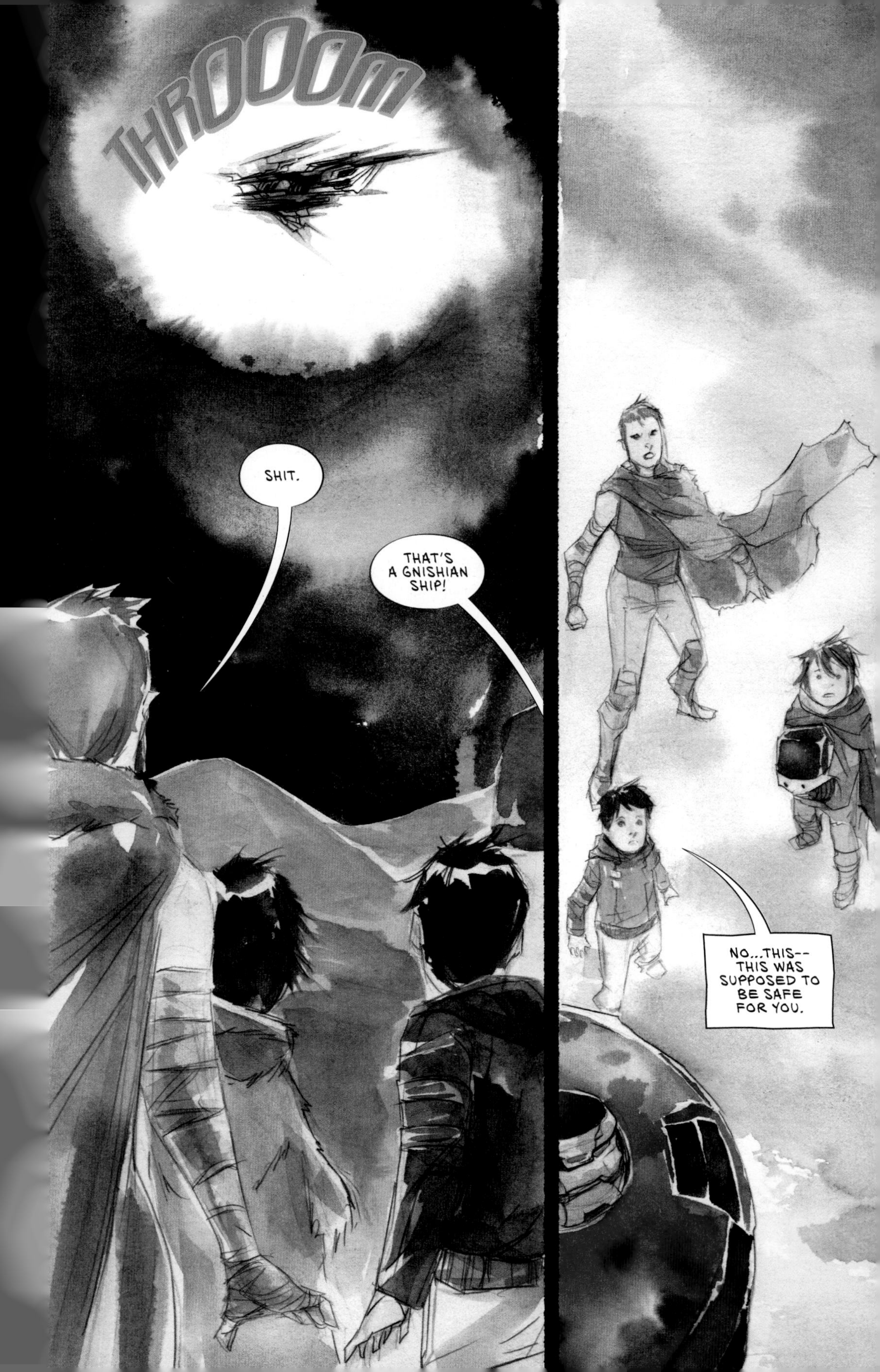
THROOOM
SHIT.
THAT'S A GNISHIAN SHIP!
NO...THIS--THIS WAS SUPPOSED TO BE SAFE FOR YOU.

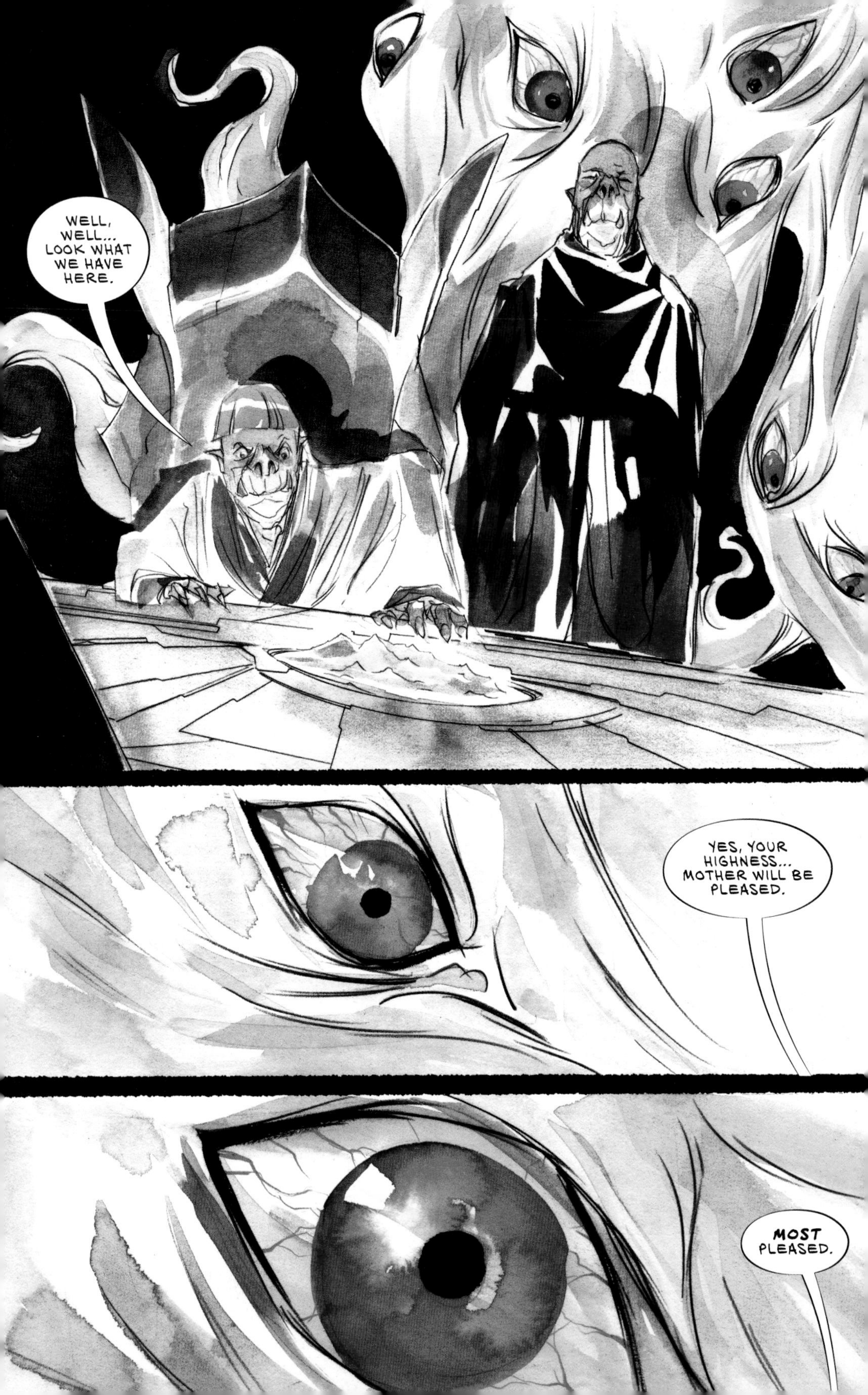
WELL, WELL... LOOK WHAT WE HAVE HERE.
YES, YOUR HIGHNESS... MOTHER WILL BE PLEASED.
MOST PLEASED.

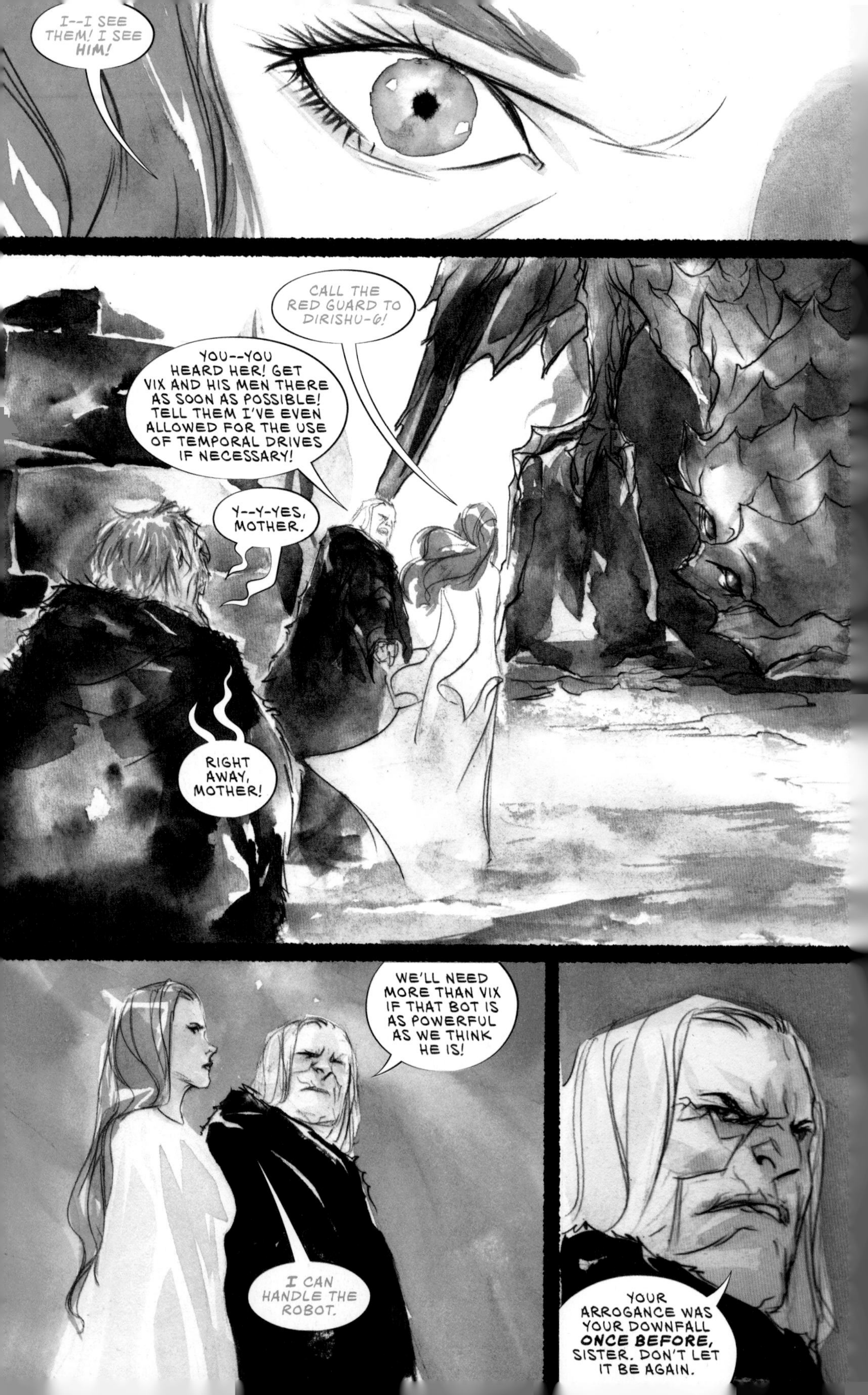
I--I SEE THEM! I SEE HIM!
CALL THE RED GUARD TO DIRISHU-6!
YOU--YOU HEARD HER! GET VIX AND HIS MEN THERE AS SOON AS POSSIBLE! TELL THEM I'VE EVEN ALLOWED FOR THE USE OF TEMPORAL DRIVES IF NECESSARY!
Y--Y-YES, MOTHER.
RIGHT AWAY, MOTHER!
WE'LL NEED MORE THAN VIX IF THAT BOT IS AS POWERFUL AS WE THINK HE IS!
I CAN HANDLE THE ROBOT.
YOUR ARROGANCE WAS YOUR DOWNFALL ONCE BEFORE, SISTER. DON'T LET IT BE AGAIN.

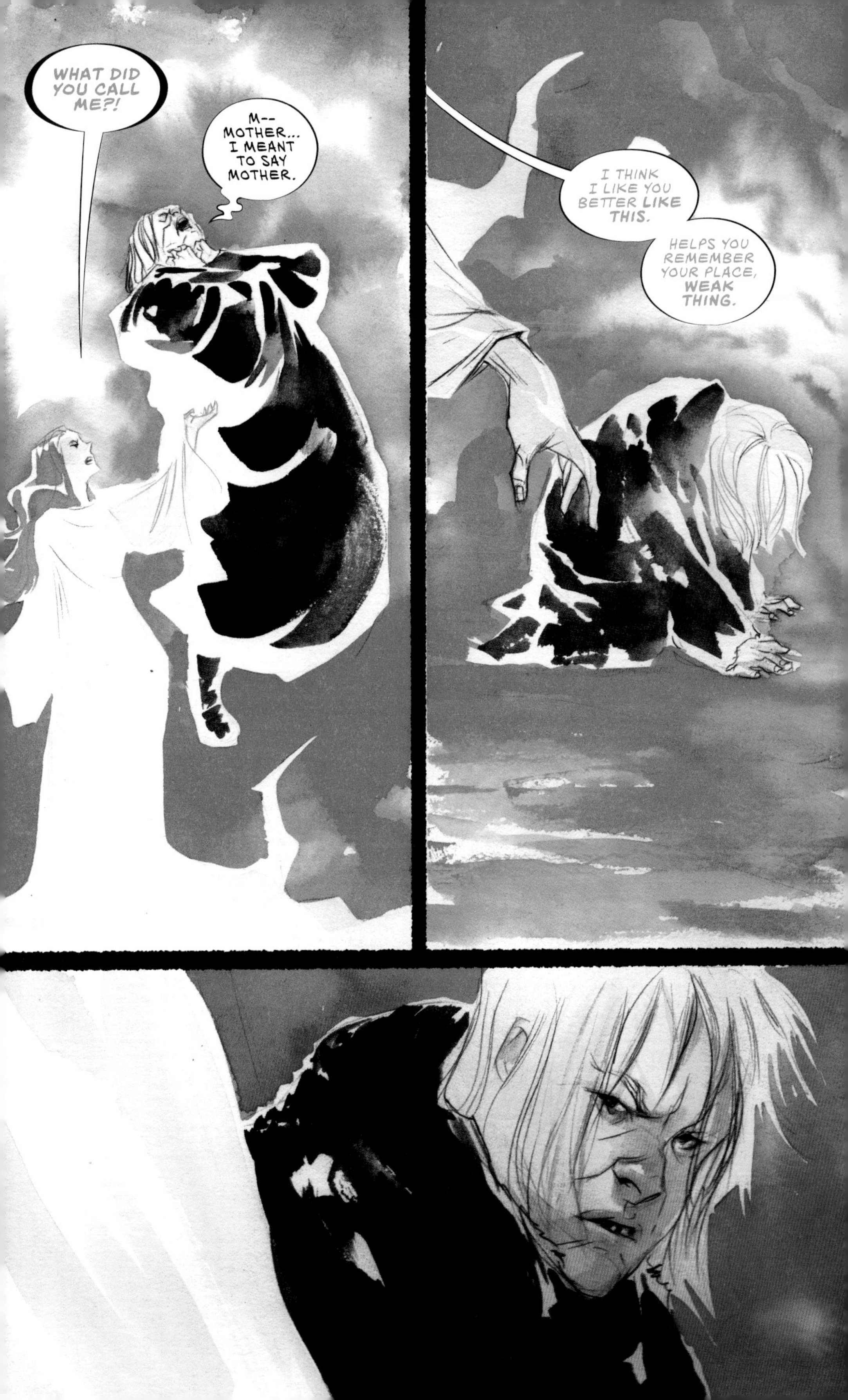
WHAT DID YOU CALL ME?!
M-- MOTHER... I MEANT TO SAY MOTHER.
I THINK I LIKE YOU BETTER LIKE THIS.
HELPS YOU REMEMBER YOUR PLACE, WEAK THING.

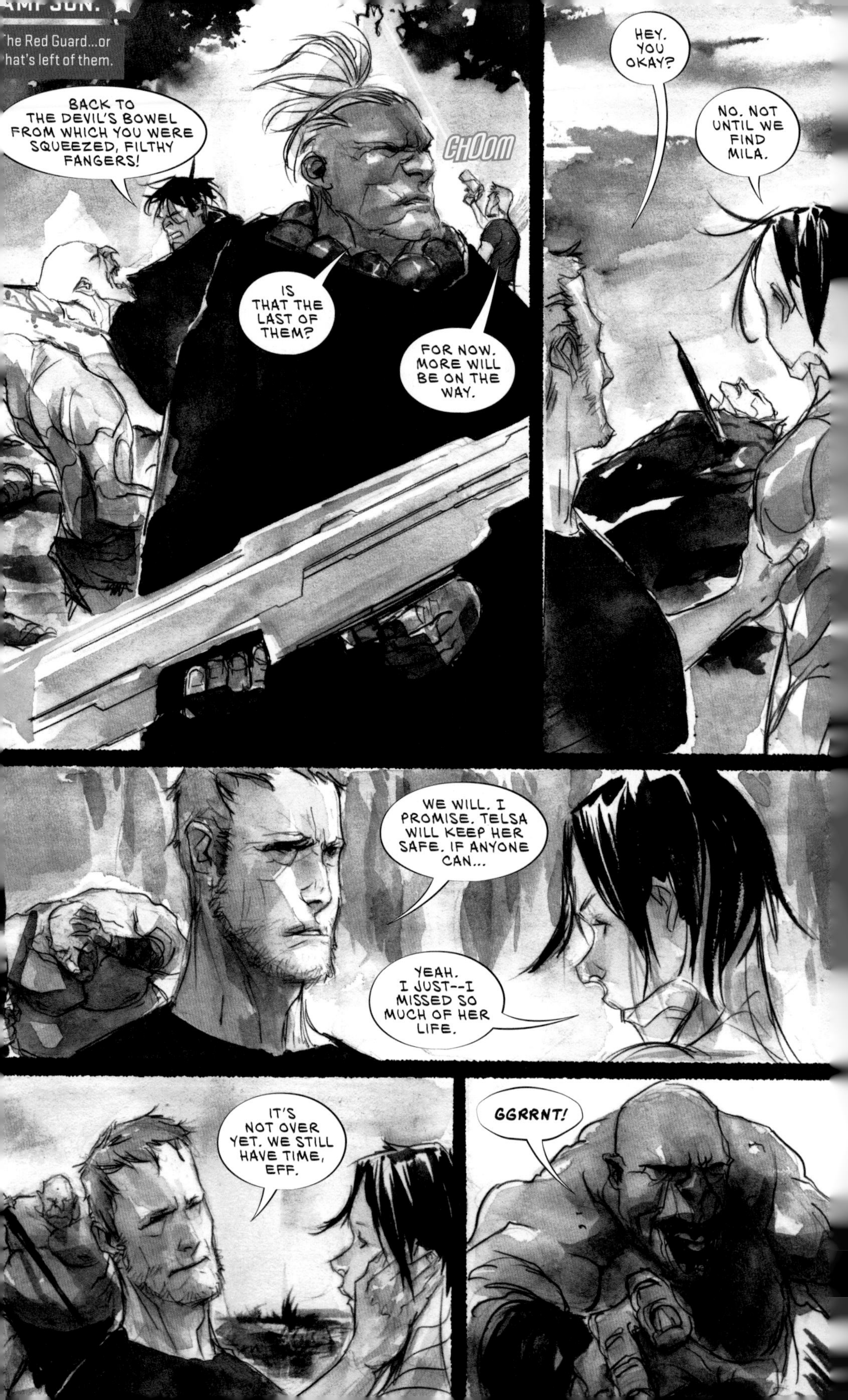

The Red Guard...or what's left of them.
BACK TO THE DEVIL'S BOWEL FROM WHICH YOU WERE SQUEEZED, FILTHY FANGERS!
CHOOM
IS THAT THE LAST OF THEM?
FOR NOW. MORE WILL BE ON THE WAY.
HEY. YOU OKAY?
NO. NOT UNTIL WE FIND MILA.
WE WILL. I PROMISE. TELSA WILL KEEP HER SAFE. IF ANYONE CAN...
YEAH. I JUST--I MISSED SO MUCH OF HER LIFE.
IT'S NOT OVER YET. WE STILL HAVE TIME, EFF.
GGRRNT!

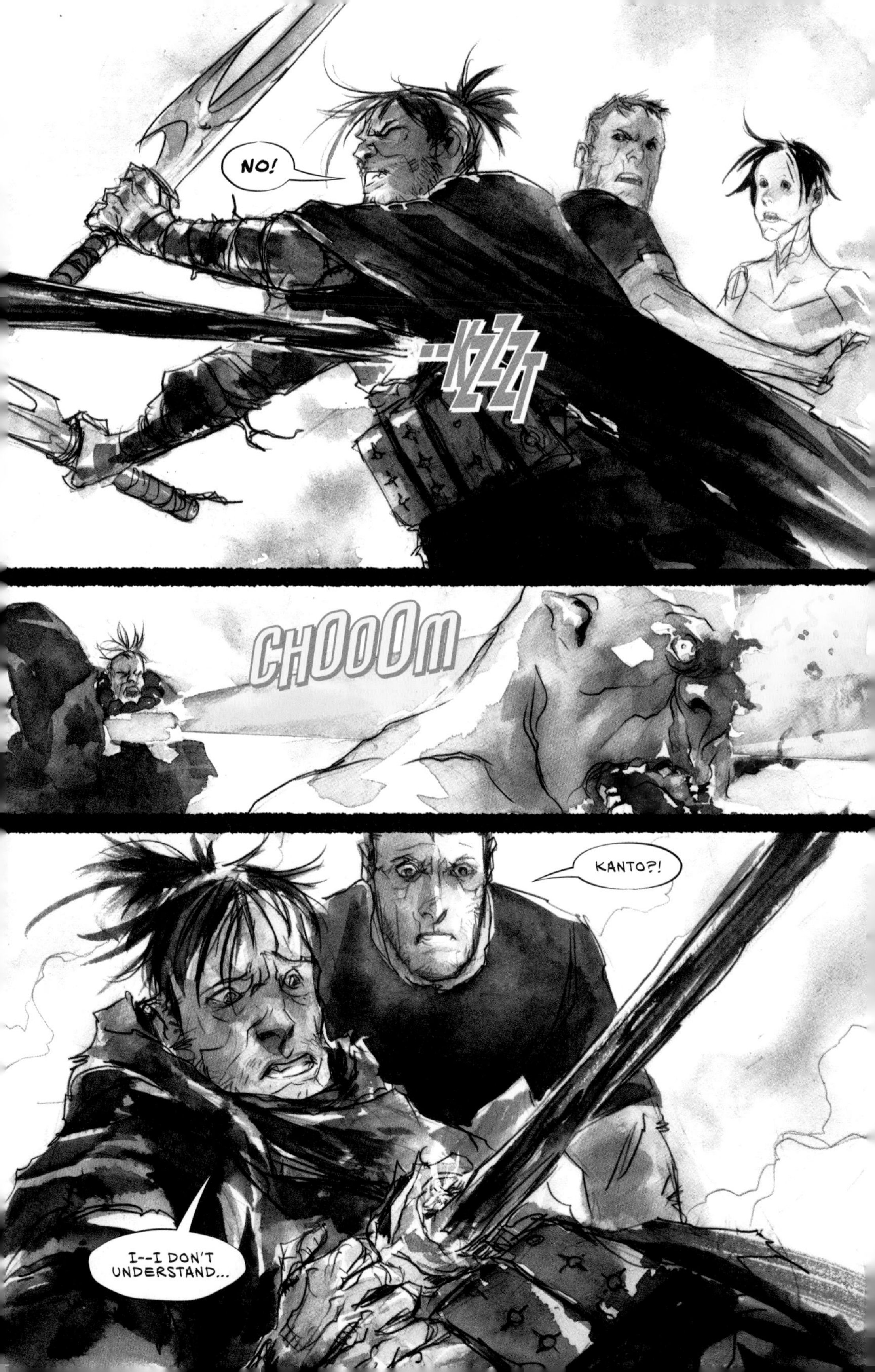
NO!
...KZZZT
CHOOOM
KANTO?!
I--I DON'T UNDERSTAND...

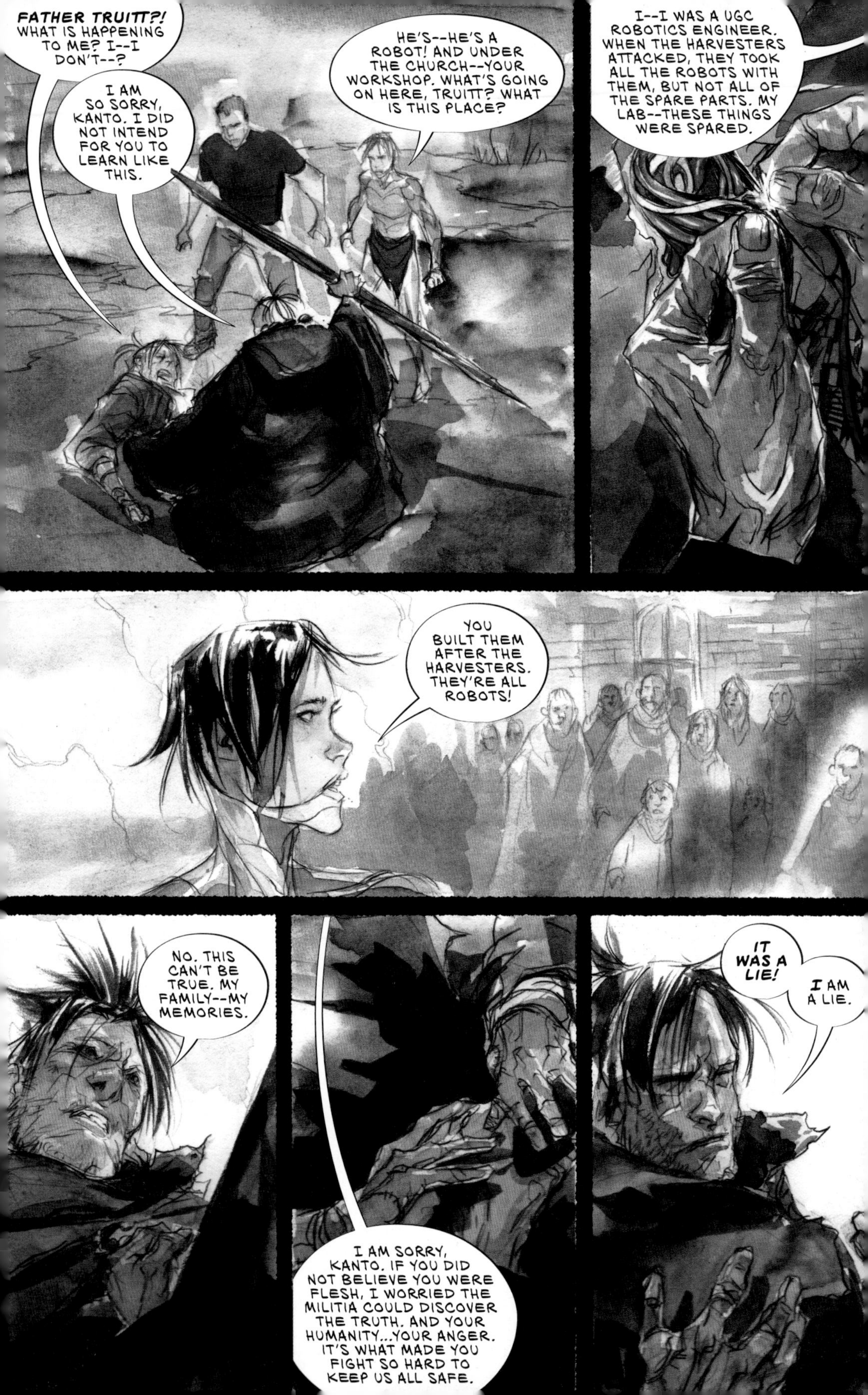
FATHER TRUITT?! WHAT IS HAPPENING TO ME? I--I DON'T--?
I AM SO SORRY, KANTO. I DID NOT INTEND FOR YOU TO LEARN LIKE THIS.
HE'S--HE'S A ROBOT! AND UNDER THE CHURCH--YOUR WORKSHOP. WHAT'S GOING ON HERE, TRUITT? WHAT IS THIS PLACE?
I--I WAS A UGC ROBOTICS ENGINEER. WHEN THE HARVESTERS ATTACKED, THEY TOOK ALL THE ROBOTS WITH THEM, BUT NOT ALL OF THE SPARE PARTS. MY LAB--THESE THINGS WERE SPARED.
YOU BUILT THEM AFTER THE HARVESTERS. THEY'RE ALL ROBOTS!
NO. THIS CAN'T BE TRUE. MY FAMILY--MY MEMORIES.
I AM SORRY, KANTO. IF YOU DID NOT BELIEVE YOU WERE FLESH, I WORRIED THE MILITIA COULD DISCOVER THE TRUTH. AND YOUR HUMANITY...YOUR ANGER. IT'S WHAT MADE YOU FIGHT SO HARD TO KEEP US ALL SAFE.
IT WAS A LIE!
I AM A LIE.

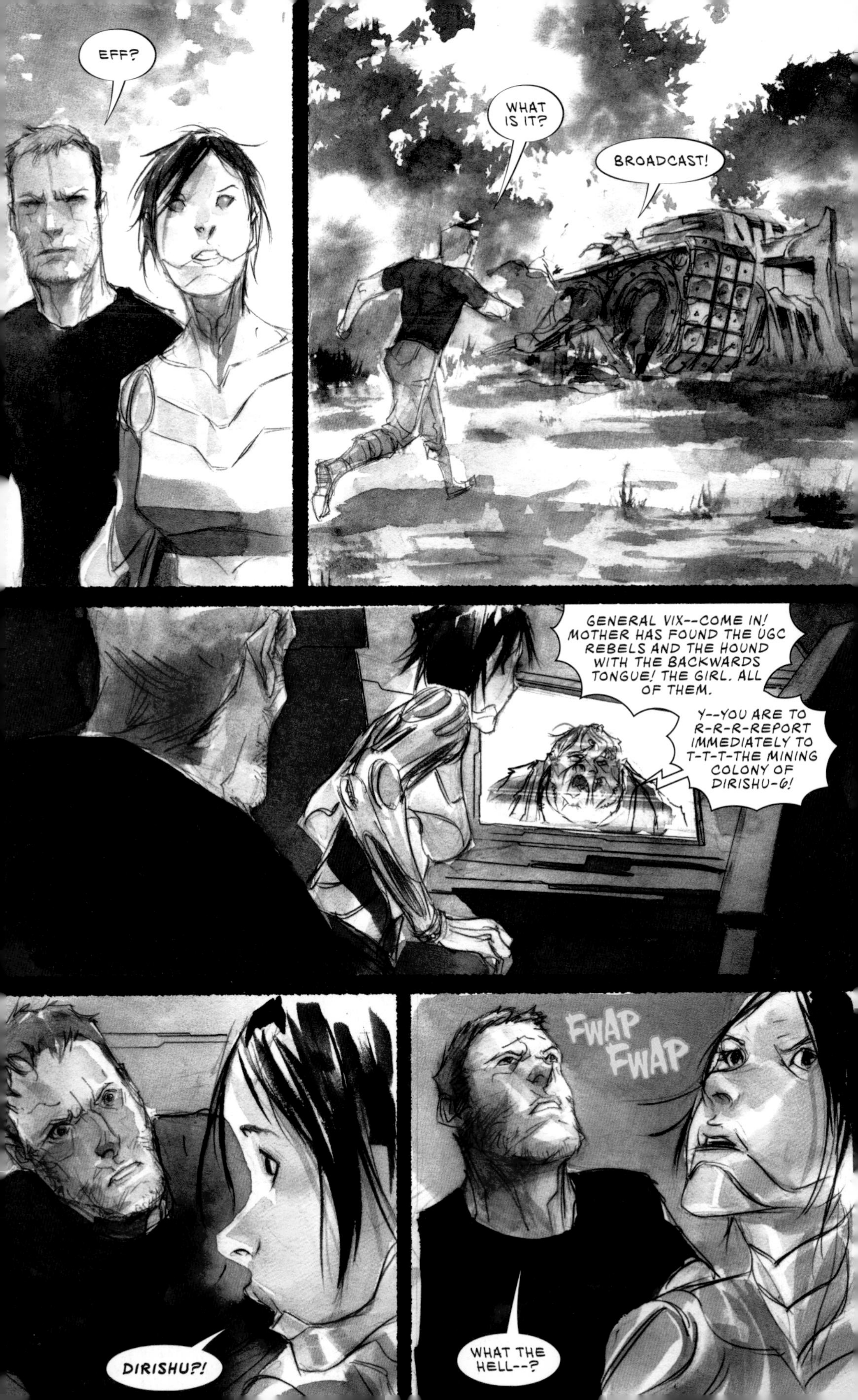
EFF?
WHAT IS IT?
BROADCAST!
GENERAL VIX--COME IN! MOTHER HAS FOUND THE UGC REBELS AND THE HOUND WITH THE BACKWARDS TONGUE! THE GIRL. ALL OF THEM.
Y--YOU ARE TO R-R-R-REPORT IMMEDIATELY TO T-T-T-THE MINING COLONY OF DIRISHU-6!
DIRISHU?!
FWAP FWAP
WHAT THE HELL--?

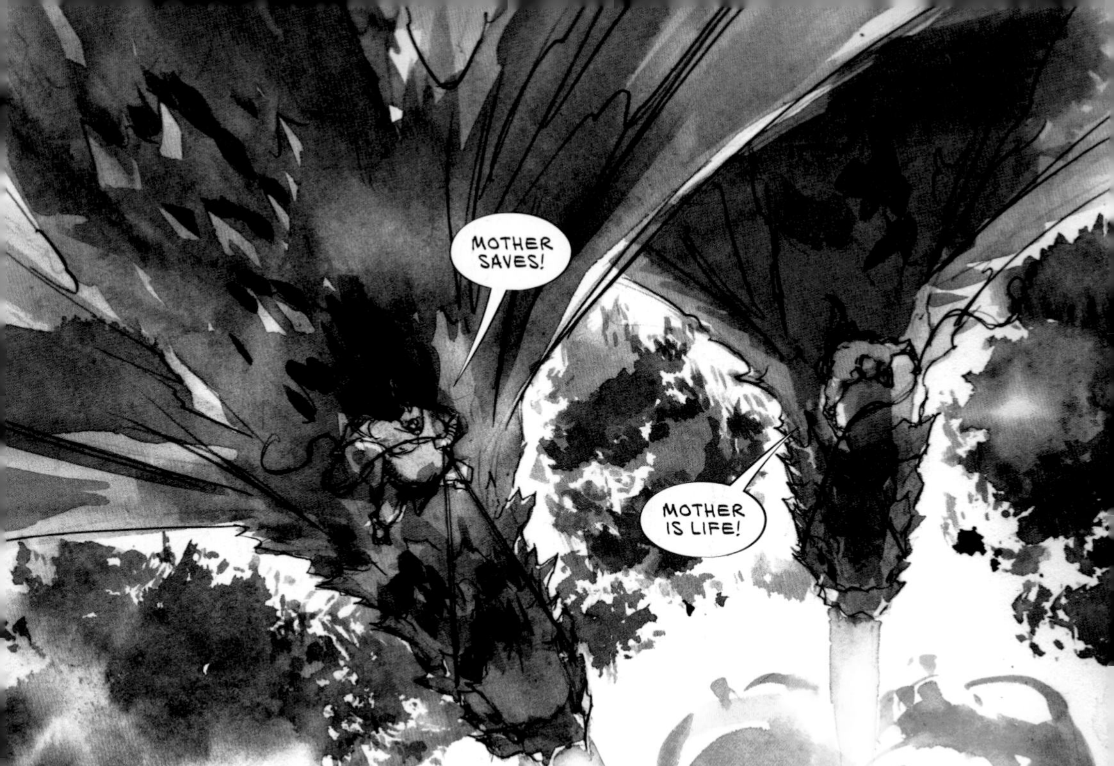
MOTHER SAVES!
MOTHER IS LIFE!
FWOOOSH

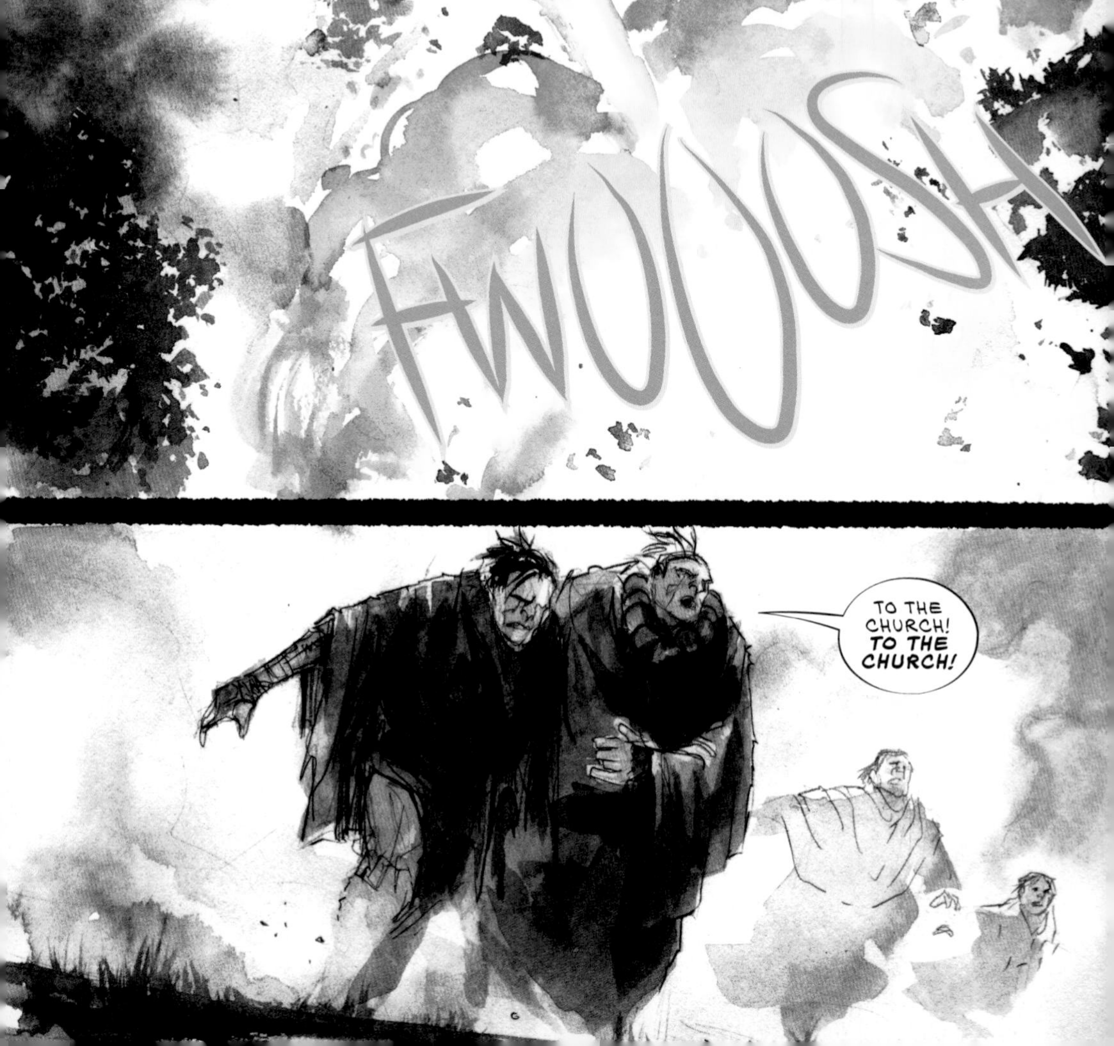
TO THE CHURCH! **TO THE CHURCH!**

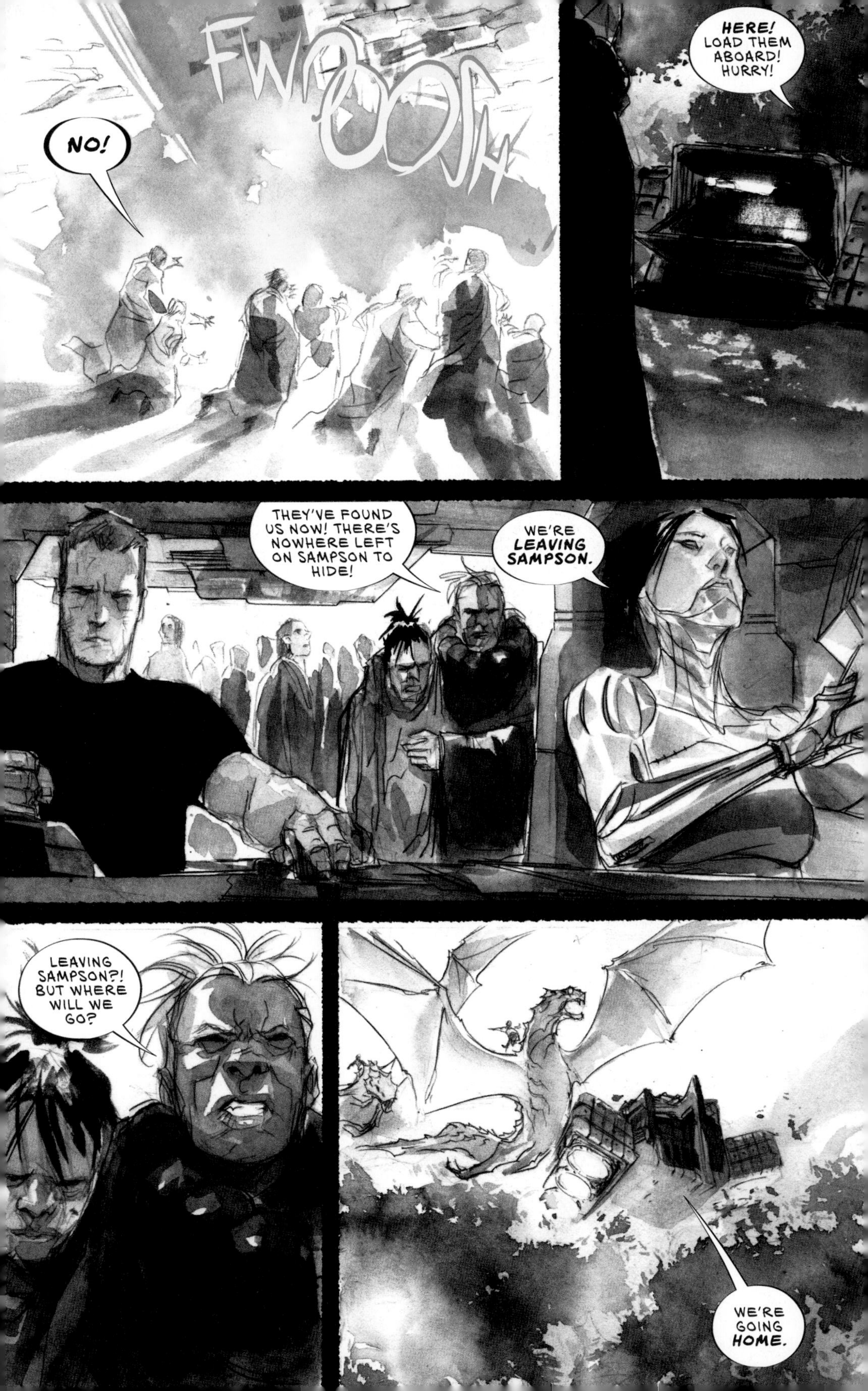
FWOOOM
NO!
HERE! LOAD THEM ABOARD! HURRY!
THEY'VE FOUND US NOW! THERE'S NOWHERE LEFT ON SAMPSON TO HIDE!
WE'RE LEAVING SAMPSON.
LEAVING SAMPSON?! BUT WHERE WILL WE GO?
WE'RE GOING HOME.

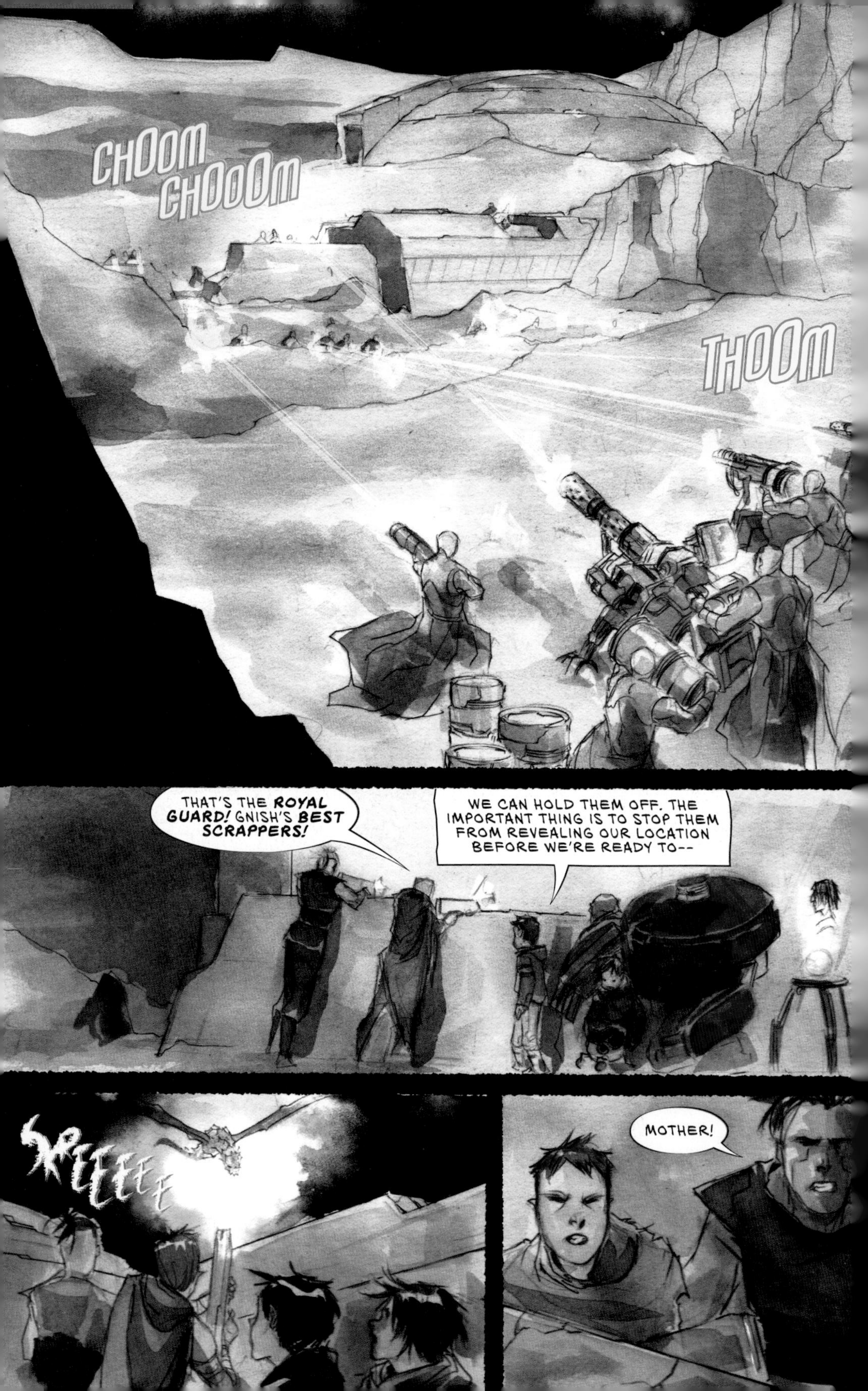
CHOOM CHOOOM
THOOM
THAT'S THE ROYAL GUARD! GNISH'S BEST SCRAPPERS!
WE CAN HOLD THEM OFF. THE IMPORTANT THING IS TO STOP THEM FROM REVEALING OUR LOCATION BEFORE WE'RE READY TO--
SKREEEEE
MOTHER!

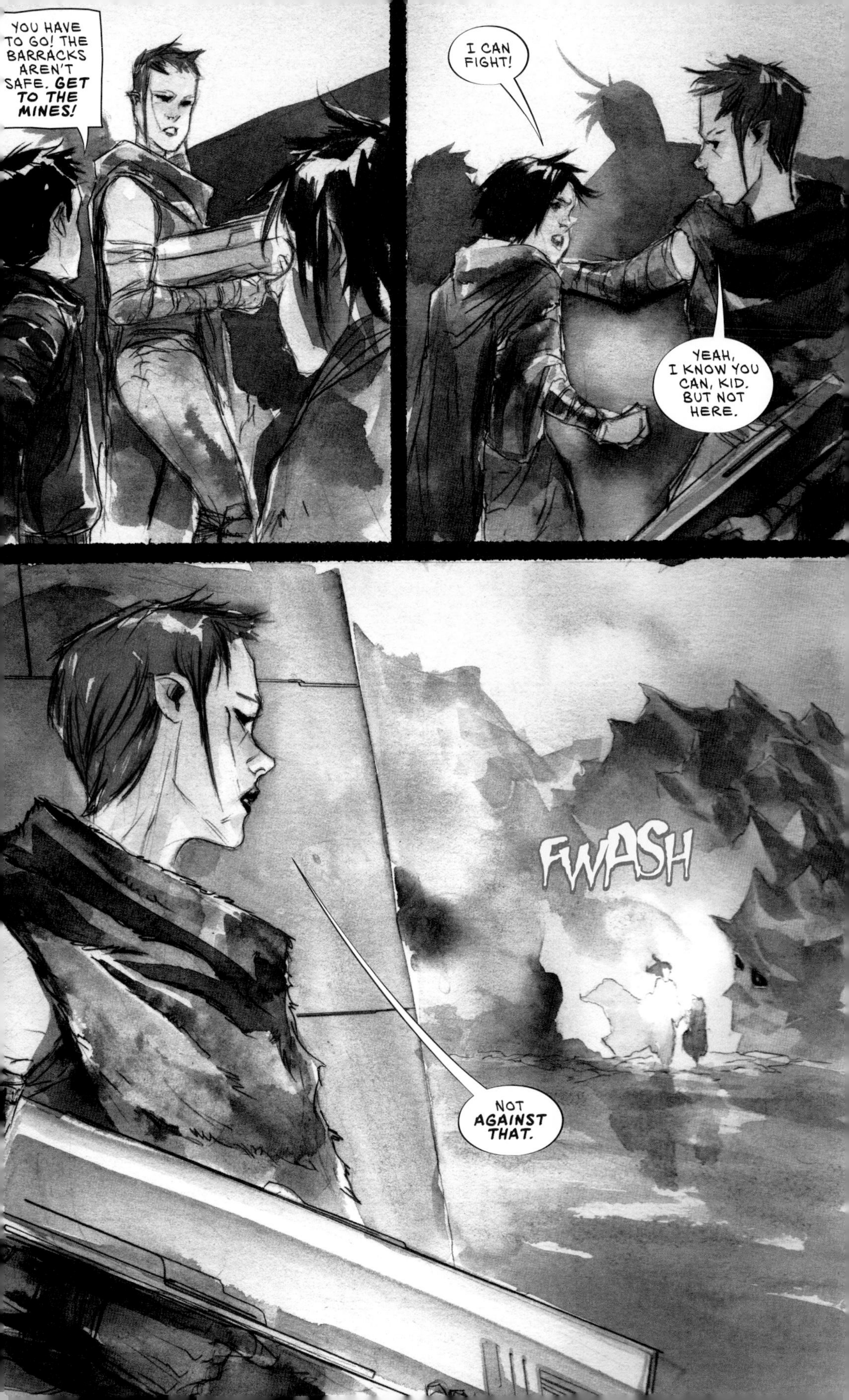
YOU HAVE TO GO! THE BARRACKS AREN'T SAFE. **GET TO THE MINES!**
I CAN FIGHT!
YEAH, I KNOW YOU CAN, KID. BUT NOT HERE.
FWASH
NOT **AGAINST** THAT.

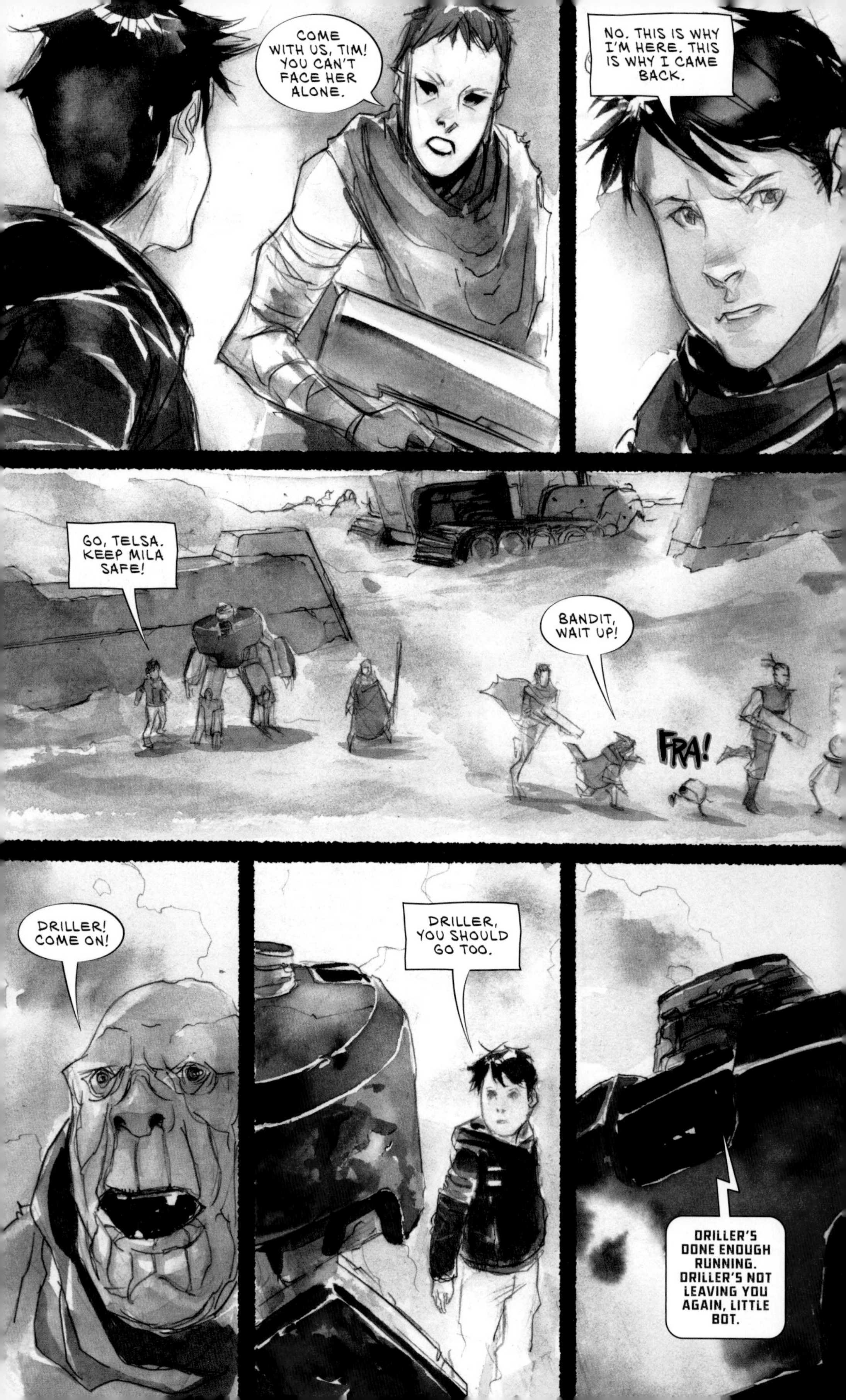
COME WITH US, TIM! YOU CAN'T FACE HER ALONE.
NO. THIS IS WHY I'M HERE. THIS IS WHY I CAME BACK.
GO, TELSA. KEEP MILA SAFE!
BANDIT, WAIT UP!
FRA!
DRILLER! COME ON!
DRILLER, YOU SHOULD GO TOO.
DRILLER'S DONE ENOUGH RUNNING. DRILLER'S NOT LEAVING YOU AGAIN, LITTLE BOT.

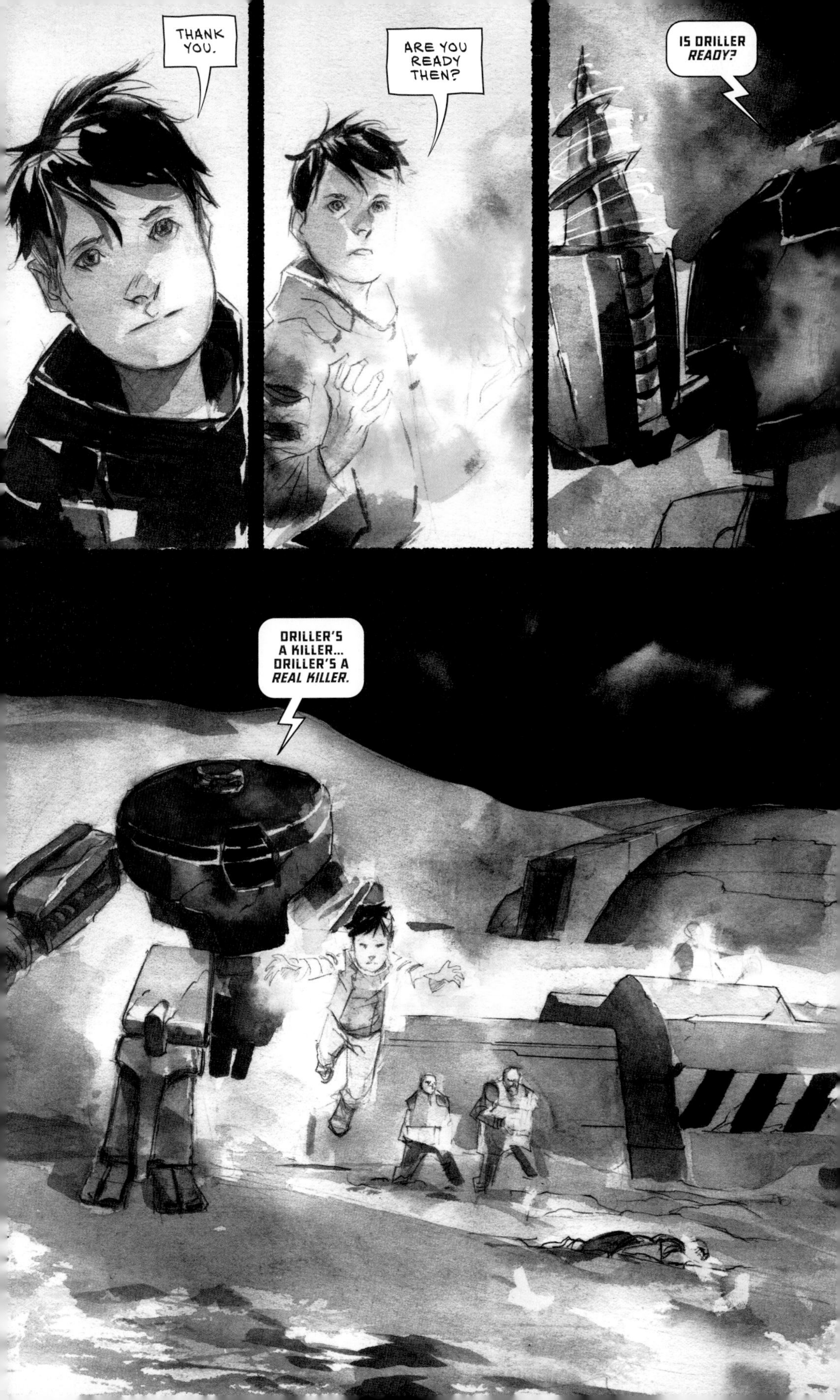
THANK YOU.
ARE YOU READY THEN?
IS DRILLER *READY?*
DRILLER'S A KILLER... DRILLER'S A *REAL KILLER.*

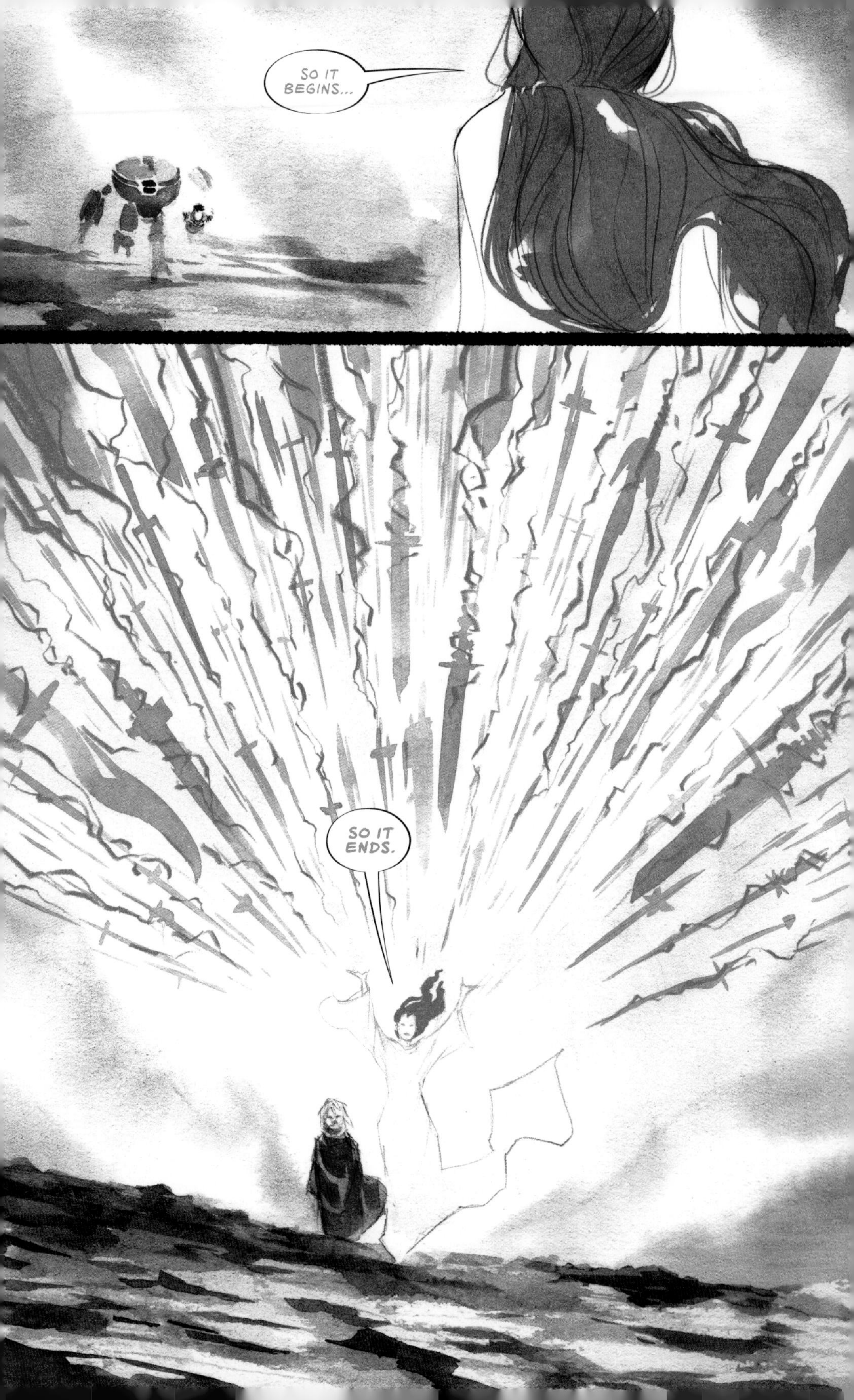

SO IT BEGINS...
SO IT ENDS.

17

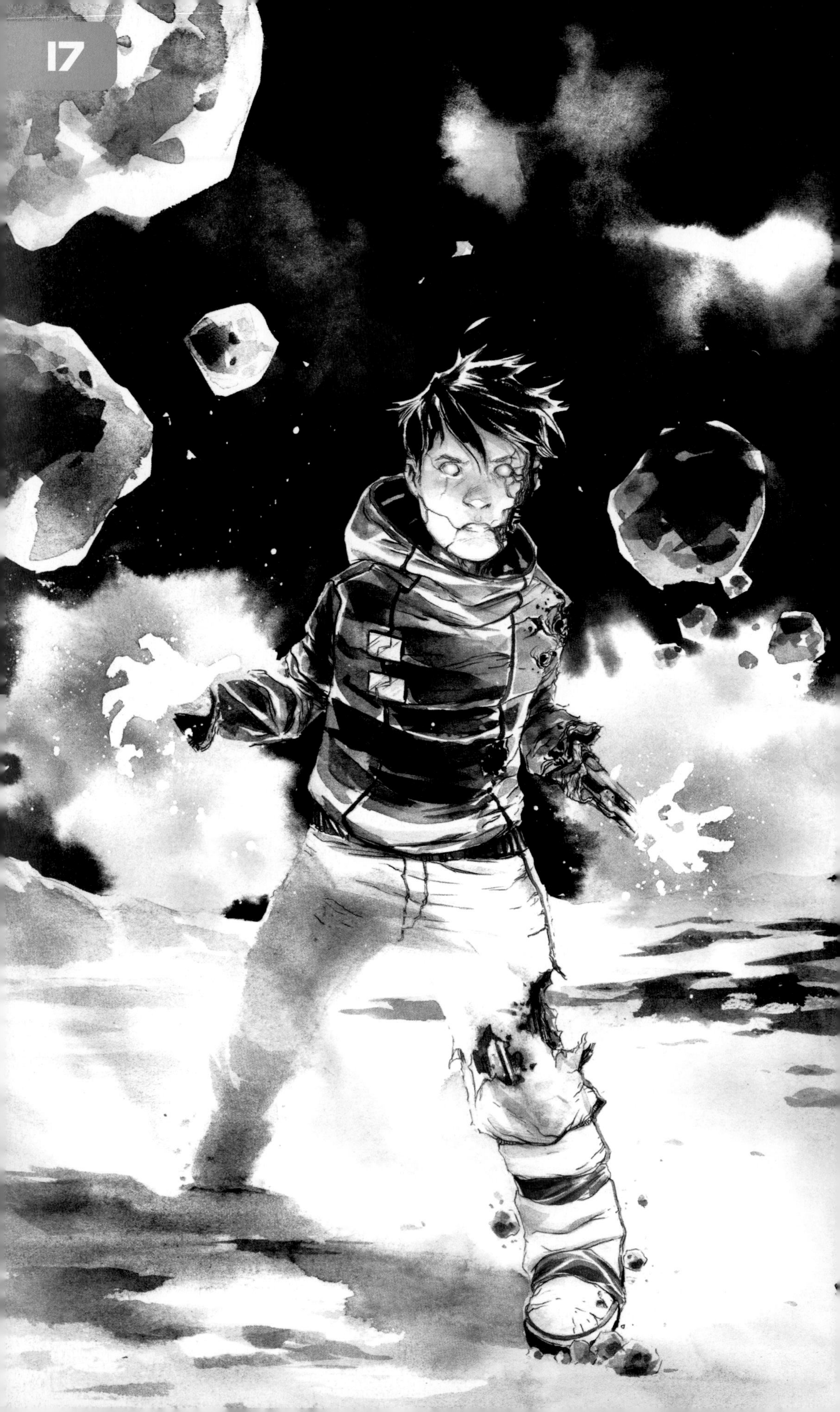

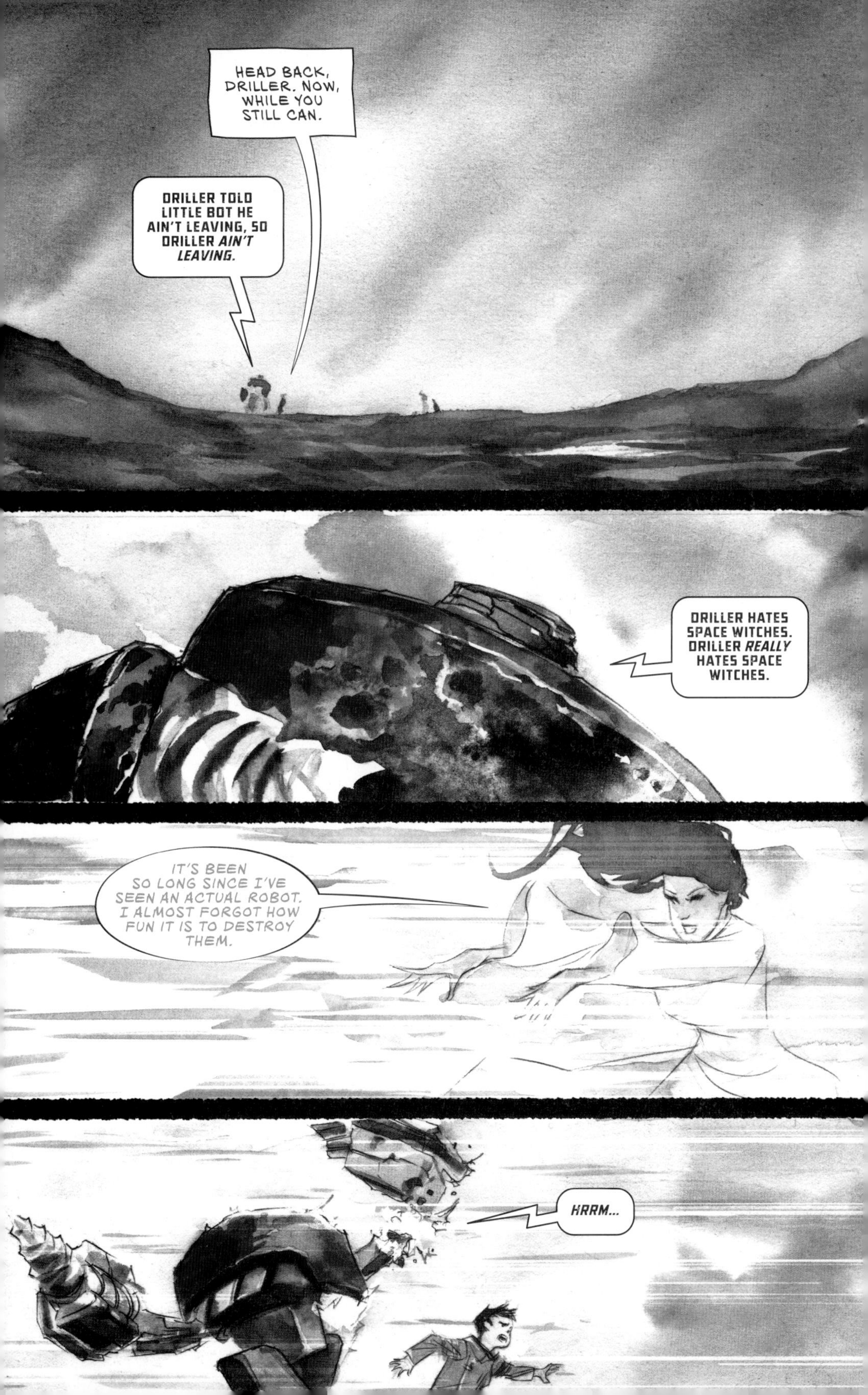
HEAD BACK, DRILLER. NOW, WHILE YOU STILL CAN.
DRILLER TOLD LITTLE BOT HE AIN'T LEAVING, SO DRILLER *AIN'T LEAVING.*
DRILLER HATES SPACE WITCHES. DRILLER *REALLY* HATES SPACE WITCHES.
IT'S BEEN SO LONG SINCE I'VE SEEN AN ACTUAL ROBOT. I ALMOST FORGOT HOW FUN IT IS TO DESTROY THEM.
HRRM...

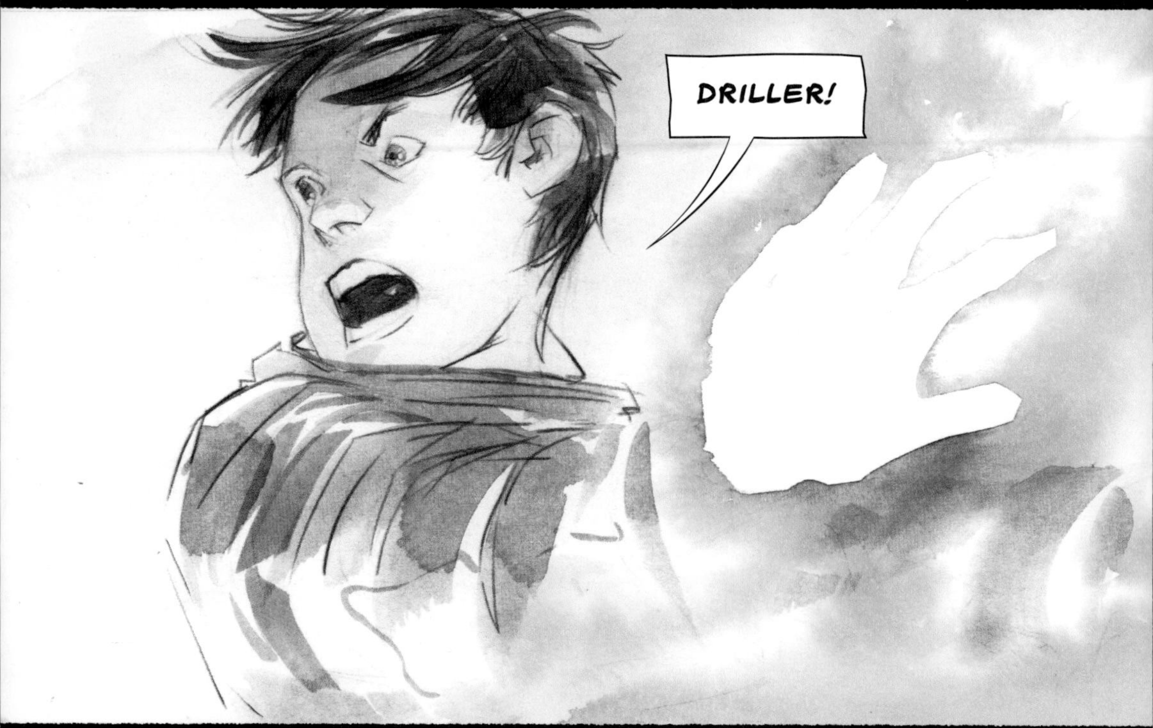
DRILLER!

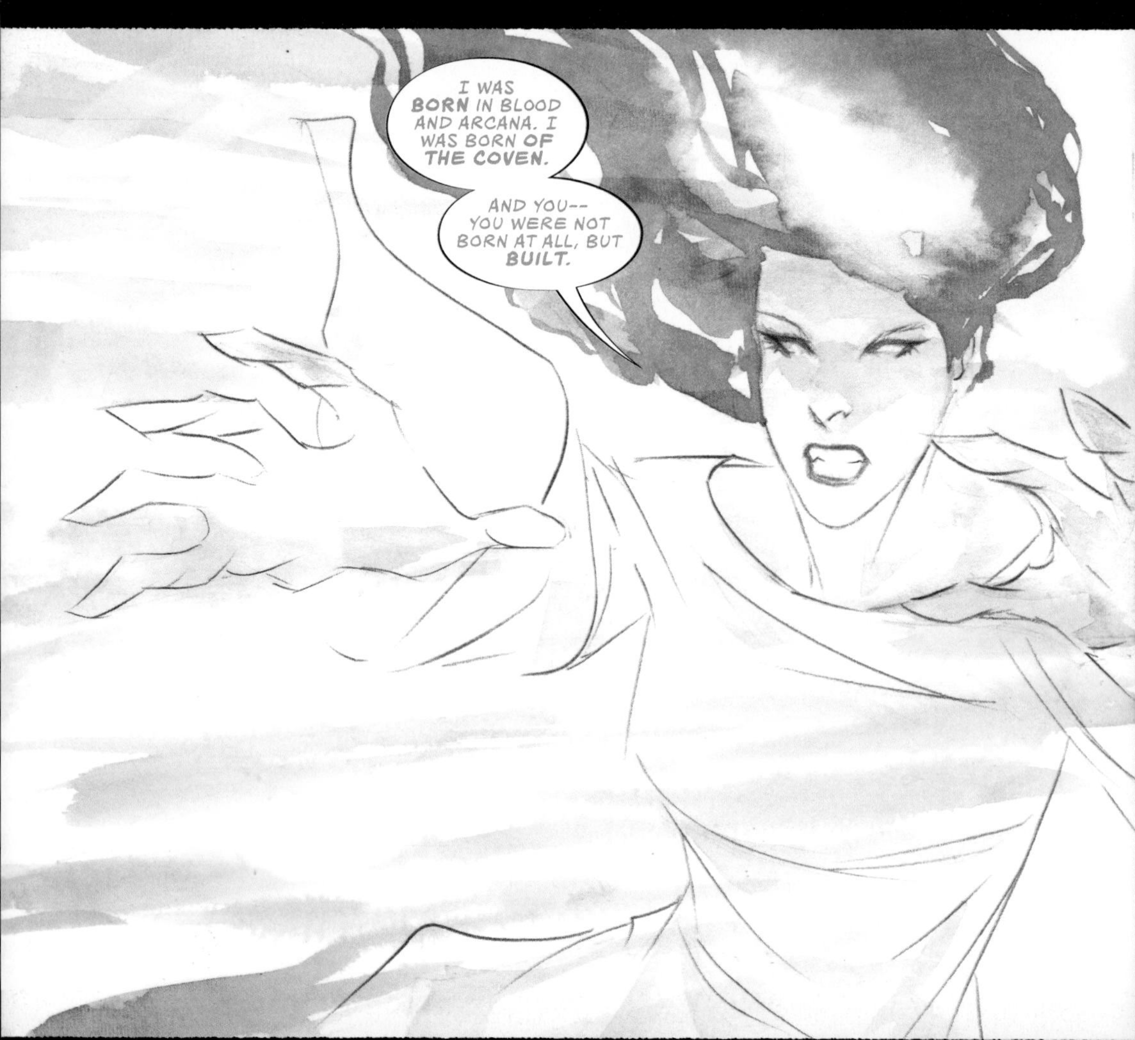
I WAS BORN IN BLOOD AND ARCANA. I WAS BORN OF THE COVEN.
AND YOU-- YOU WERE NOT BORN AT ALL, BUT BUILT.

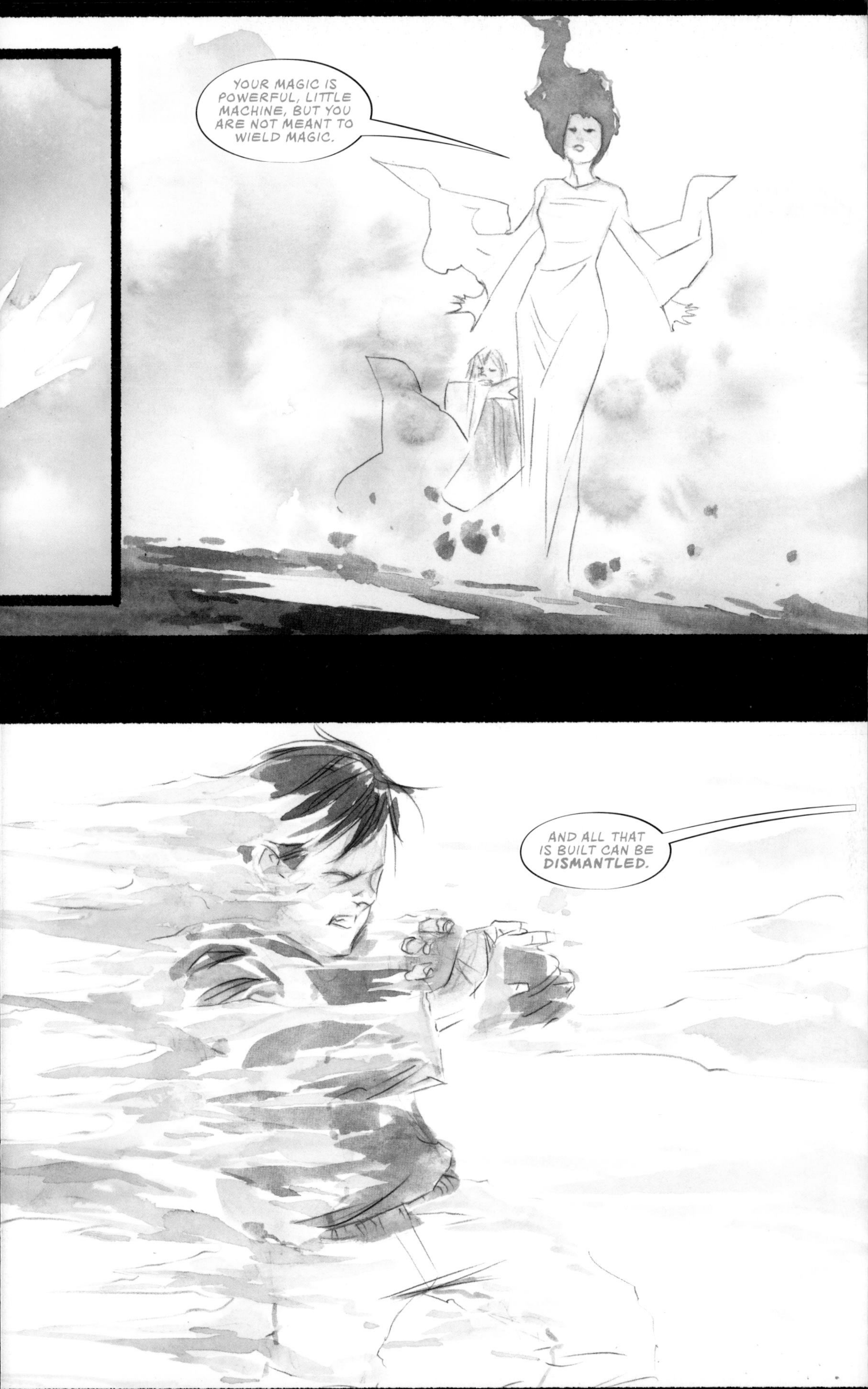
YOUR MAGIC IS POWERFUL, LITTLE MACHINE, BUT YOU ARE NOT MEANT TO WIELD MAGIC.
AND ALL THAT IS BUILT CAN BE DISMANTLED.

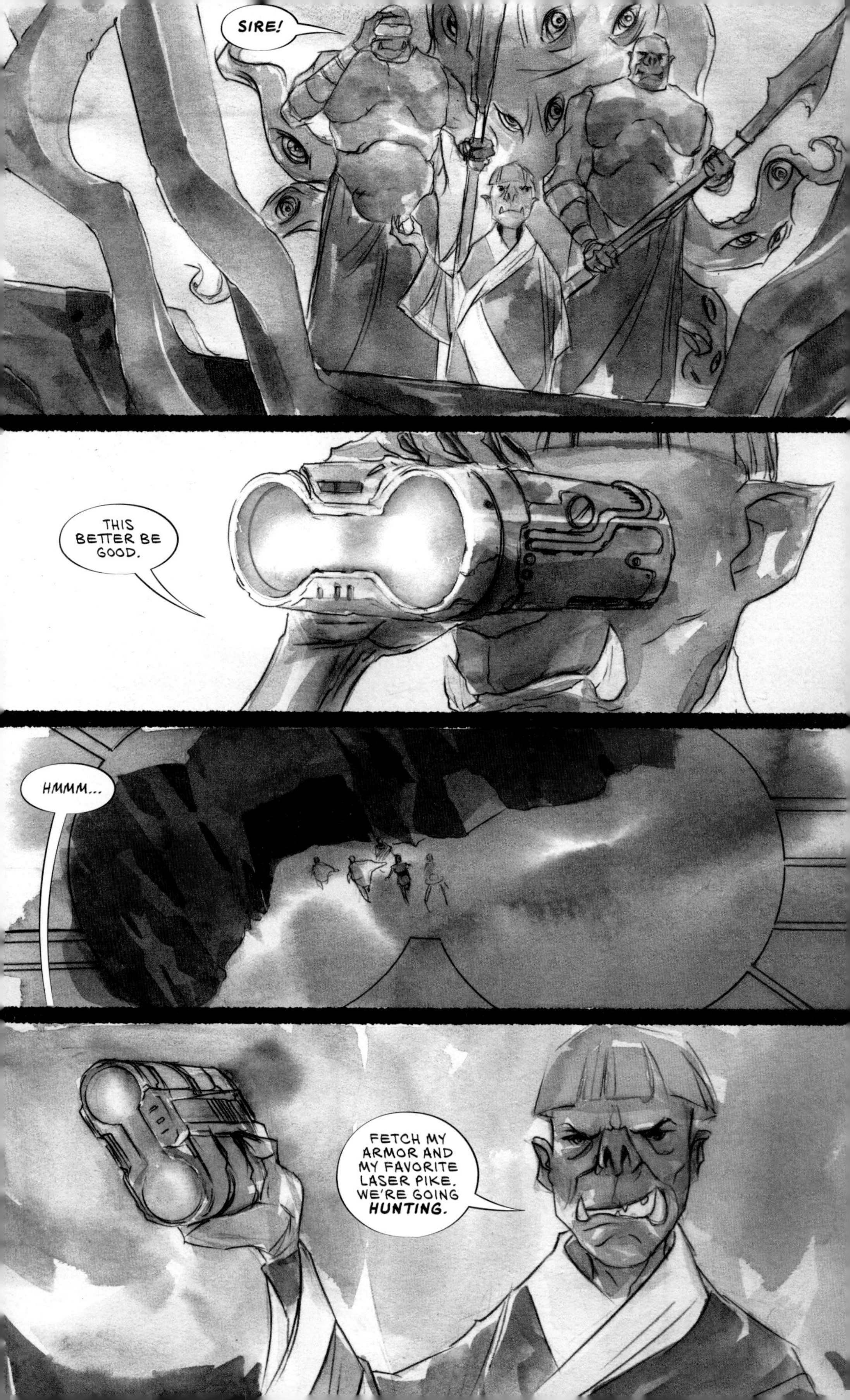
SIRE!
THIS BETTER BE GOOD.
HMMM...
FETCH MY ARMOR AND MY FAVORITE LASER PIKE. WE'RE GOING **HUNTING**.

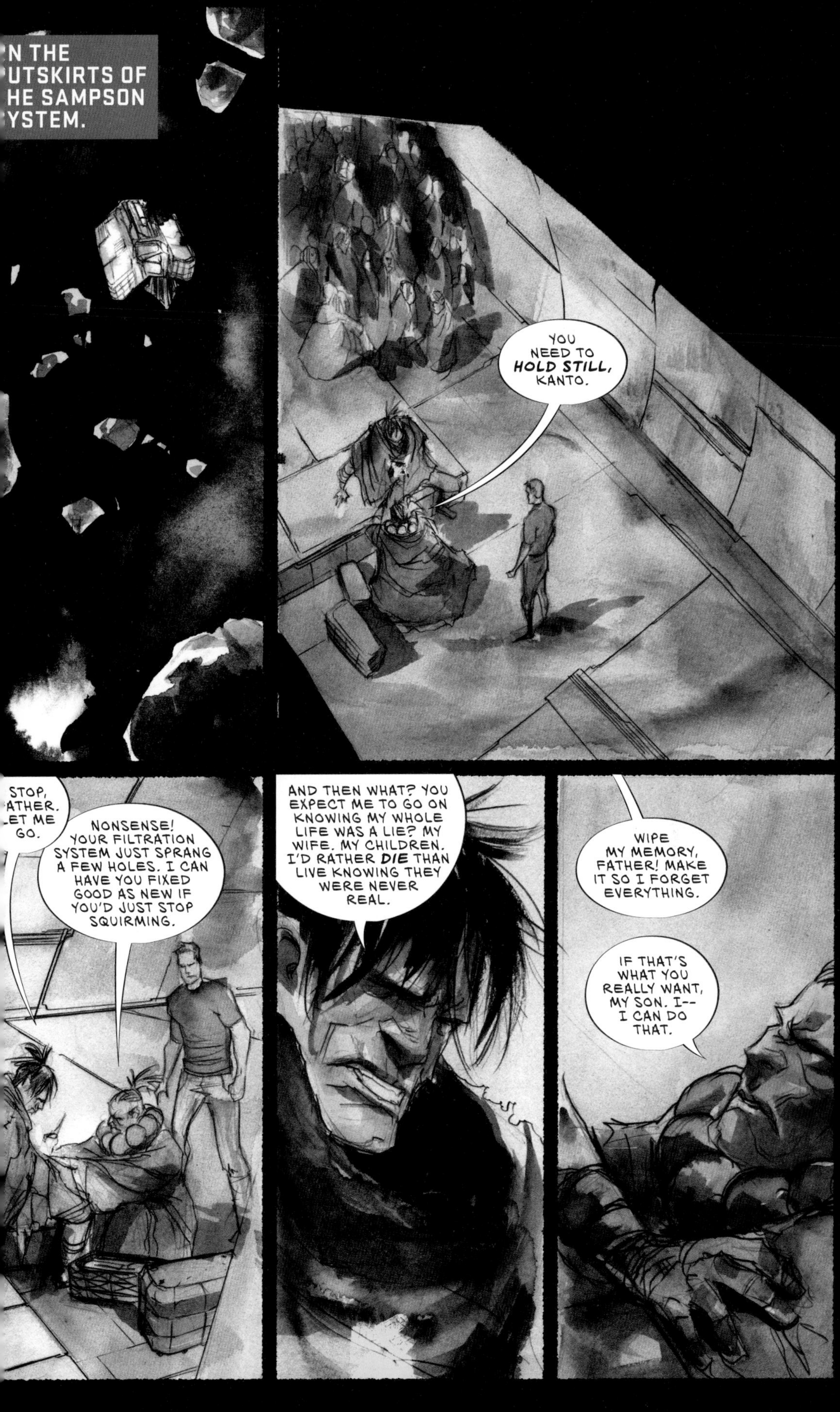
N THE
UTSKIRTS OF
HE SAMPSON
YSTEM.
YOU NEED TO HOLD STILL, KANTO.
STOP, ATHER. ET ME GO.
NONSENSE! YOUR FILTRATION SYSTEM JUST SPRANG A FEW HOLES. I CAN HAVE YOU FIXED GOOD AS NEW IF YOU'D JUST STOP SQUIRMING.
AND THEN WHAT? YOU EXPECT ME TO GO ON KNOWING MY WHOLE LIFE WAS A LIE? MY WIFE. MY CHILDREN. I'D RATHER DIE THAN LIVE KNOWING THEY WERE NEVER REAL.
WIPE MY MEMORY, FATHER! MAKE IT SO I FORGET EVERYTHING.
IF THAT'S WHAT YOU REALLY WANT, MY SON. I-- I CAN DO THAT.

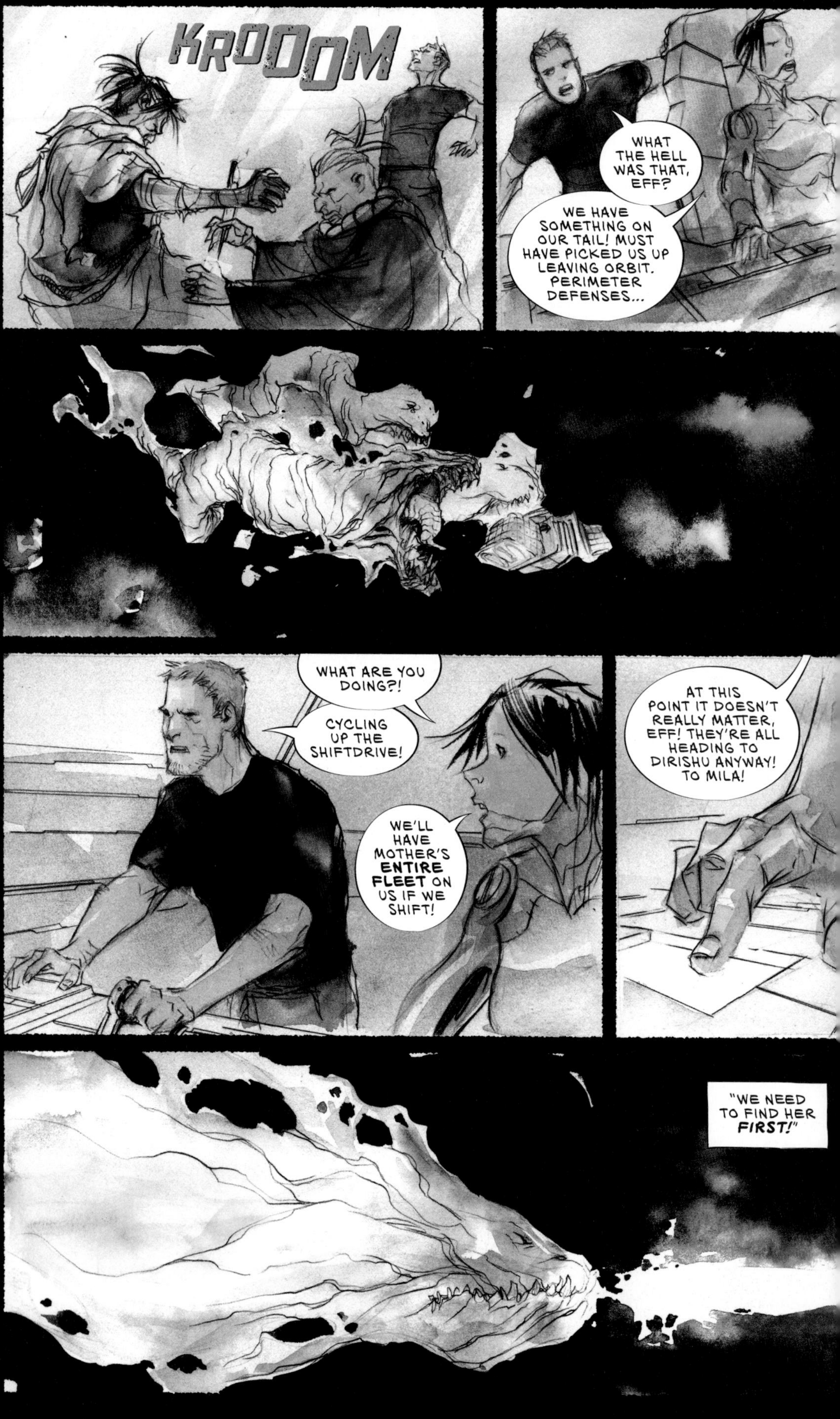
KROOOM
WHAT THE HELL WAS THAT, EFF?
WE HAVE SOMETHING ON OUR TAIL! MUST HAVE PICKED US UP LEAVING ORBIT. PERIMETER DEFENSES...
WHAT ARE YOU DOING?!
CYCLING UP THE SHIFTDRIVE!
WE'LL HAVE MOTHER'S **ENTIRE FLEET** ON US IF WE SHIFT!
AT THIS POINT IT DOESN'T REALLY MATTER, EFF! THEY'RE ALL HEADING TO DIRISHU ANYWAY! TO MILA!
"WE NEED TO FIND HER ***FIRST!***"

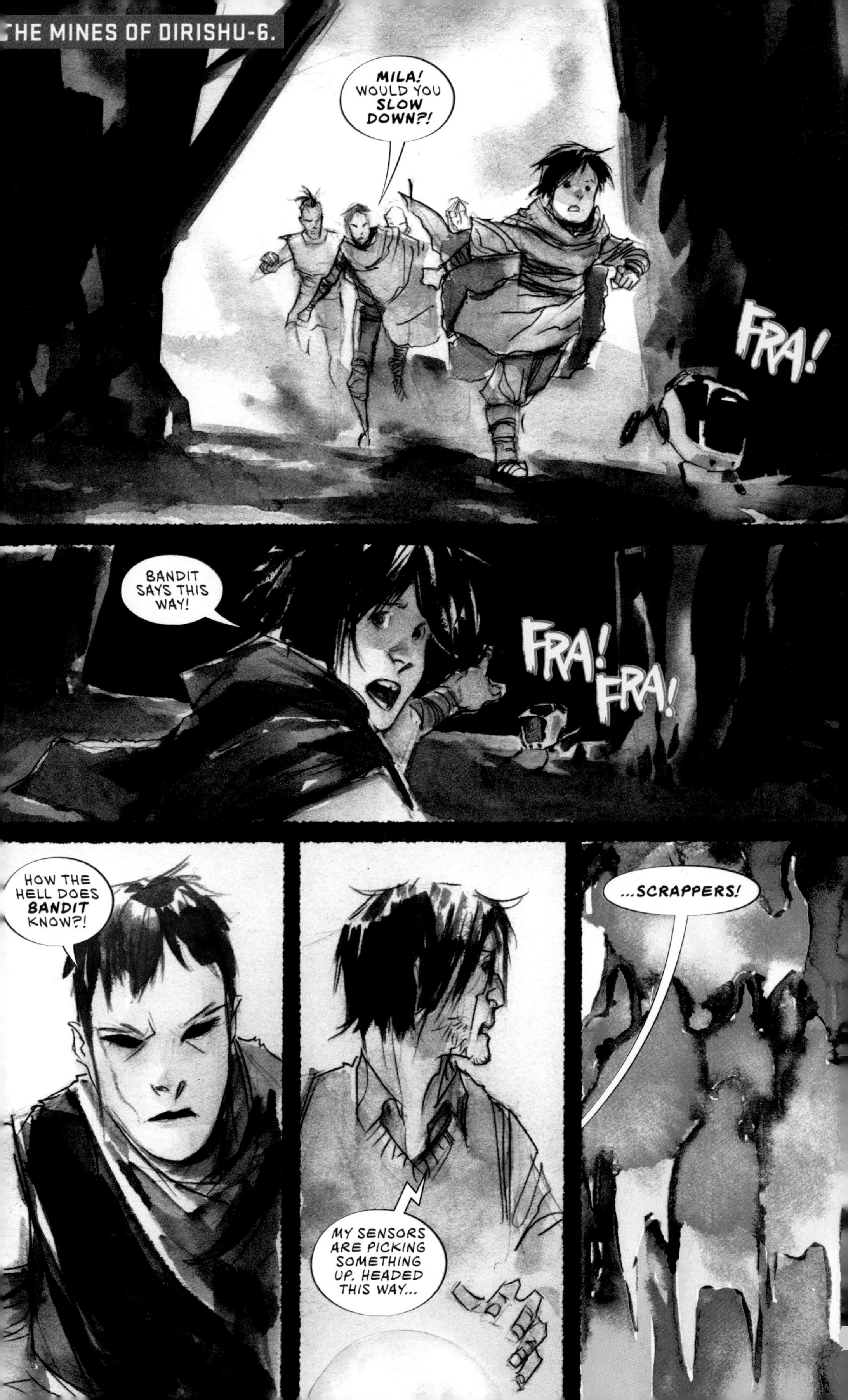
THE MINES OF DIRISHU-6.
MILA! WOULD YOU SLOW DOWN?!
FRA!
BANDIT SAYS THIS WAY!
FRA! FRA!
HOW THE HELL DOES BANDIT KNOW?!
MY SENSORS ARE PICKING SOMETHING UP. HEADED THIS WAY...
...SCRAPPERS!

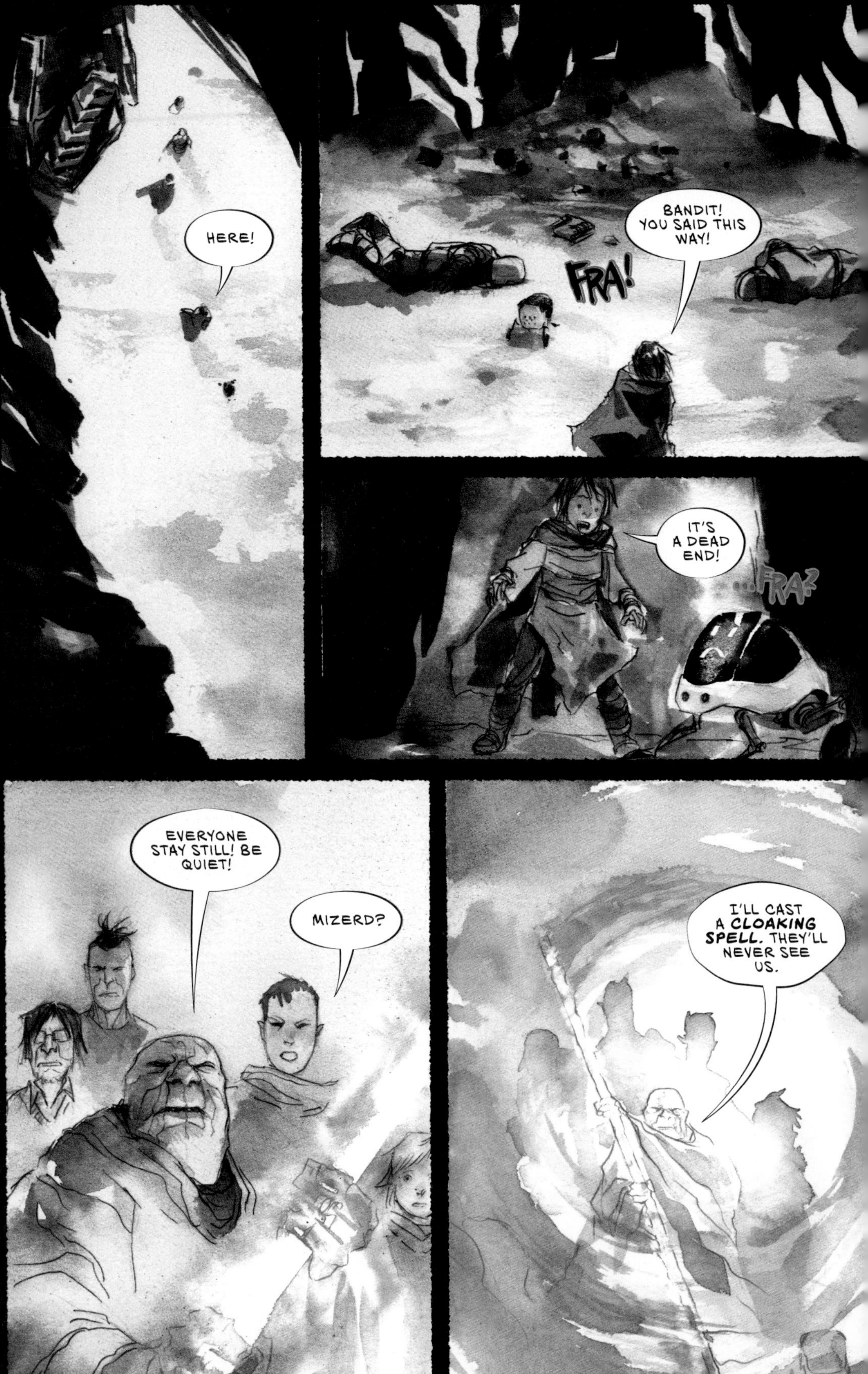
HERE!
BANDIT! YOU SAID THIS WAY!
FRA!
IT'S A DEAD END!
...FRA?
EVERYONE STAY STILL! BE QUIET!
MIZERD?
I'LL CAST A **CLOAKING SPELL.** THEY'LL NEVER SEE US.

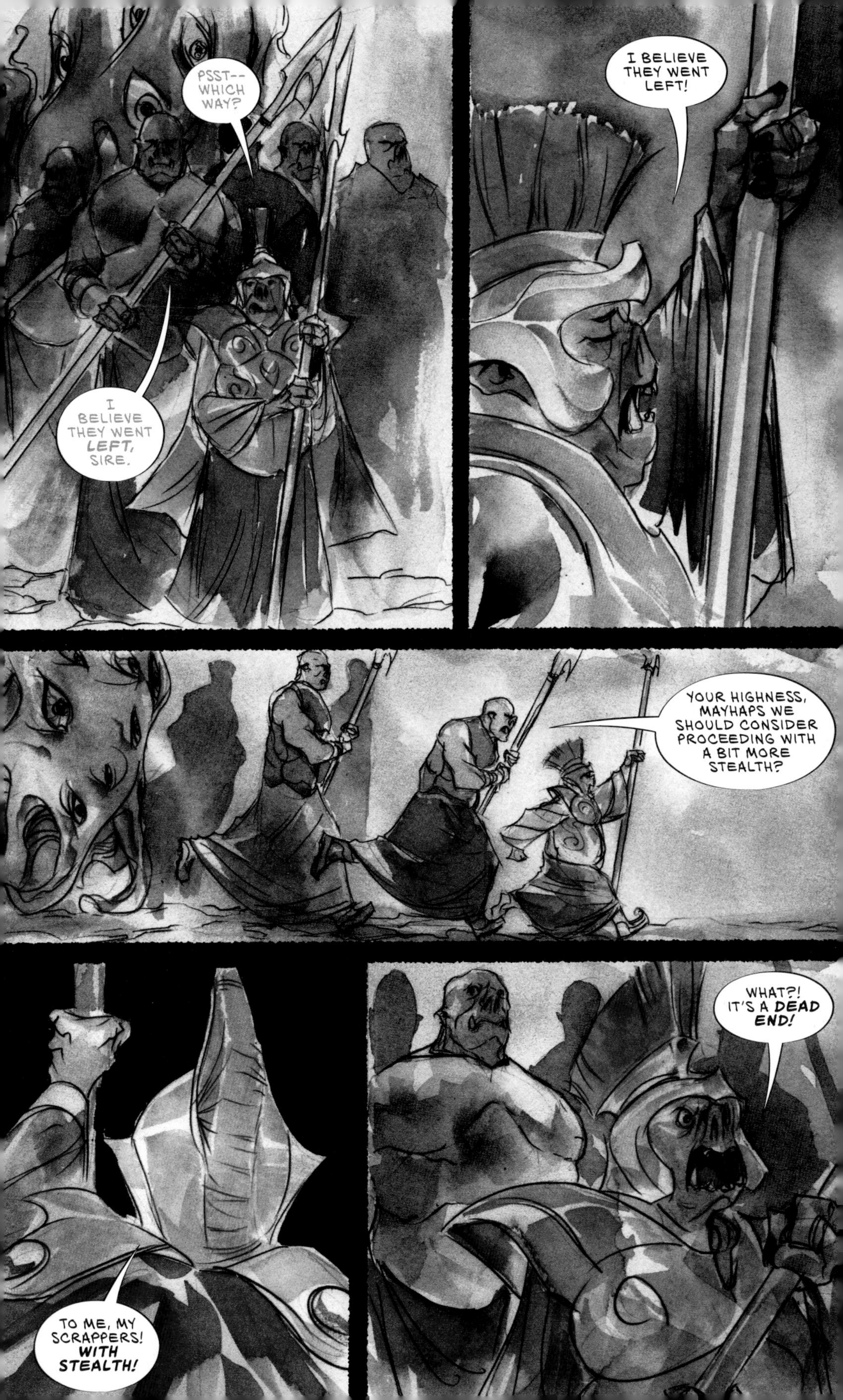
PSST-- WHICH WAY?
I BELIEVE THEY WENT LEFT, SIRE.
I BELIEVE THEY WENT LEFT!
YOUR HIGHNESS, MAYHAPS WE SHOULD CONSIDER PROCEEDING WITH A BIT MORE STEALTH?
TO ME, MY SCRAPPERS! WITH STEALTH!
WHAT?! IT'S A DEAD END!

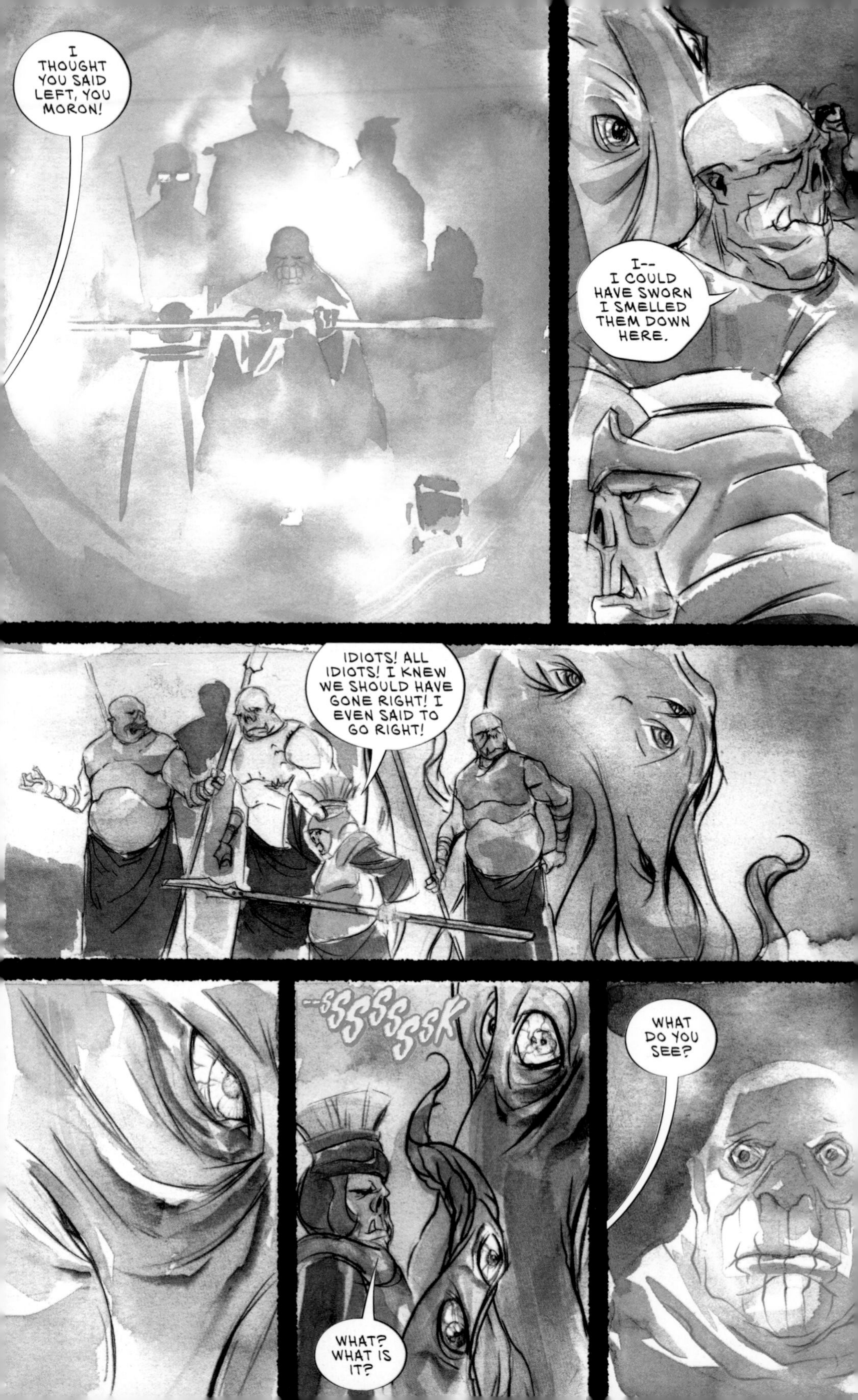
I THOUGHT YOU SAID LEFT, YOU MORON!
I-- I COULD HAVE SWORN I SMELLED THEM DOWN HERE.
IDIOTS! ALL IDIOTS! I KNEW WE SHOULD HAVE GONE RIGHT! I EVEN SAID TO GO RIGHT!
--SSSSSSK
WHAT? WHAT IS IT?
WHAT DO YOU SEE?

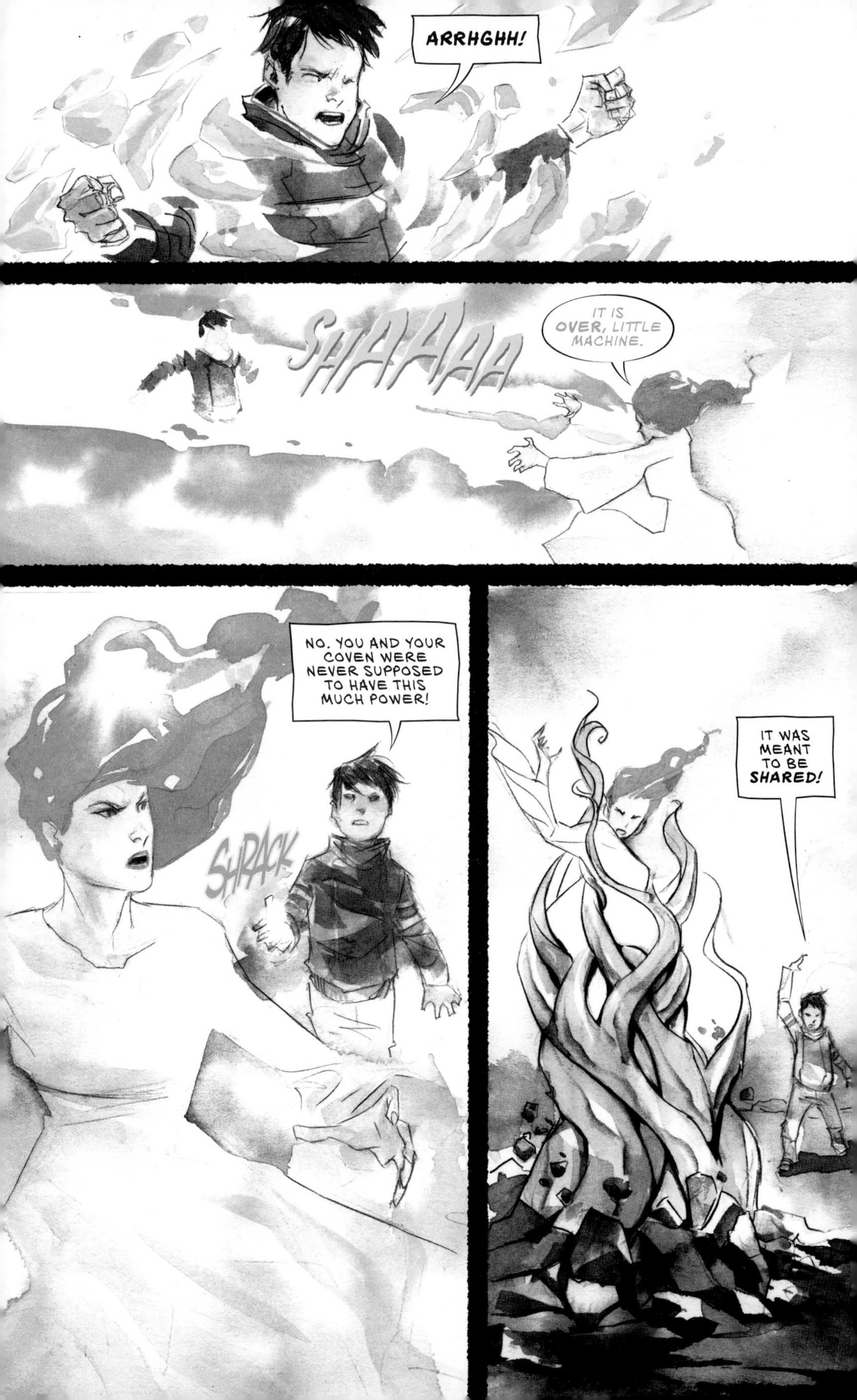
ARRHGHH!
SHAAAAA
IT IS OVER, LITTLE MACHINE.
NO. YOU AND YOUR COVEN WERE NEVER SUPPOSED TO HAVE THIS MUCH POWER!
SHRACK
IT WAS MEANT TO BE SHARED!

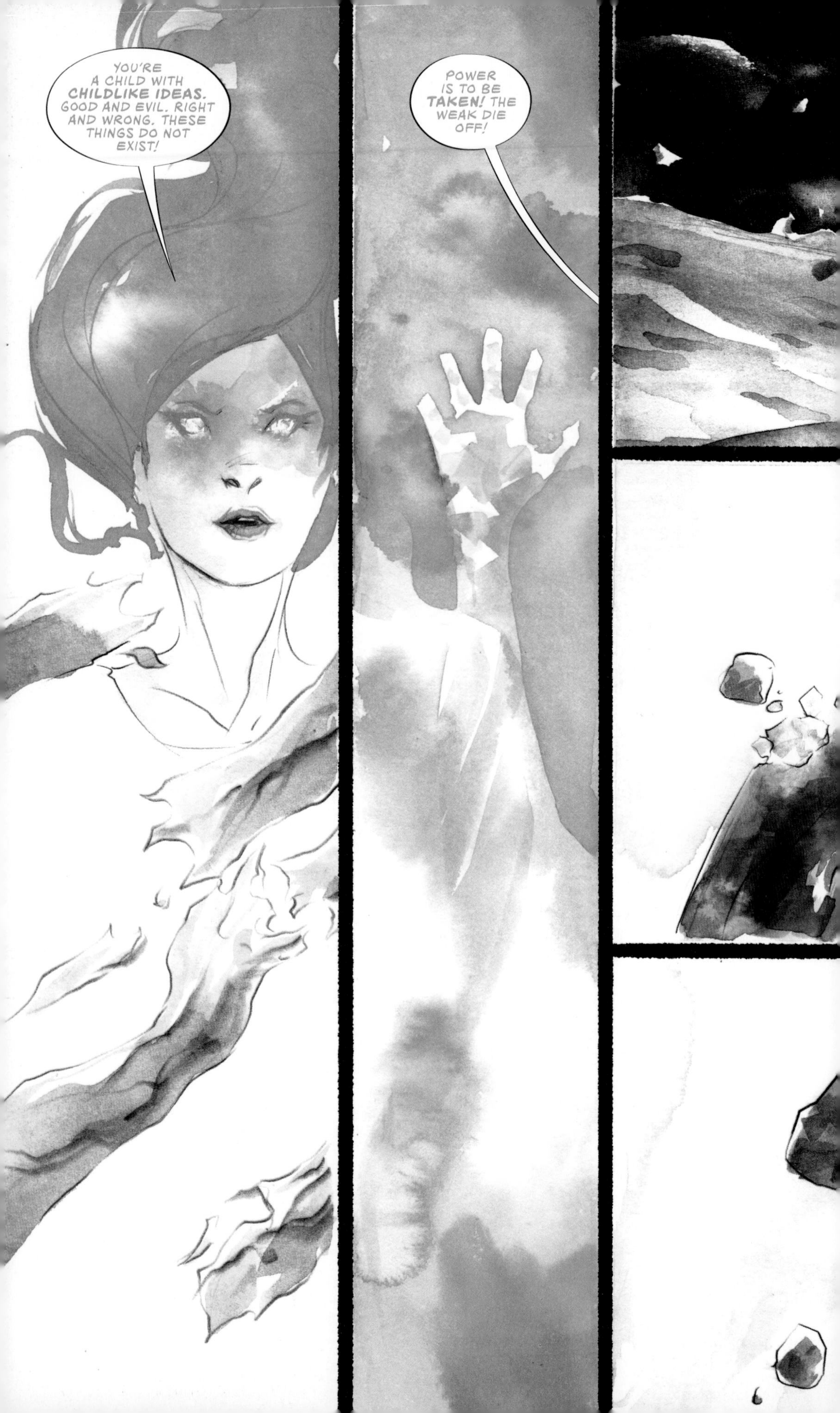
YOU'RE A CHILD WITH CHILDLIKE IDEAS. GOOD AND EVIL. RIGHT AND WRONG. THESE THINGS DO NOT EXIST!
POWER IS TO BE TAKEN! THE WEAK DIE OFF!

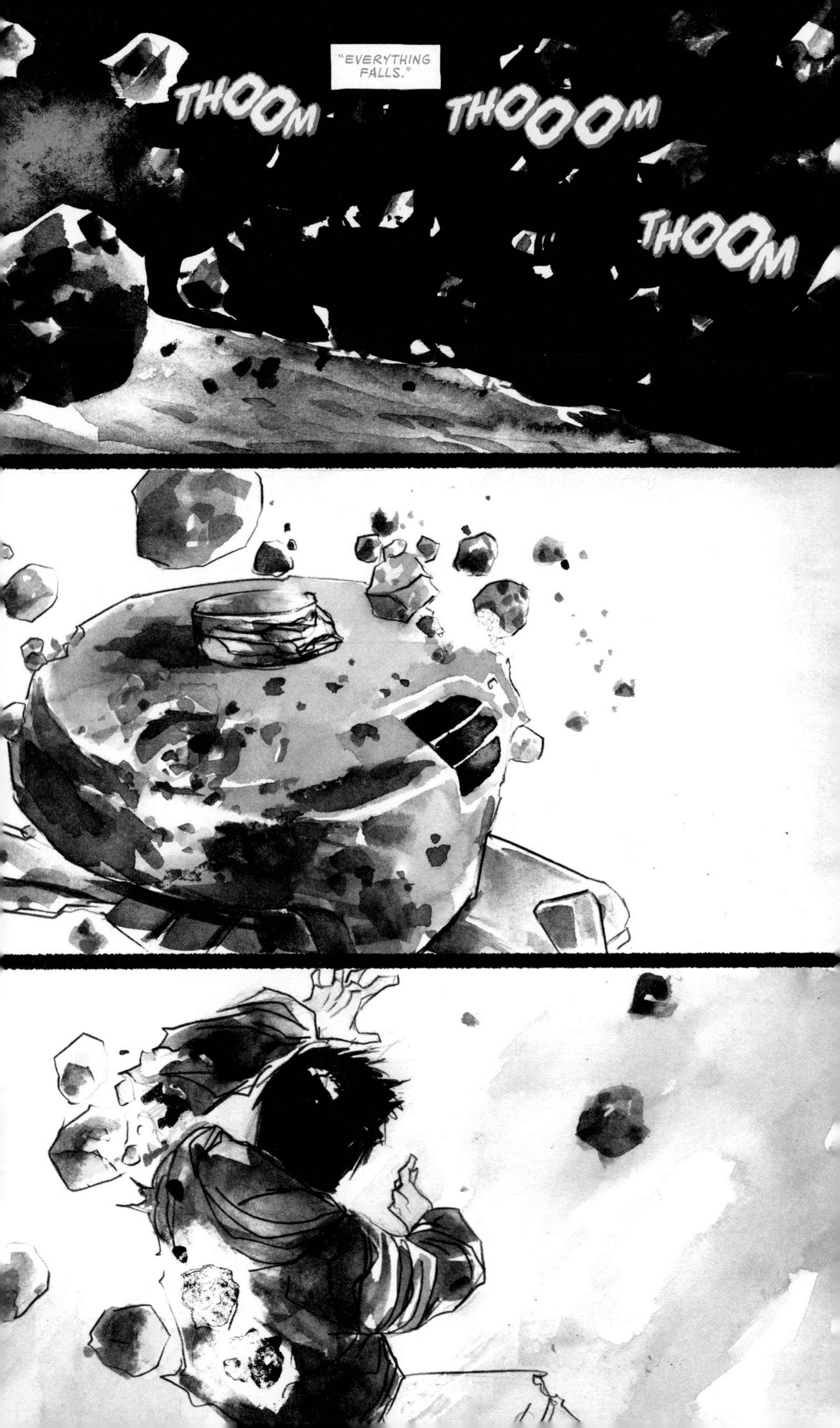
"EVERYTHING FALLS."
THOOM
THOOOM
THOOM

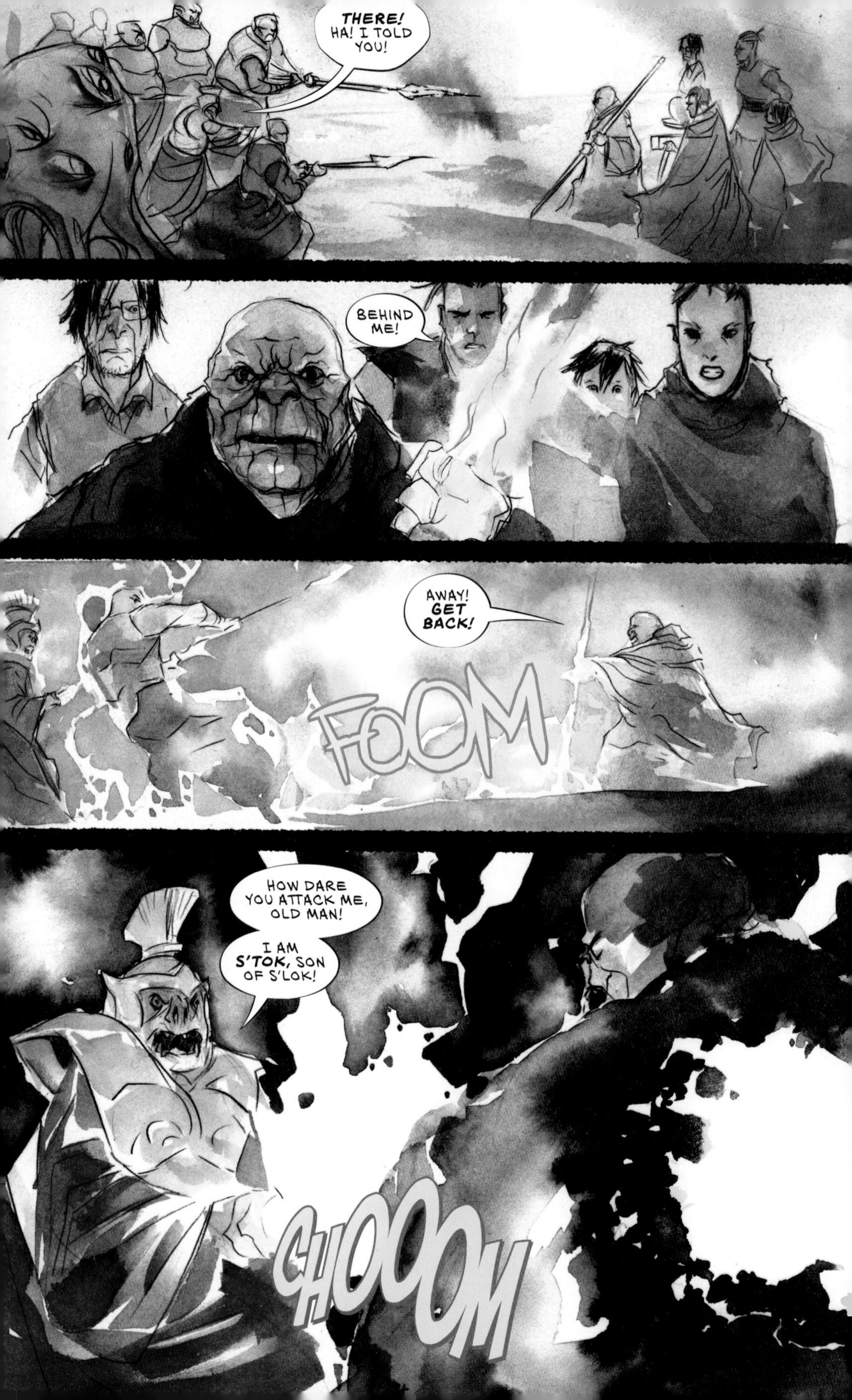
THERE! HA! I TOLD YOU!
BEHIND ME!
AWAY! GET BACK!
FOOM
HOW DARE YOU ATTACK ME, OLD MAN!
I AM S'TOK, SON OF S'LOK!
CHOOOM

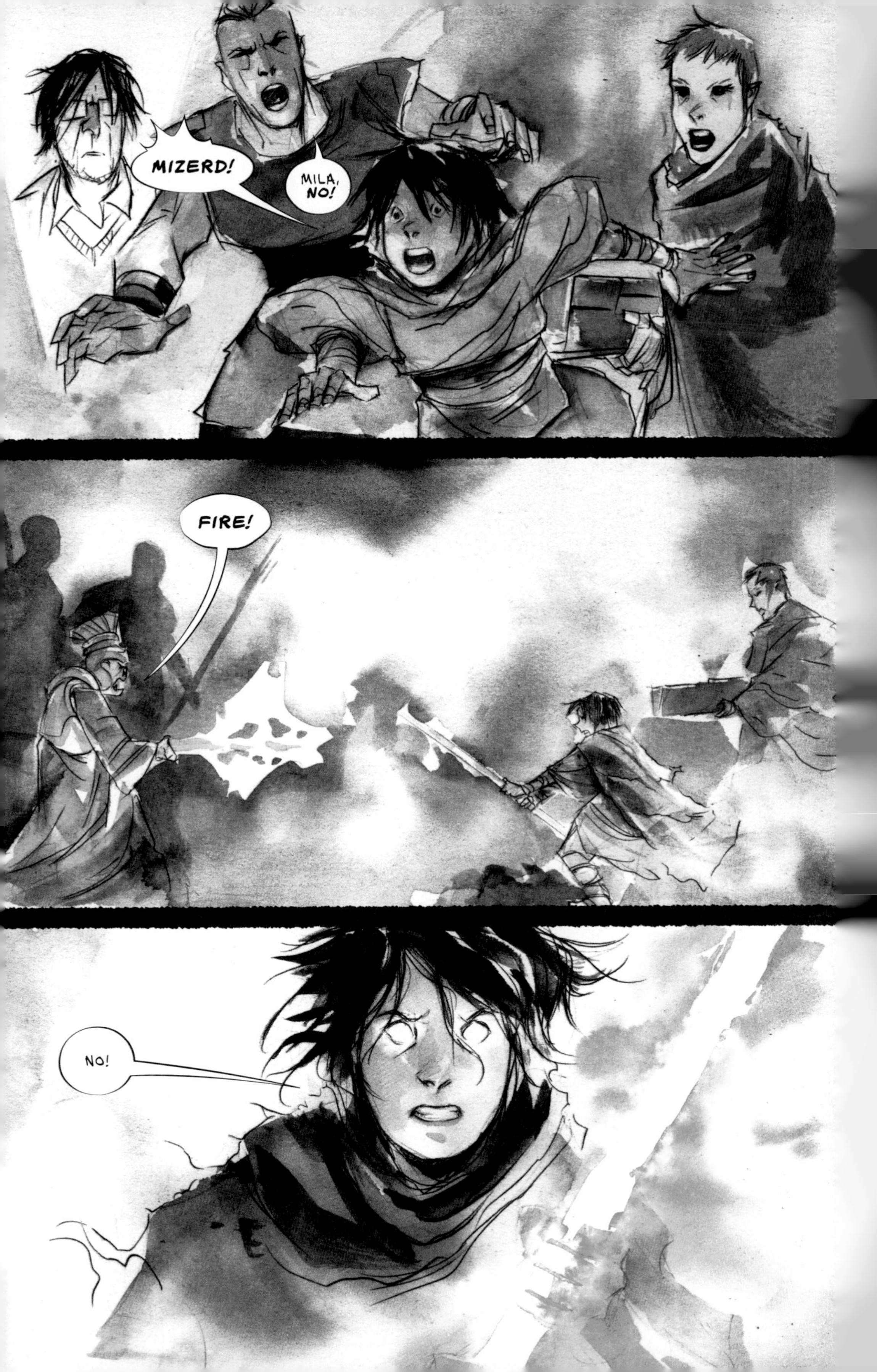
MIZERD!
MILA, NO!
FIRE!
NO!

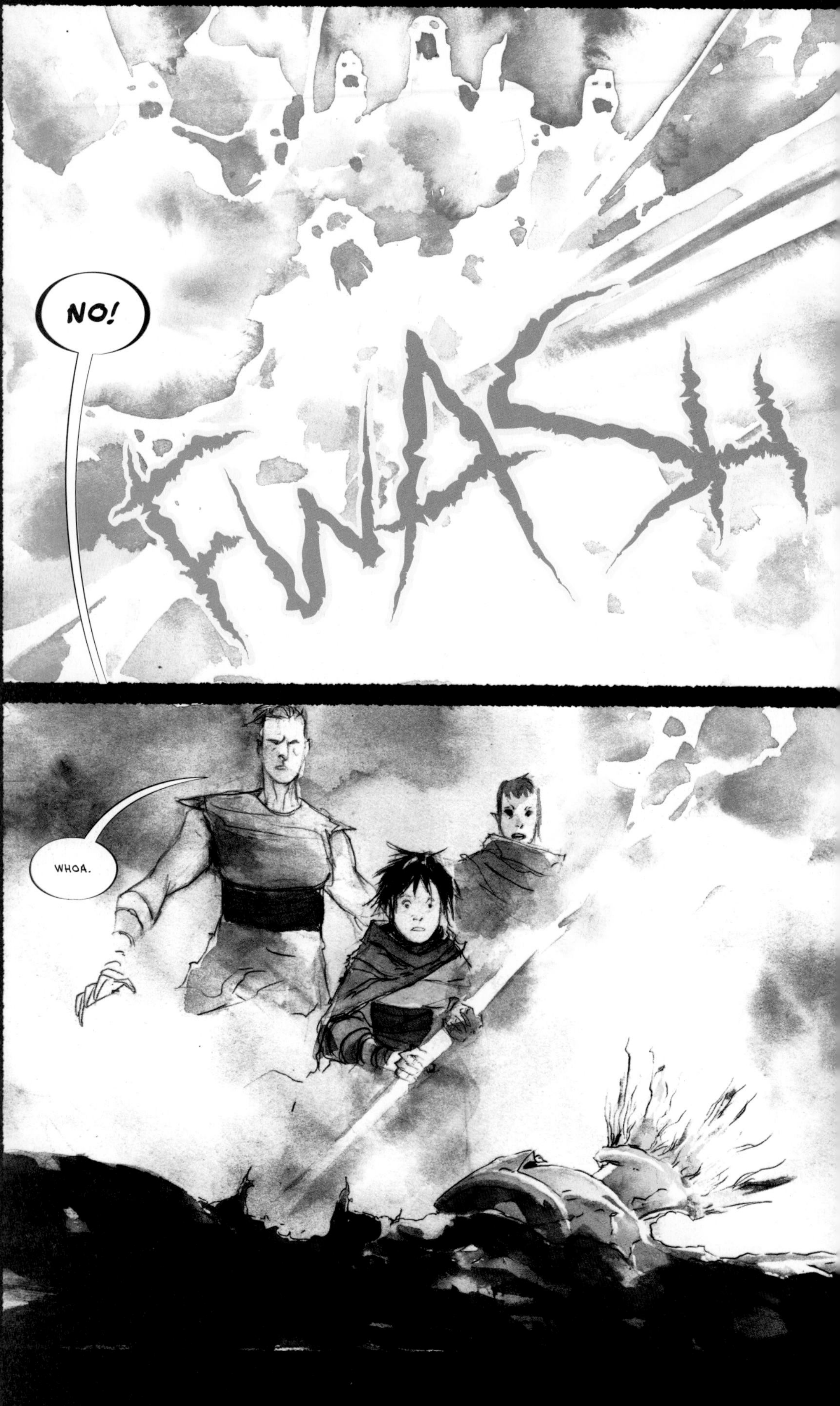
NO!
FWASH
WHOA.

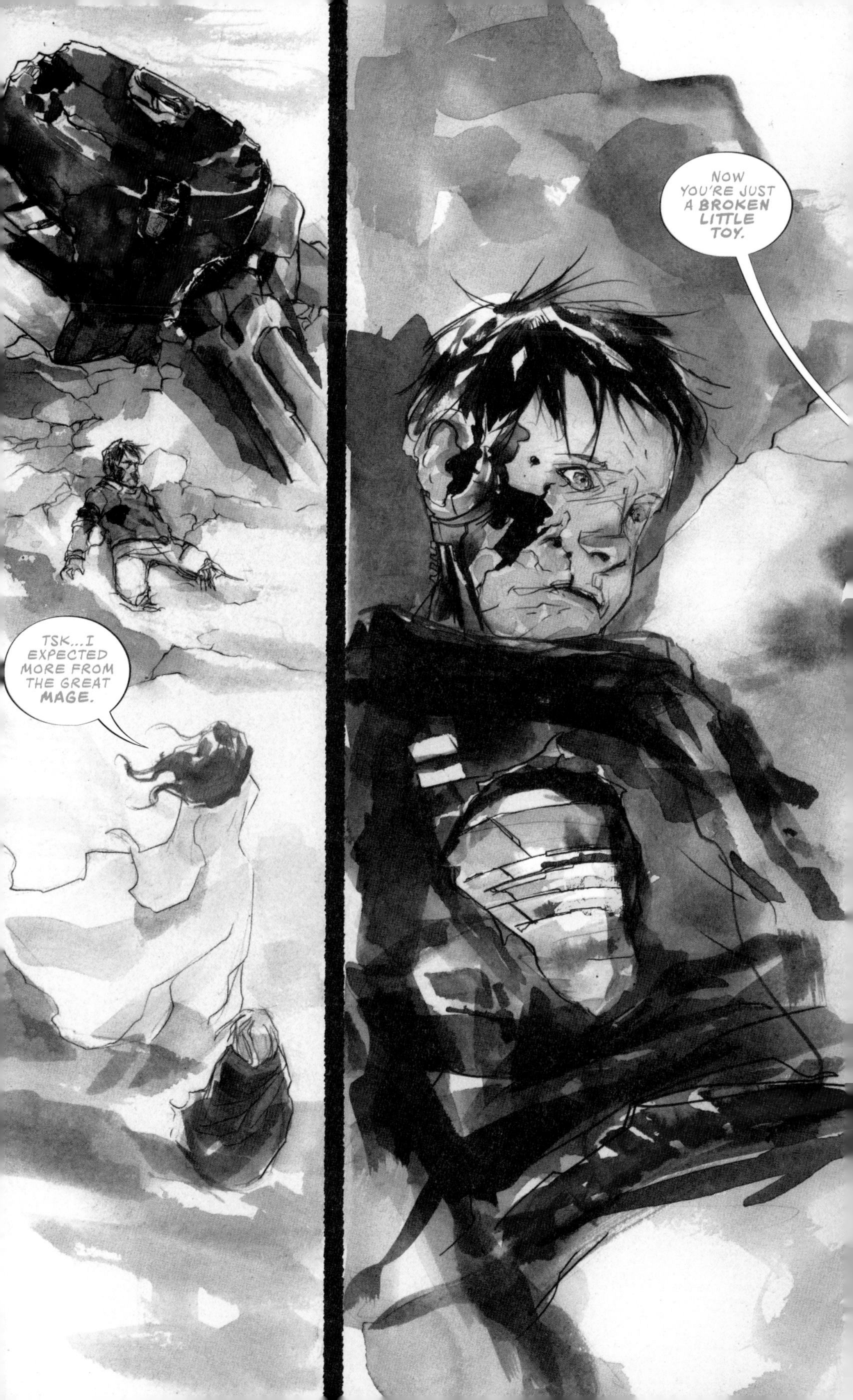
TSK...I EXPECTED MORE FROM THE GREAT MAGE.
NOW YOU'RE JUST A BROKEN LITTLE TOY.

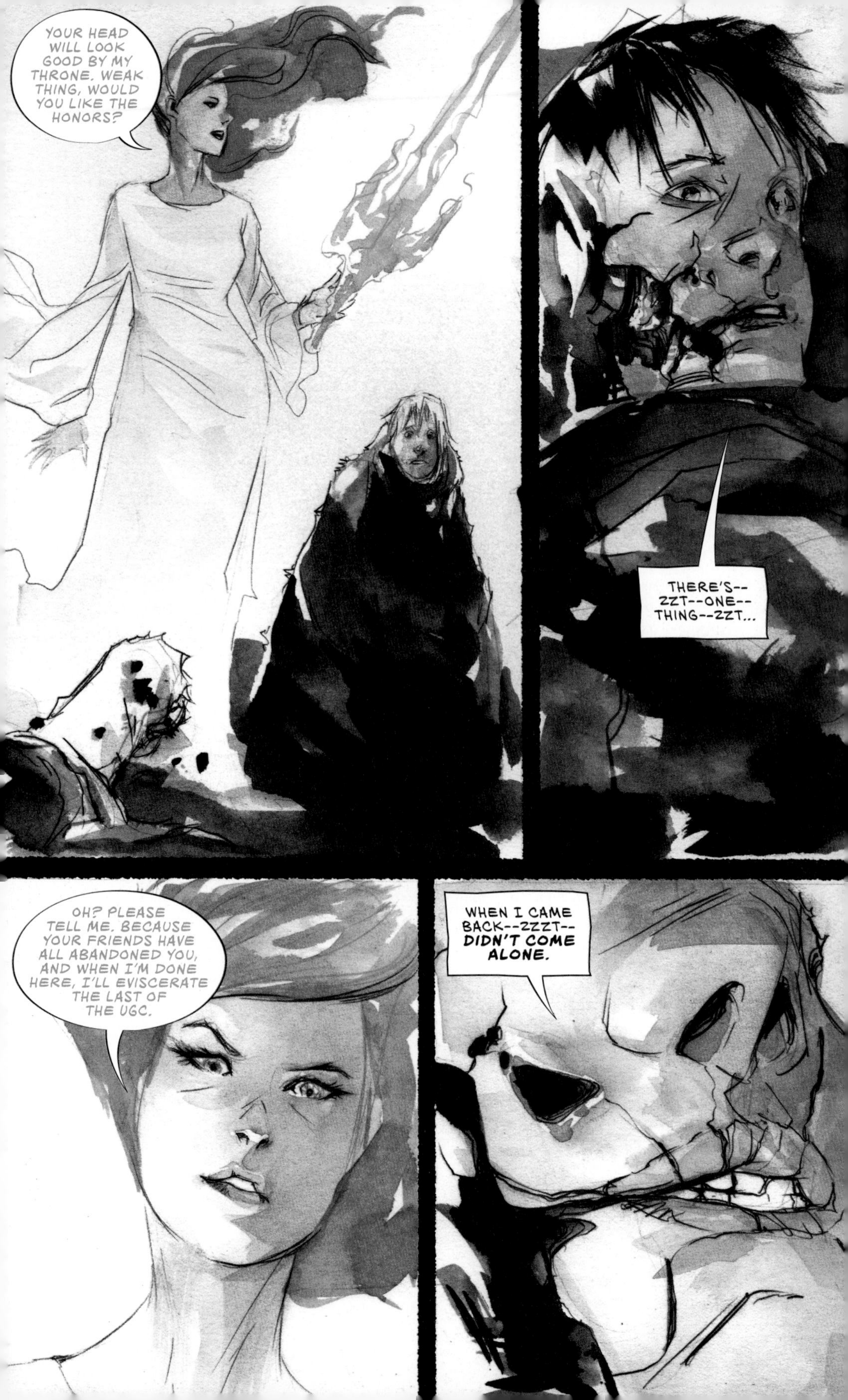
YOUR HEAD WILL LOOK GOOD BY MY THRONE. WEAK THING, WOULD YOU LIKE THE HONORS?
THERE'S--ZZT--ONE--THING--ZZT...
OH? PLEASE TELL ME. BECAUSE YOUR FRIENDS HAVE ALL ABANDONED YOU, AND WHEN I'M DONE HERE, I'LL EVISCERATE THE LAST OF THE UGC.
WHEN I CAME BACK--ZZZT--DIDN'T COME ALONE.

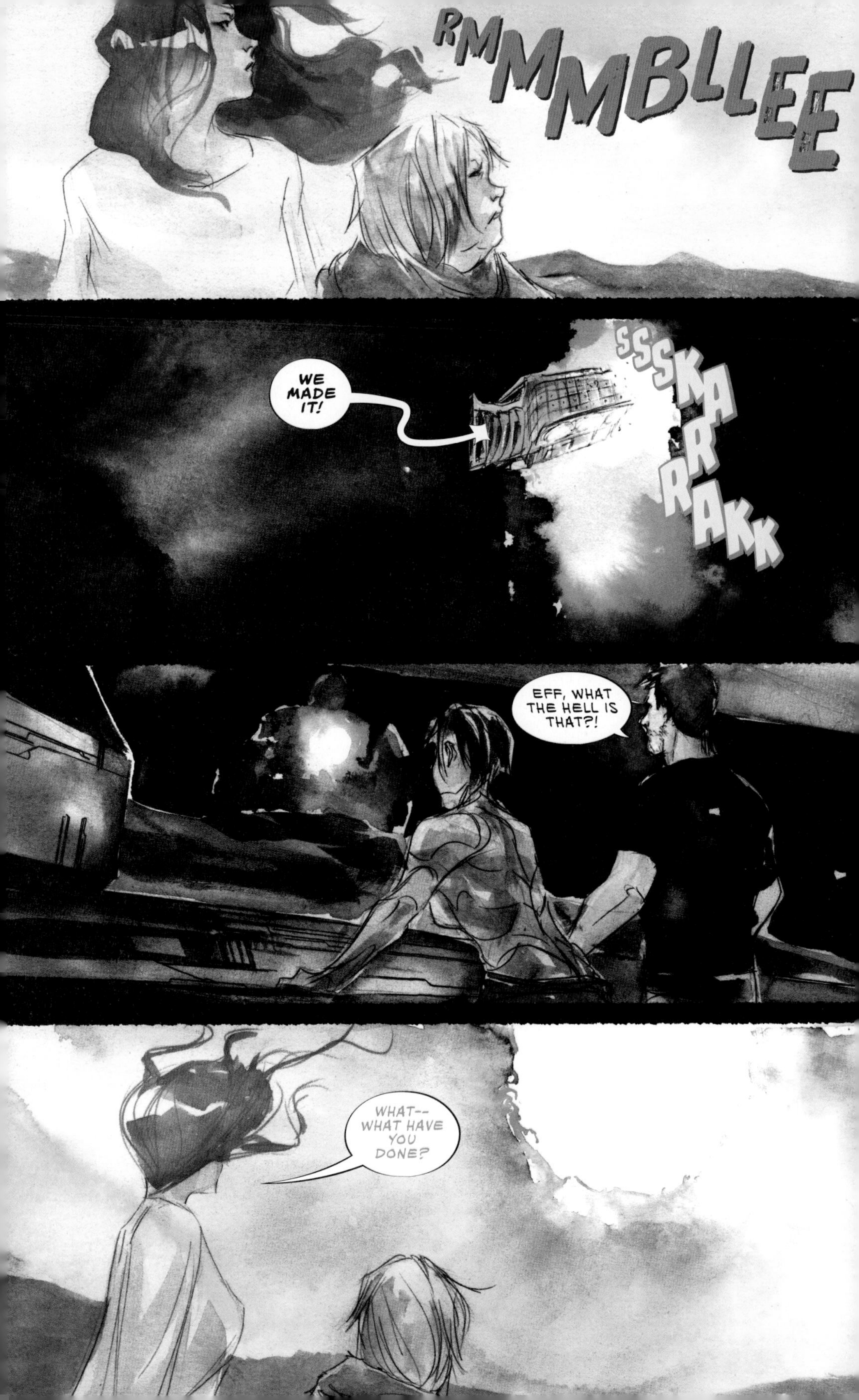
RMMMBLLEE
WE MADE IT!
SSSKARRAKK
EFF, WHAT THE HELL IS THAT?!
WHAT-- WHAT HAVE YOU DONE?

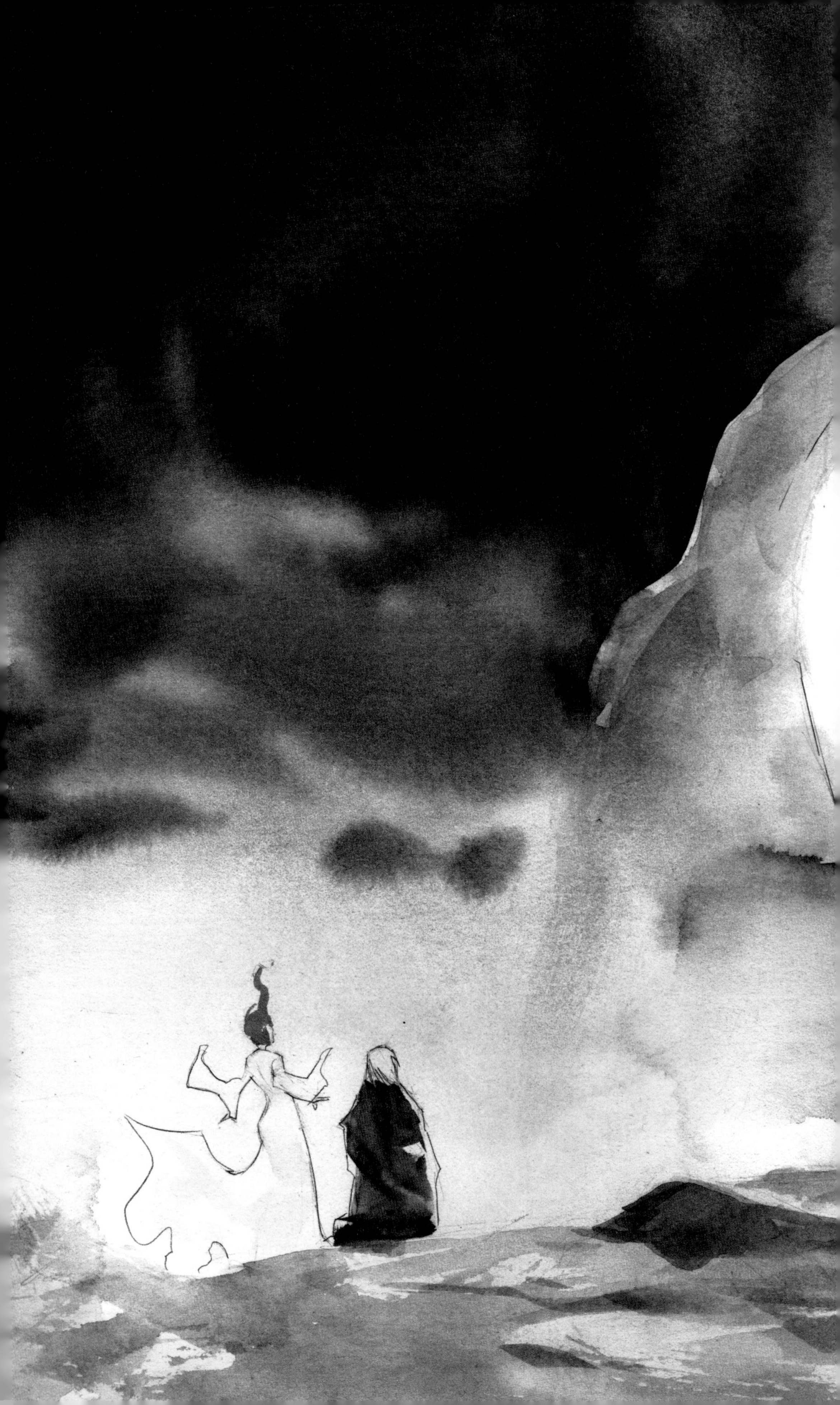

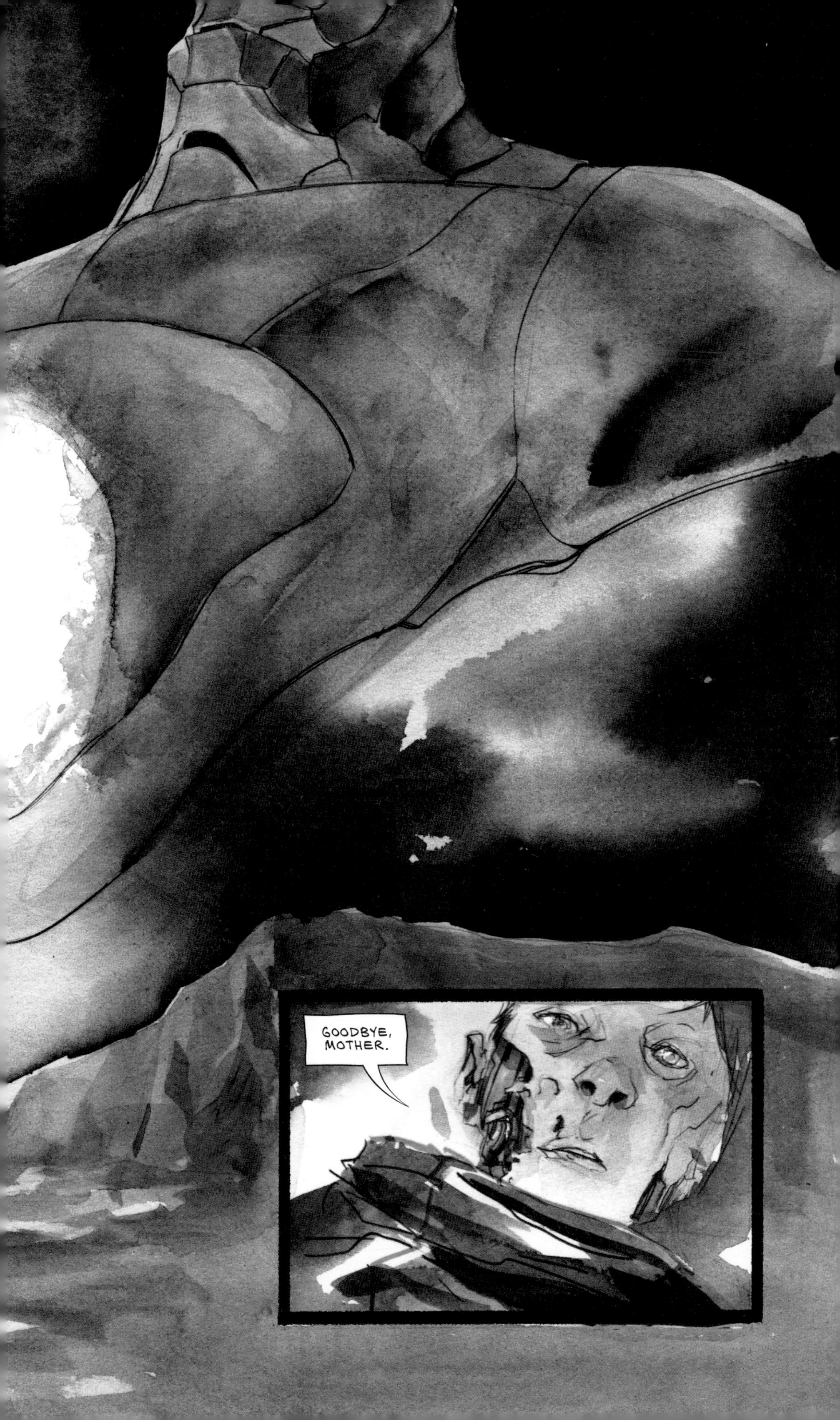
GOODBYE, MOTHER.

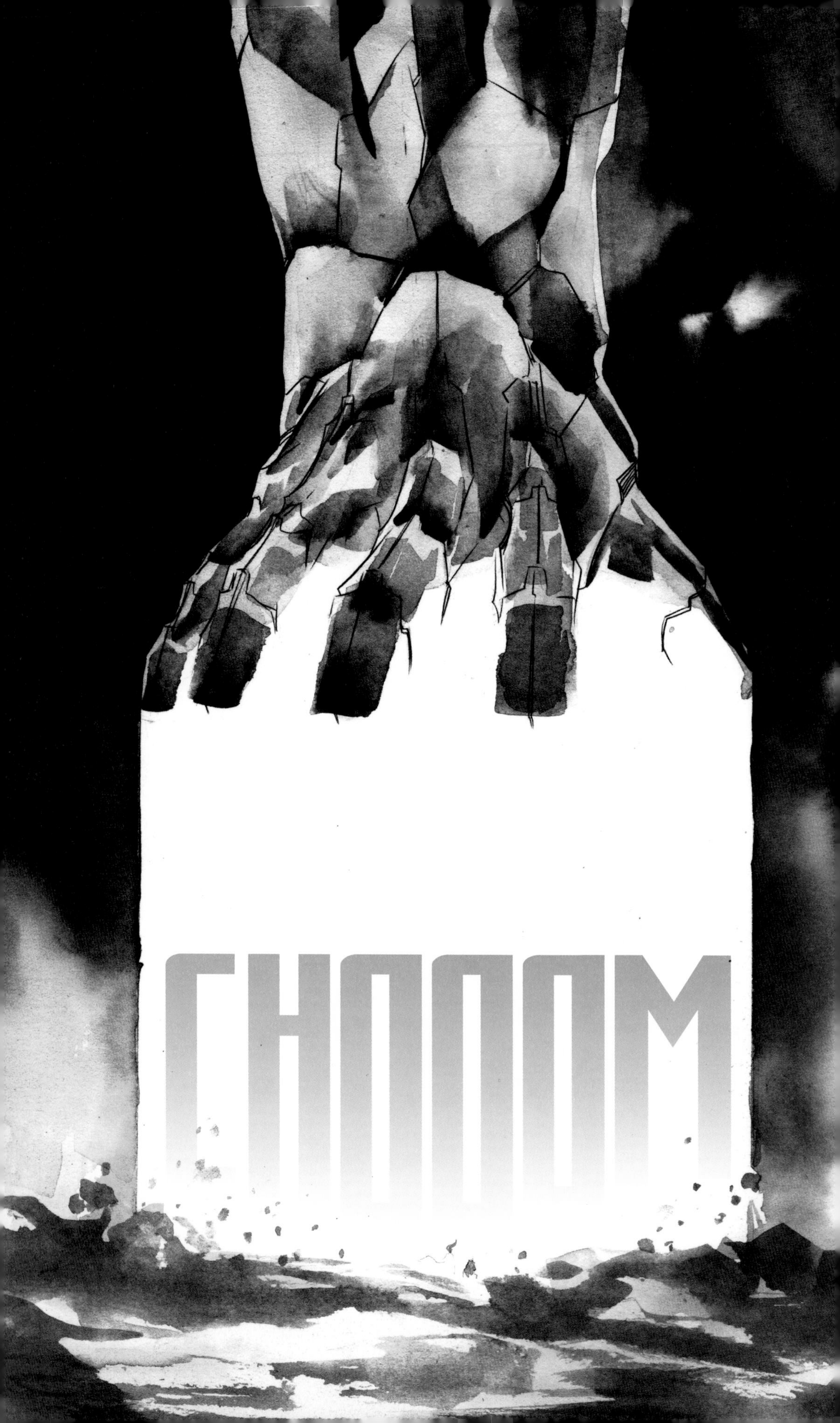
CHOOOM

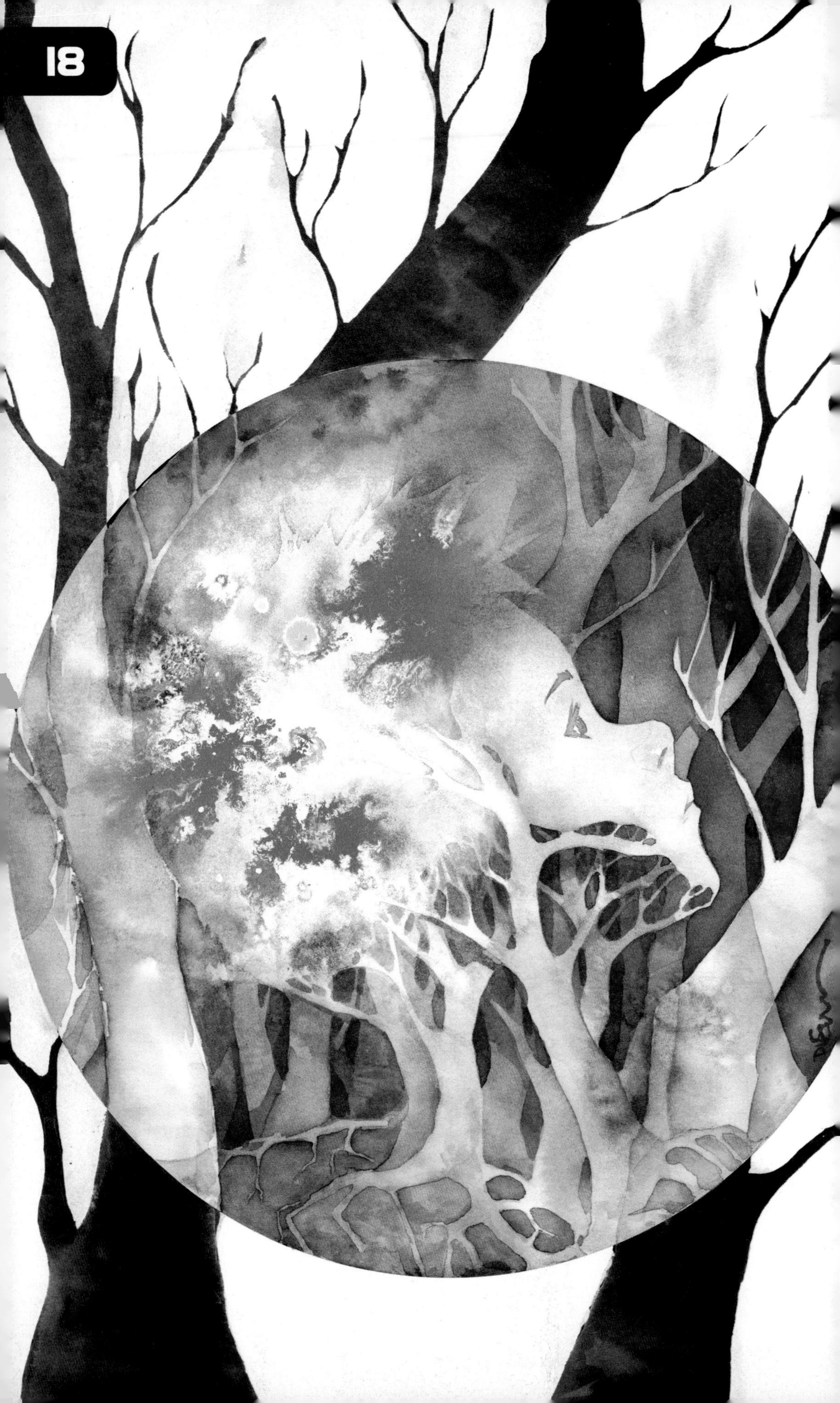
18

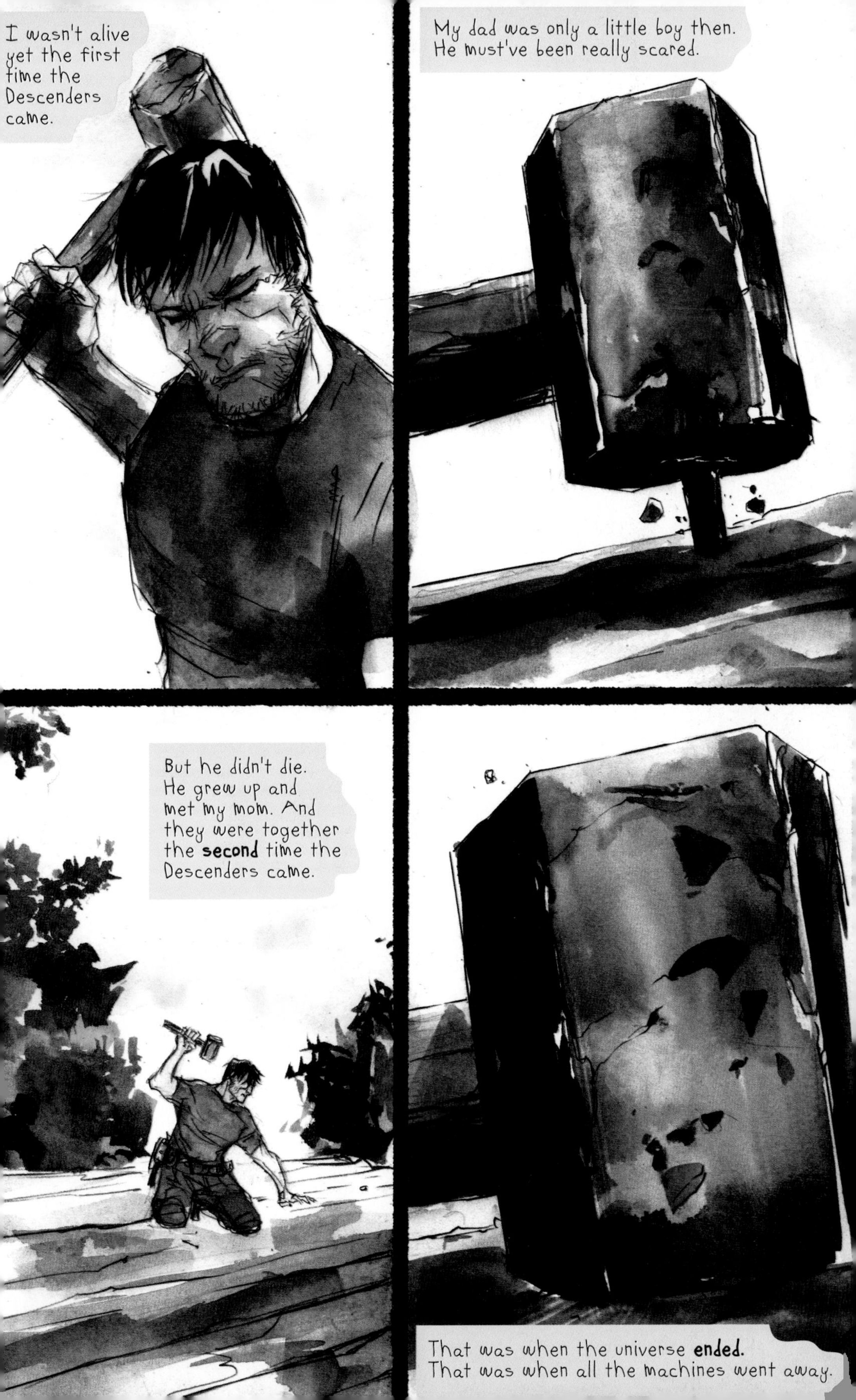
I wasn't alive yet the first time the Descenders came.
My dad was only a little boy then. He must've been really scared.
But he didn't die. He grew up and met my mom. And they were together the **second** time the Descenders came.
That was when the universe **ended.** That was when all the machines went away.

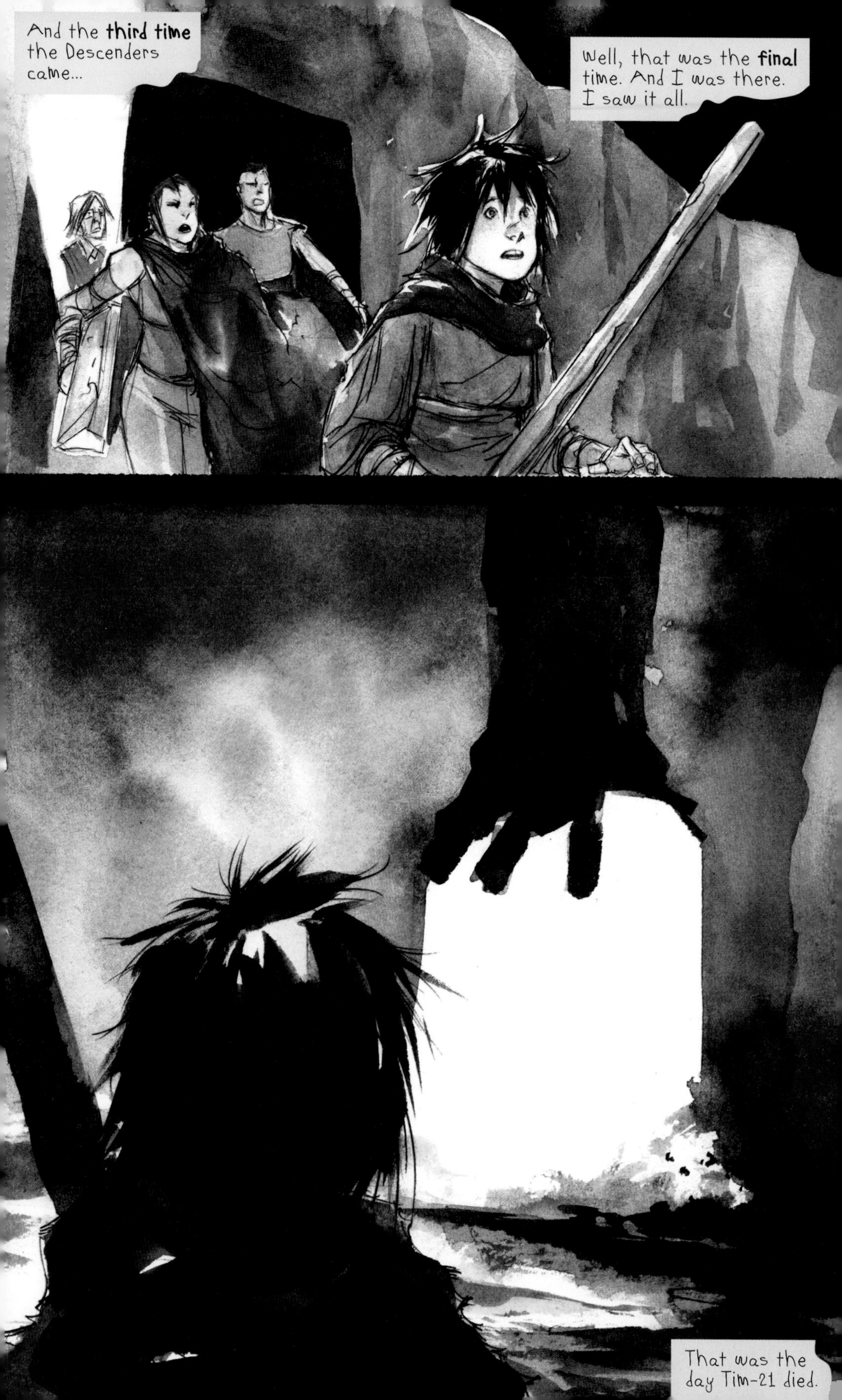

And the **third time** the Descenders came...
Well, that was the **final** time. And I was there. I saw it all.
That was the day Tim-21 died.

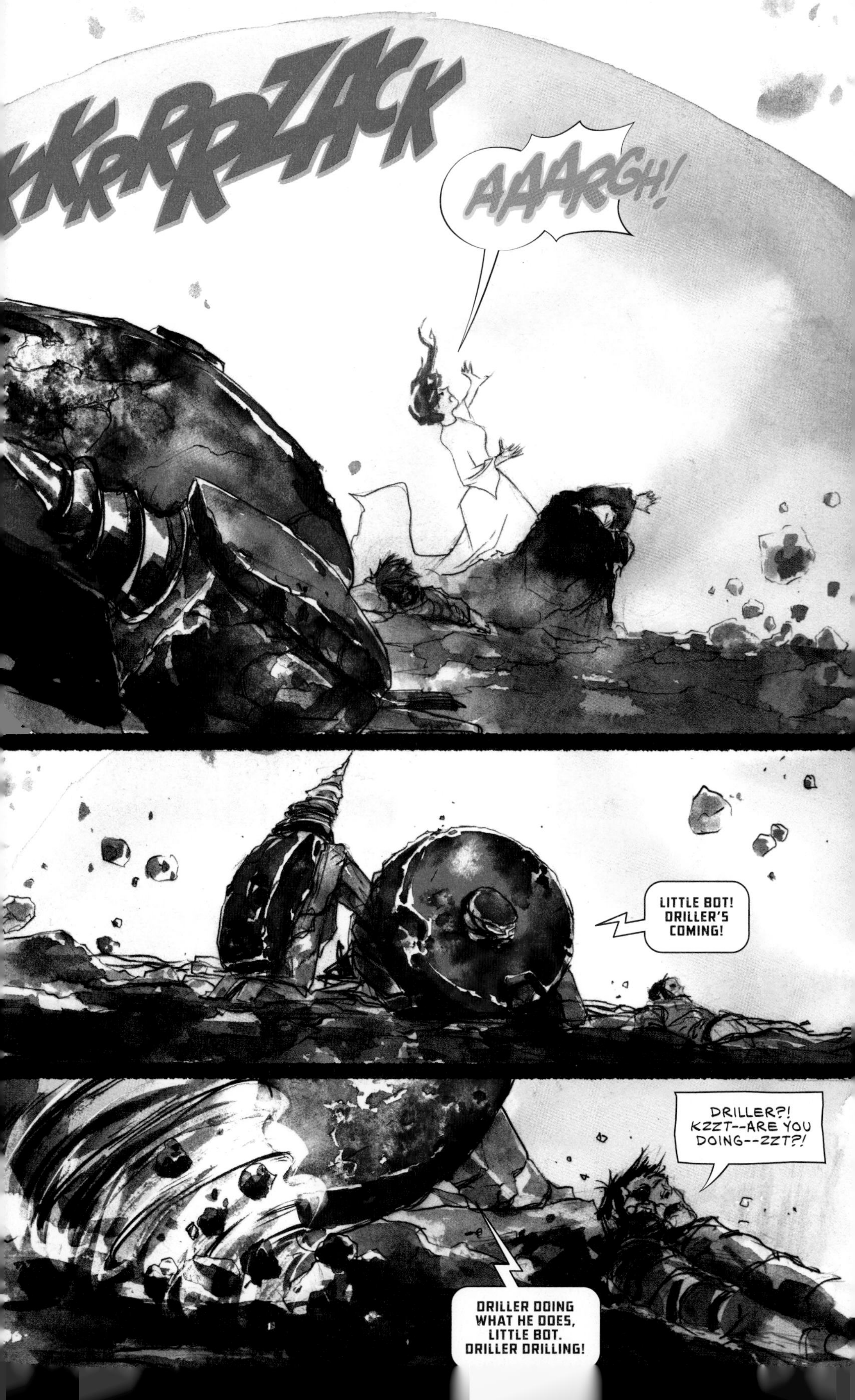
KKRRRZACK
AAAARGH!
LITTLE BOT! DRILLER'S COMING!
DRILLER?! KZZT--ARE YOU DOING--ZZT?!
DRILLER DOING WHAT HE DOES, LITTLE BOT. DRILLER DRILLING!

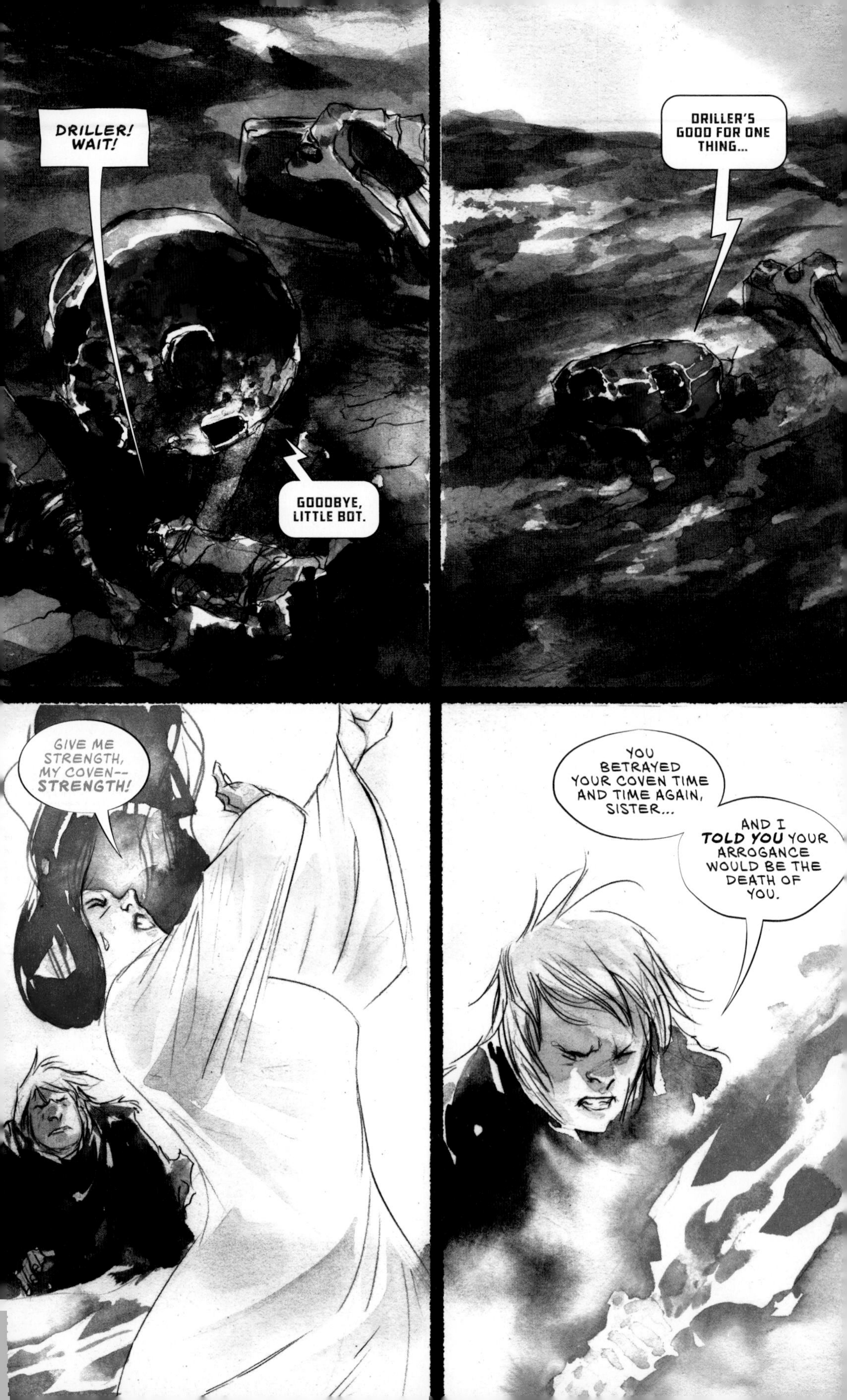
DRILLER! WAIT!
GOODBYE, LITTLE BOT.
DRILLER'S GOOD FOR ONE THING...
GIVE ME STRENGTH, MY COVEN-- STRENGTH!
YOU BETRAYED YOUR COVEN TIME AND TIME AGAIN, SISTER...
AND I TOLD YOU YOUR ARROGANCE WOULD BE THE DEATH OF YOU.

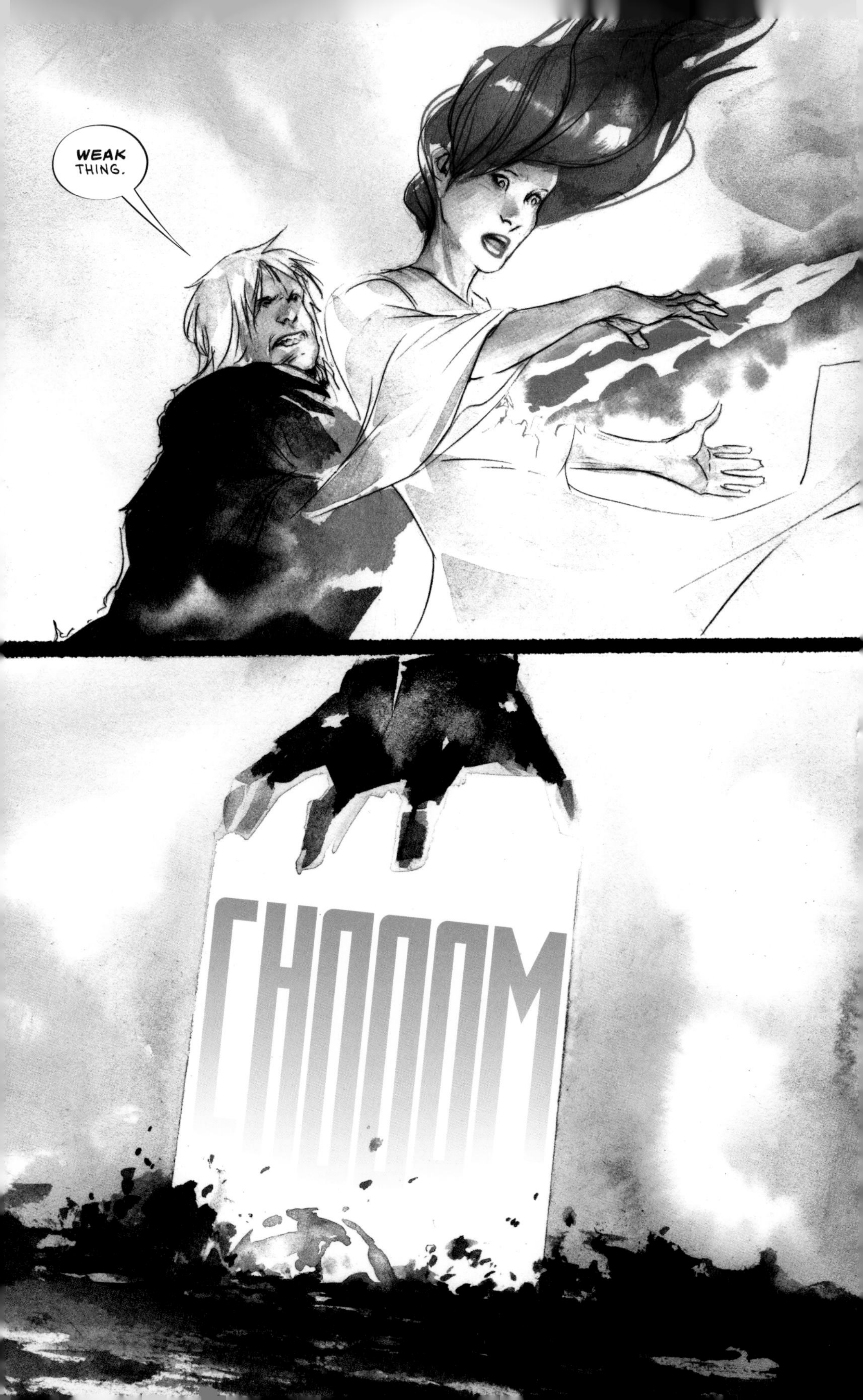
WEAK THING.
CHOOOM

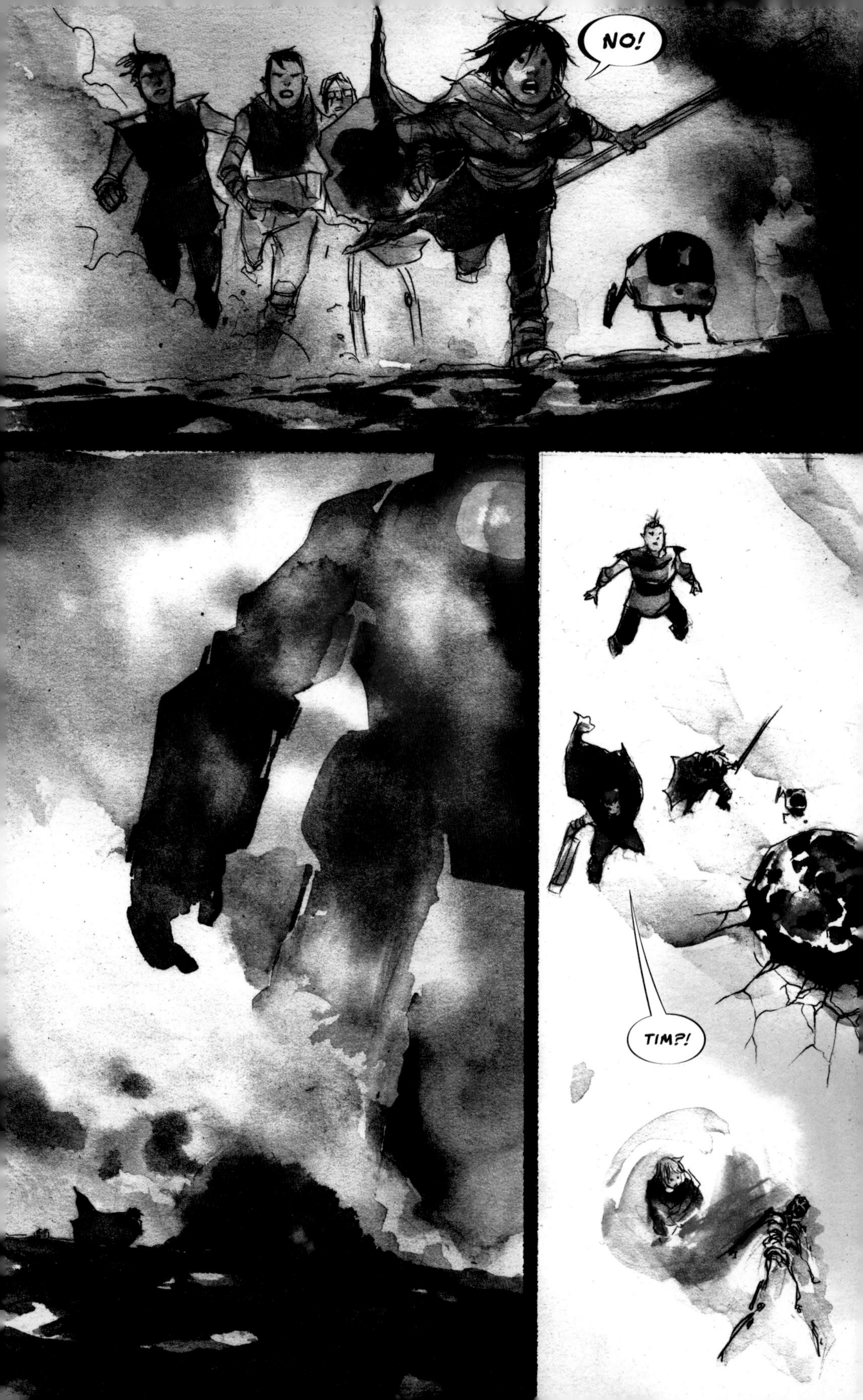
NO!
TIM?!

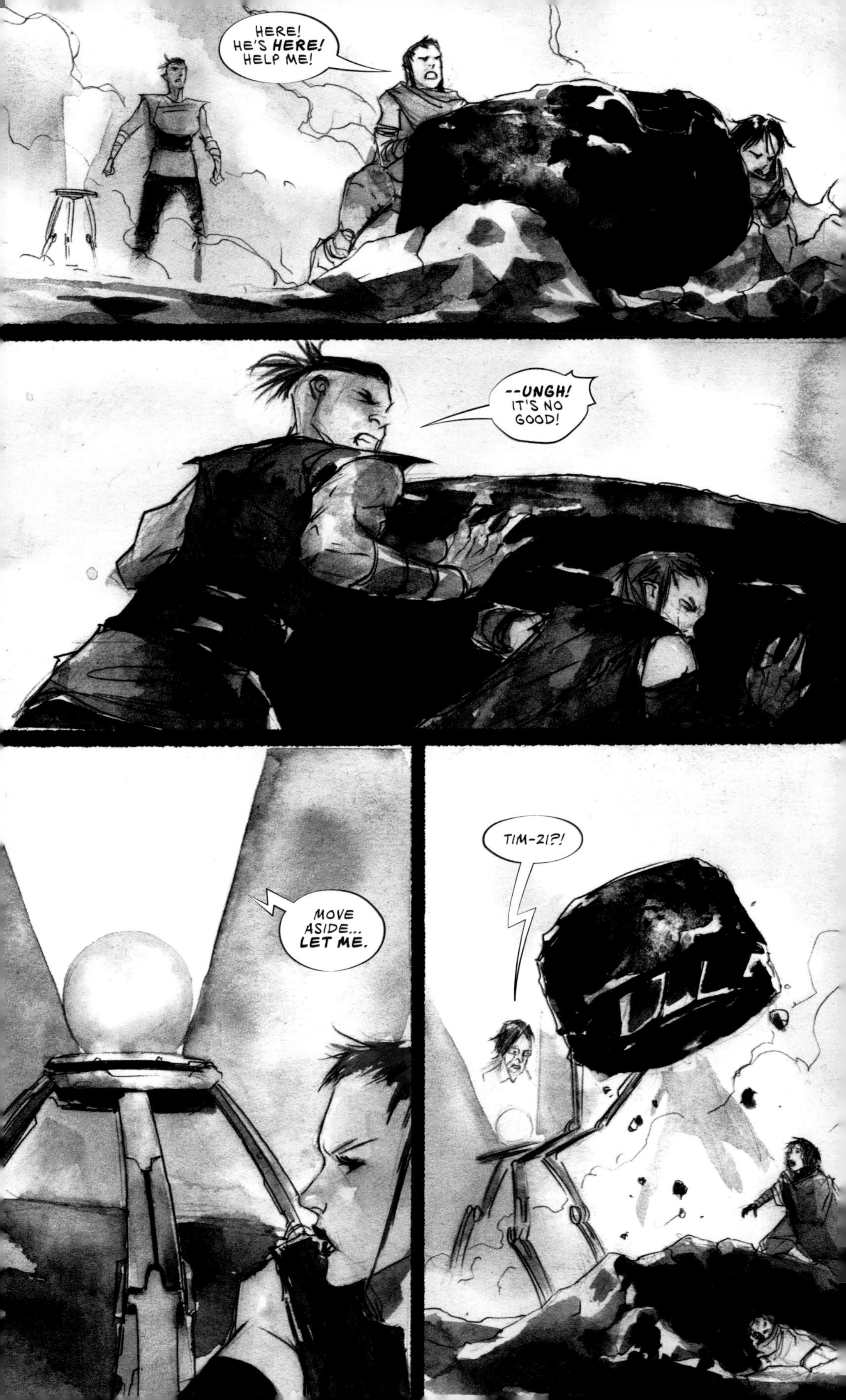
HERE! HE'S **HERE!** HELP ME!
--UNGH! IT'S NO GOOD!
MOVE ASIDE... **LET ME.**
TIM-21?!

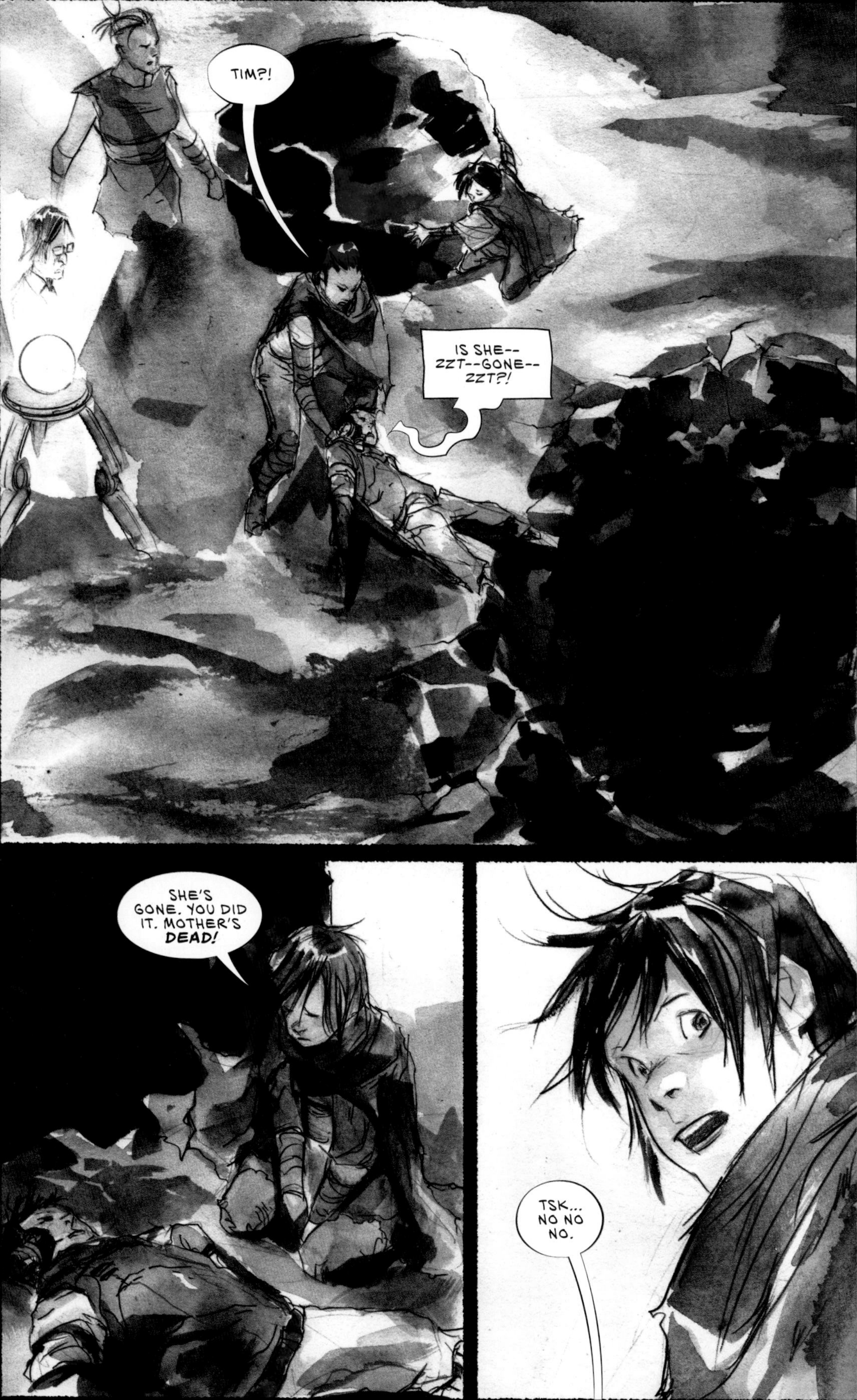
TIM?!
IS SHE-- ZZT--GONE-- ZZT?!
SHE'S GONE. YOU DID IT. MOTHER'S **DEAD!**
TSK... NO NO NO.

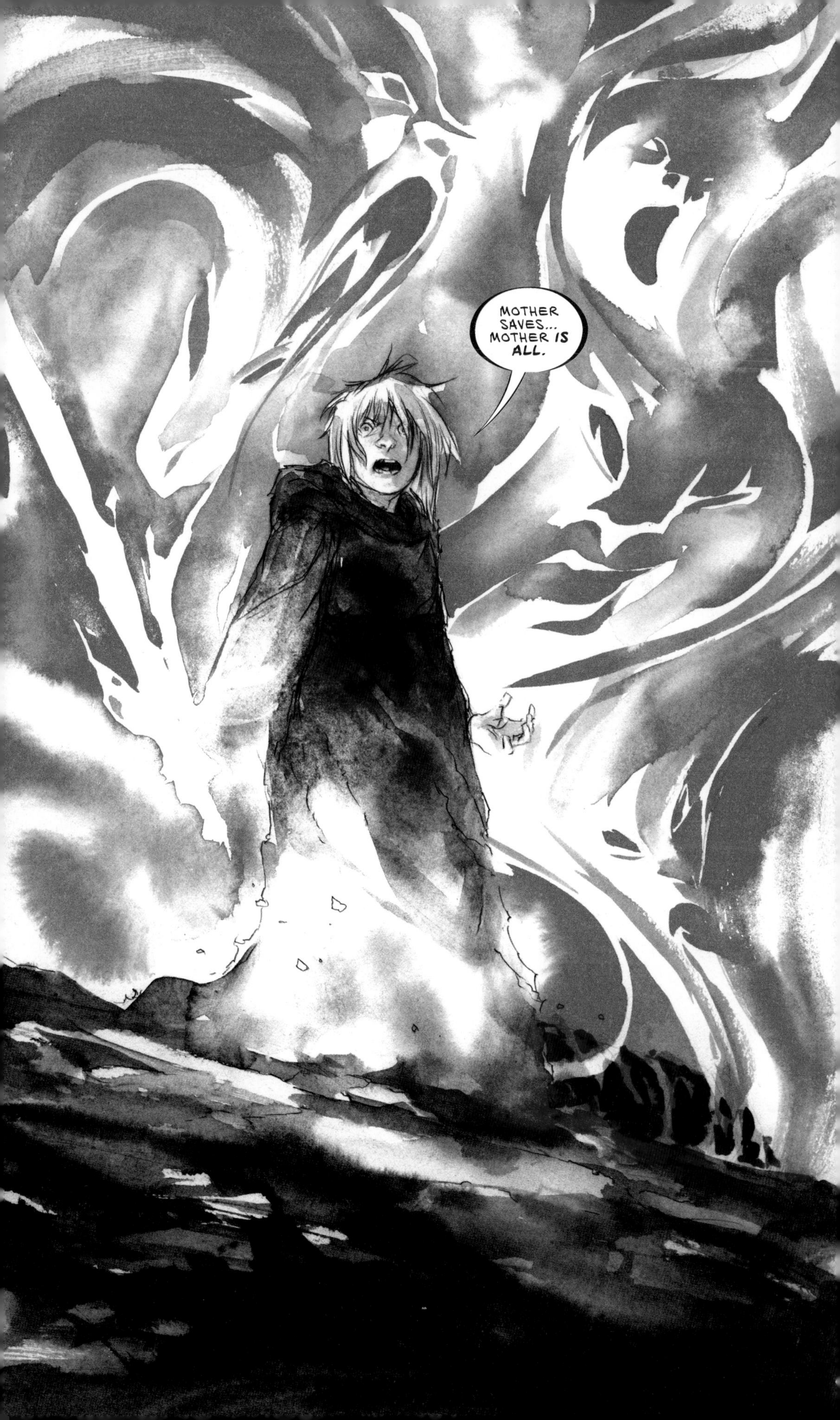
MOTHER SAVES... MOTHER IS ALL.

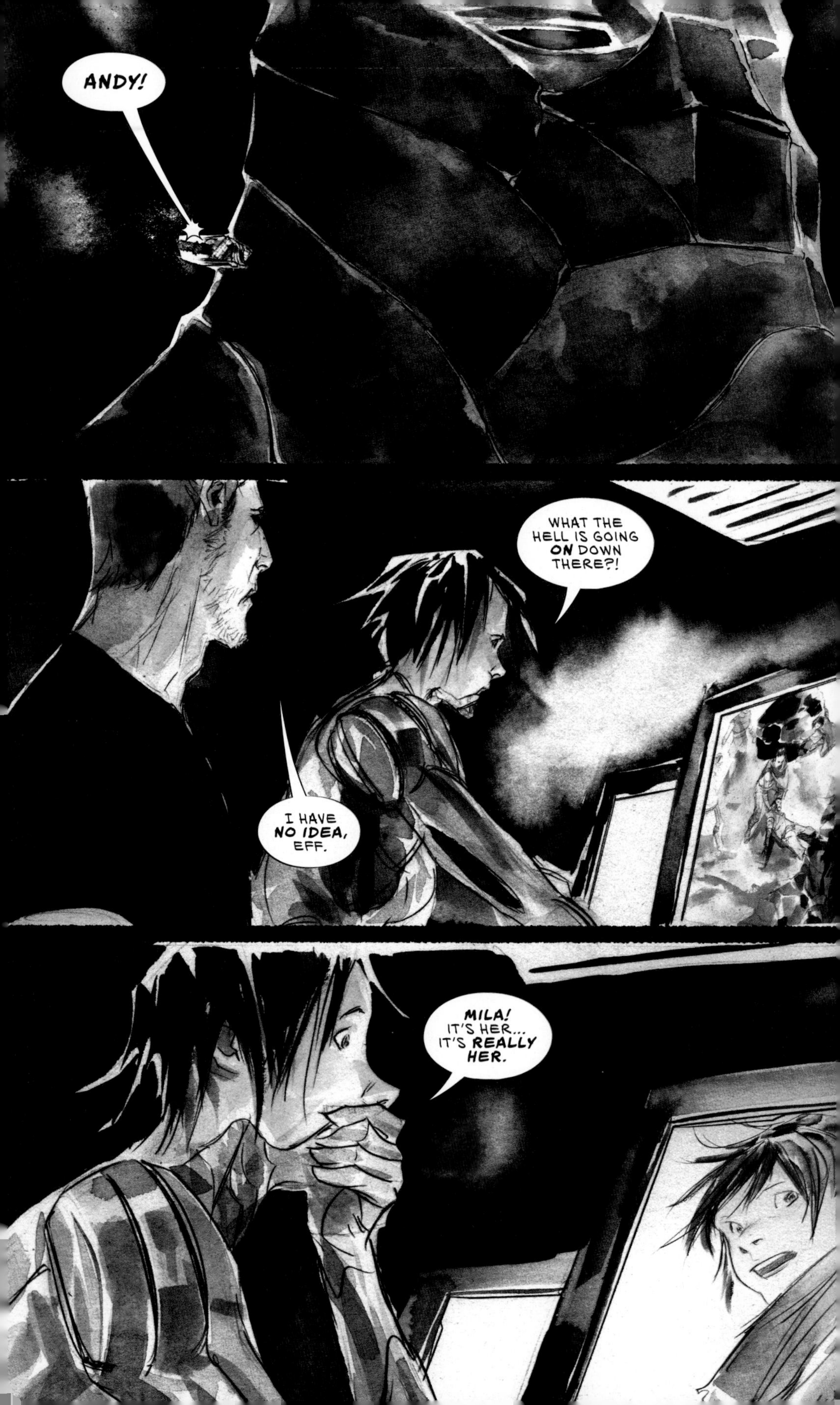
ANDY!
WHAT THE HELL IS GOING ON DOWN THERE?!
I HAVE NO IDEA, EFF.
MILA! IT'S HER... IT'S REALLY HER.

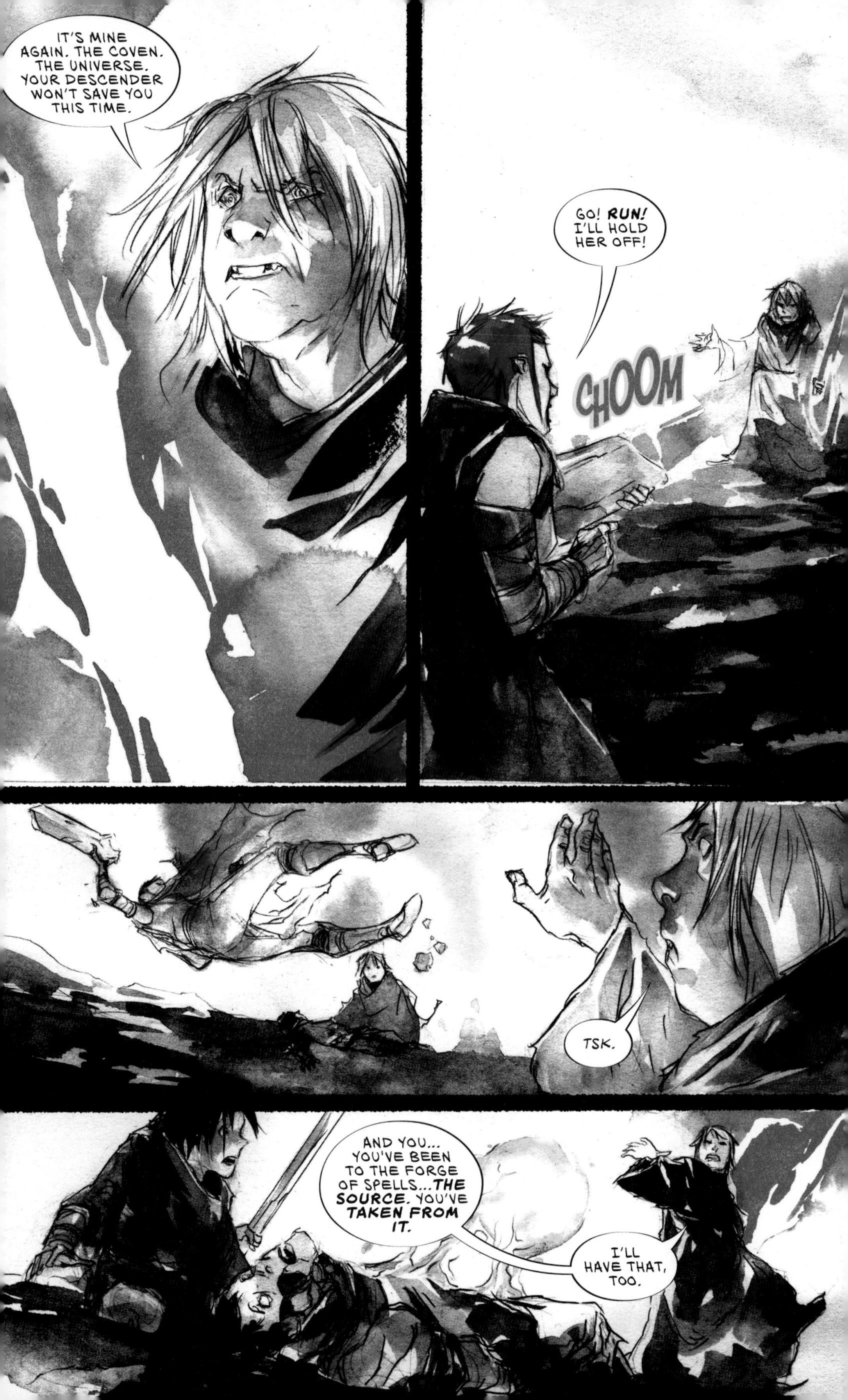
IT'S MINE AGAIN. THE COVEN. THE UNIVERSE. YOUR DESCENDER WON'T SAVE YOU THIS TIME.
GO! **RUN!** I'LL HOLD HER OFF!
CHOOM
TSK.
AND YOU... YOU'VE BEEN TO THE FORGE OF SPELLS...**THE SOURCE.** YOU'VE ***TAKEN FROM IT.***
I'LL HAVE THAT, TOO.

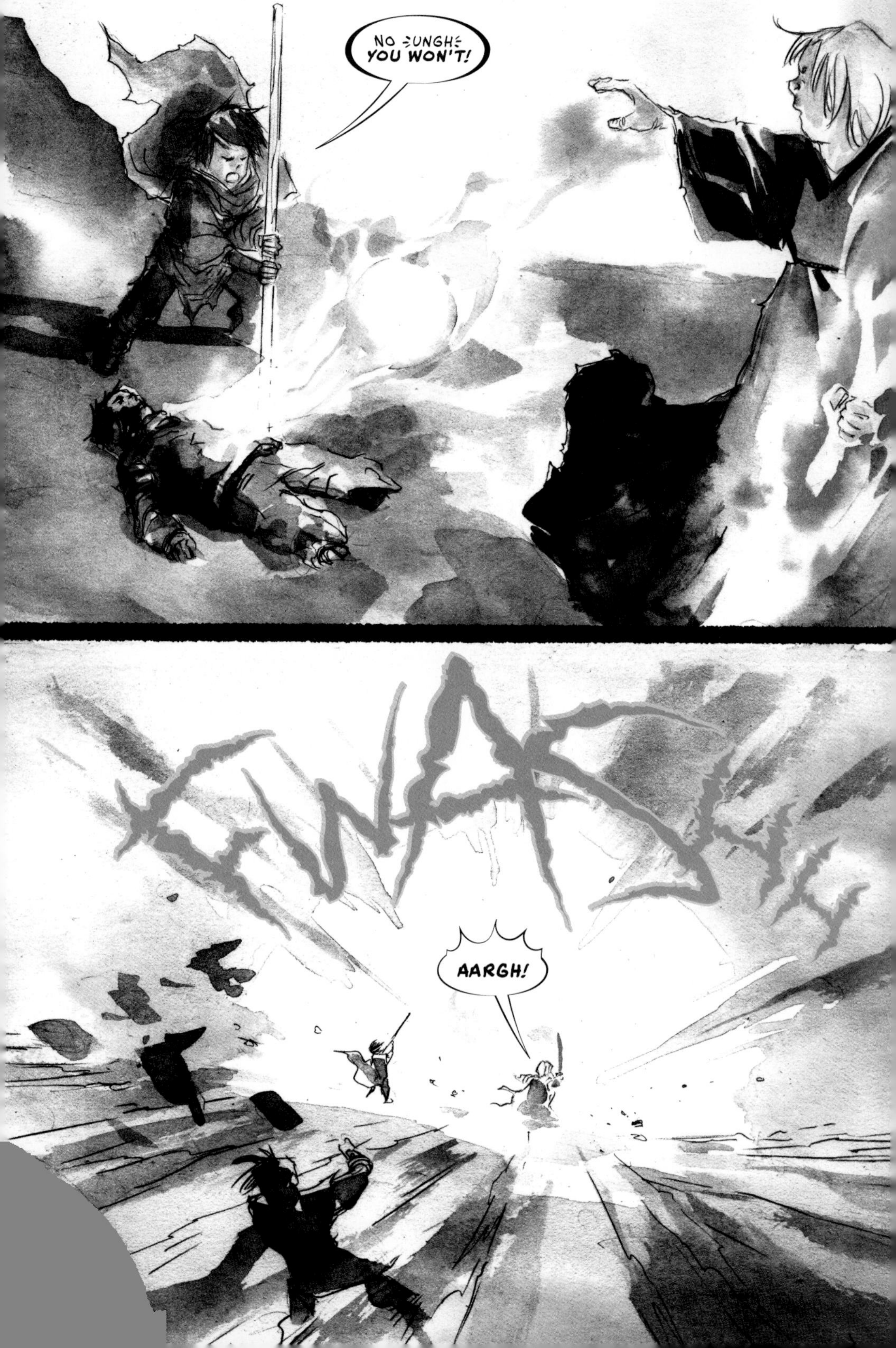
NO —UNGH— YOU WON'T!
AARGH!

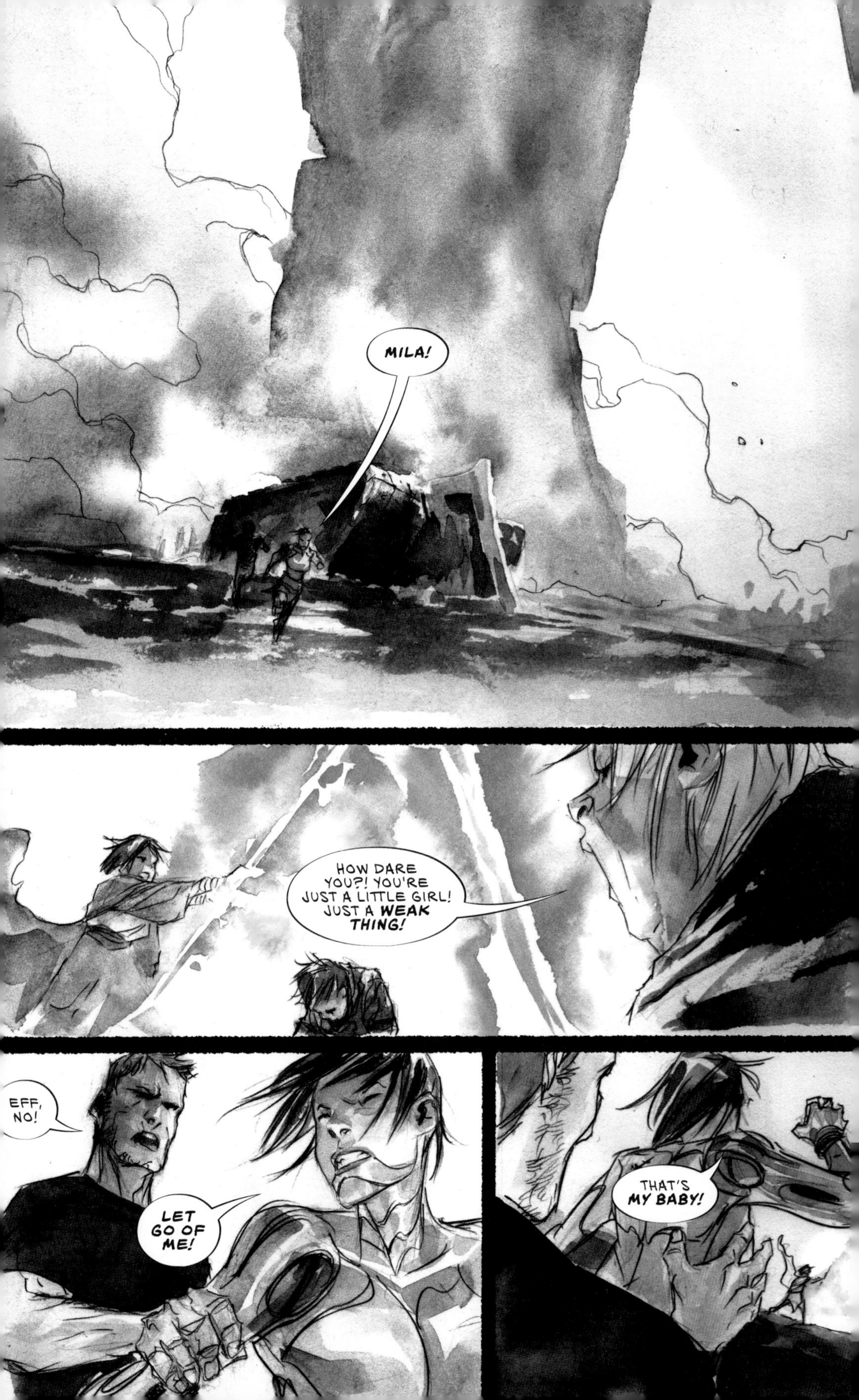
MILA!
HOW DARE YOU?! YOU'RE JUST A LITTLE GIRL! JUST A **WEAK THING!**
EFF, NO!
LET GO OF ME!
THAT'S **MY BABY!**

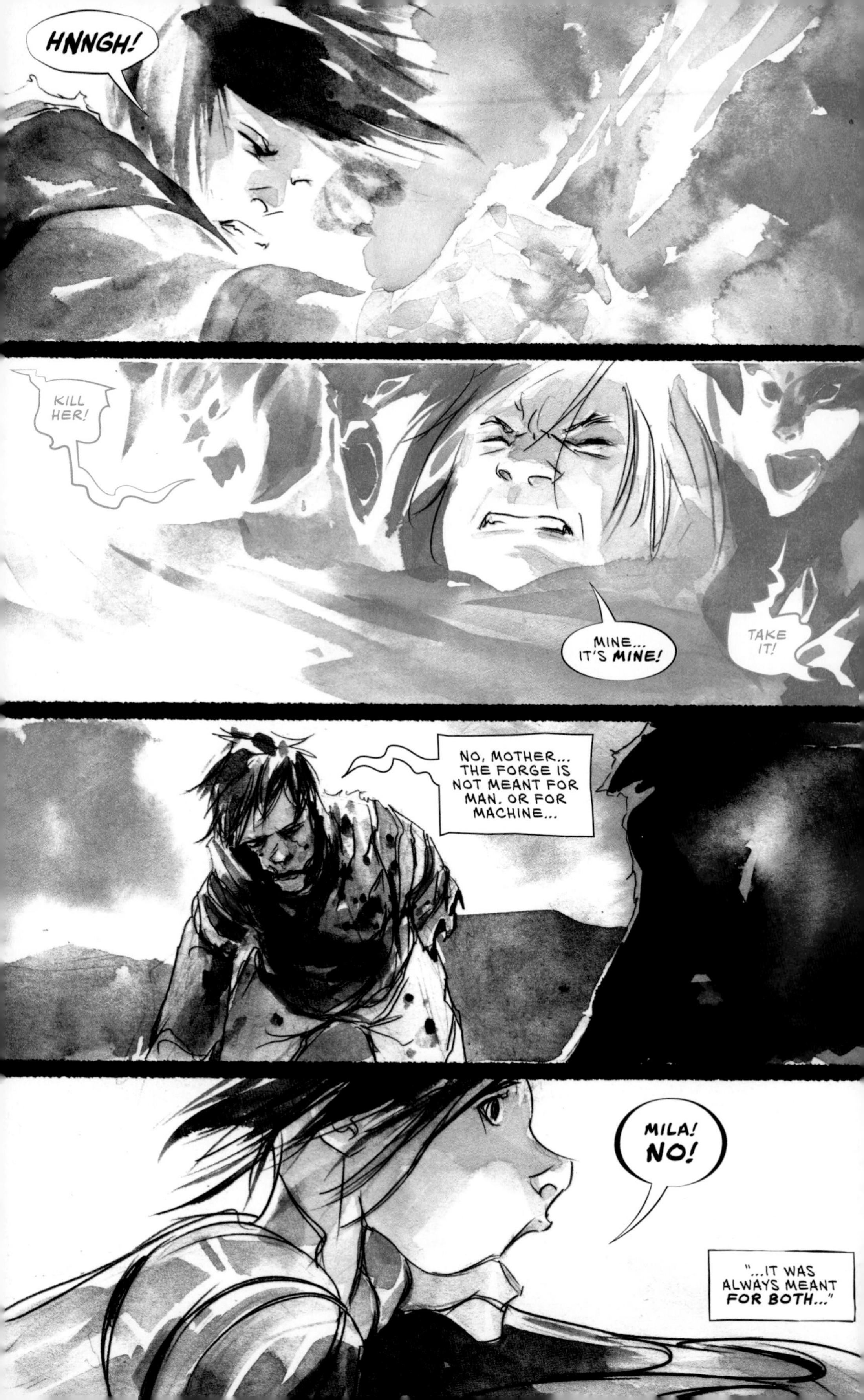
HNNGH!
KILL HER!
MINE... IT'S MINE!
TAKE IT!
NO, MOTHER... THE FORGE IS NOT MEANT FOR MAN. OR FOR MACHINE...
MILA! NO!
"...IT WAS ALWAYS MEANT FOR BOTH..."

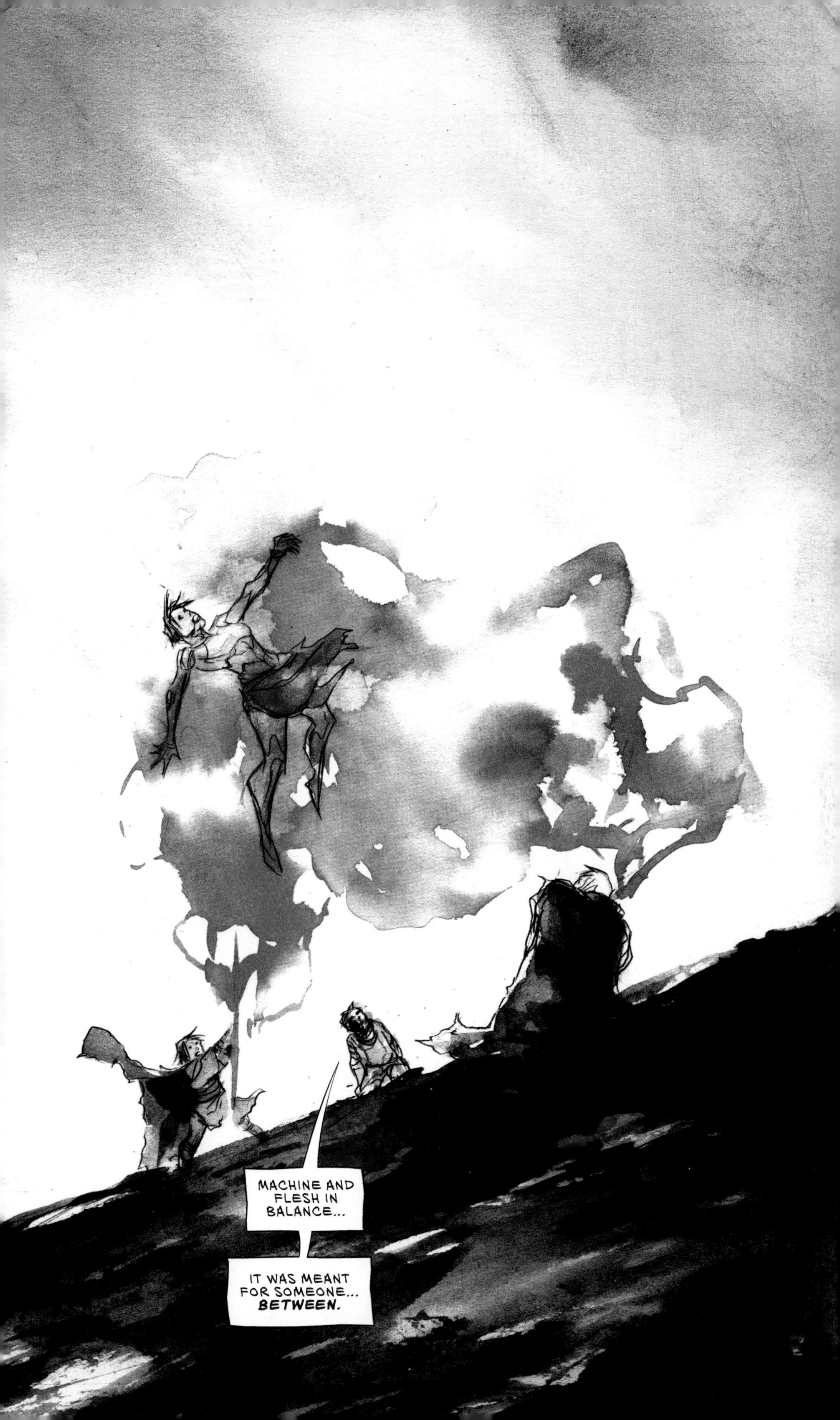
MACHINE AND FLESH IN BALANCE...
IT WAS MEANT FOR SOMEONE... **BETWEEN.**

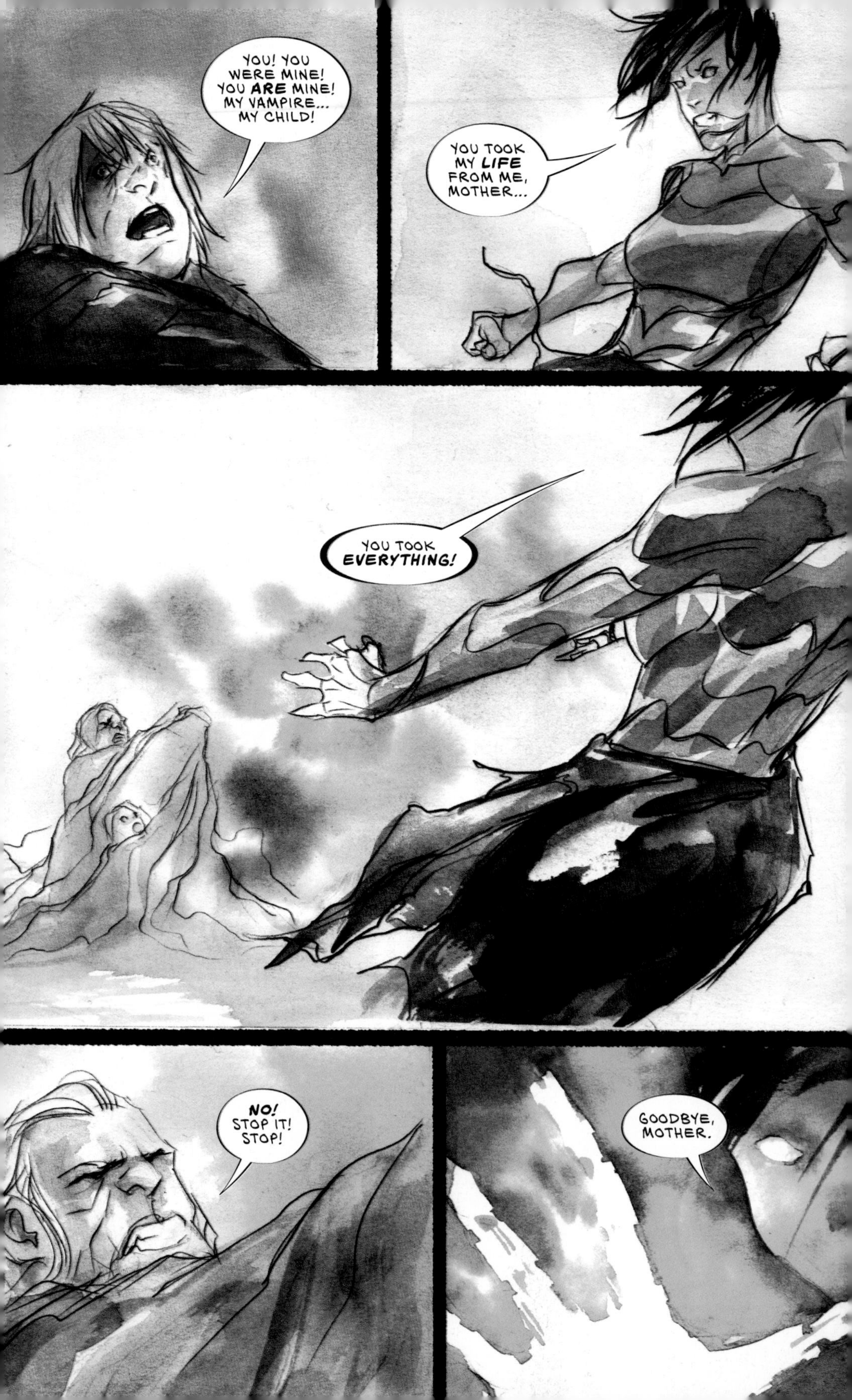
YOU! YOU WERE MINE! YOU ARE MINE! MY VAMPIRE... MY CHILD!
YOU TOOK MY LIFE FROM ME, MOTHER...
YOU TOOK EVERYTHING!
NO! STOP IT! STOP!
GOODBYE, MOTHER.

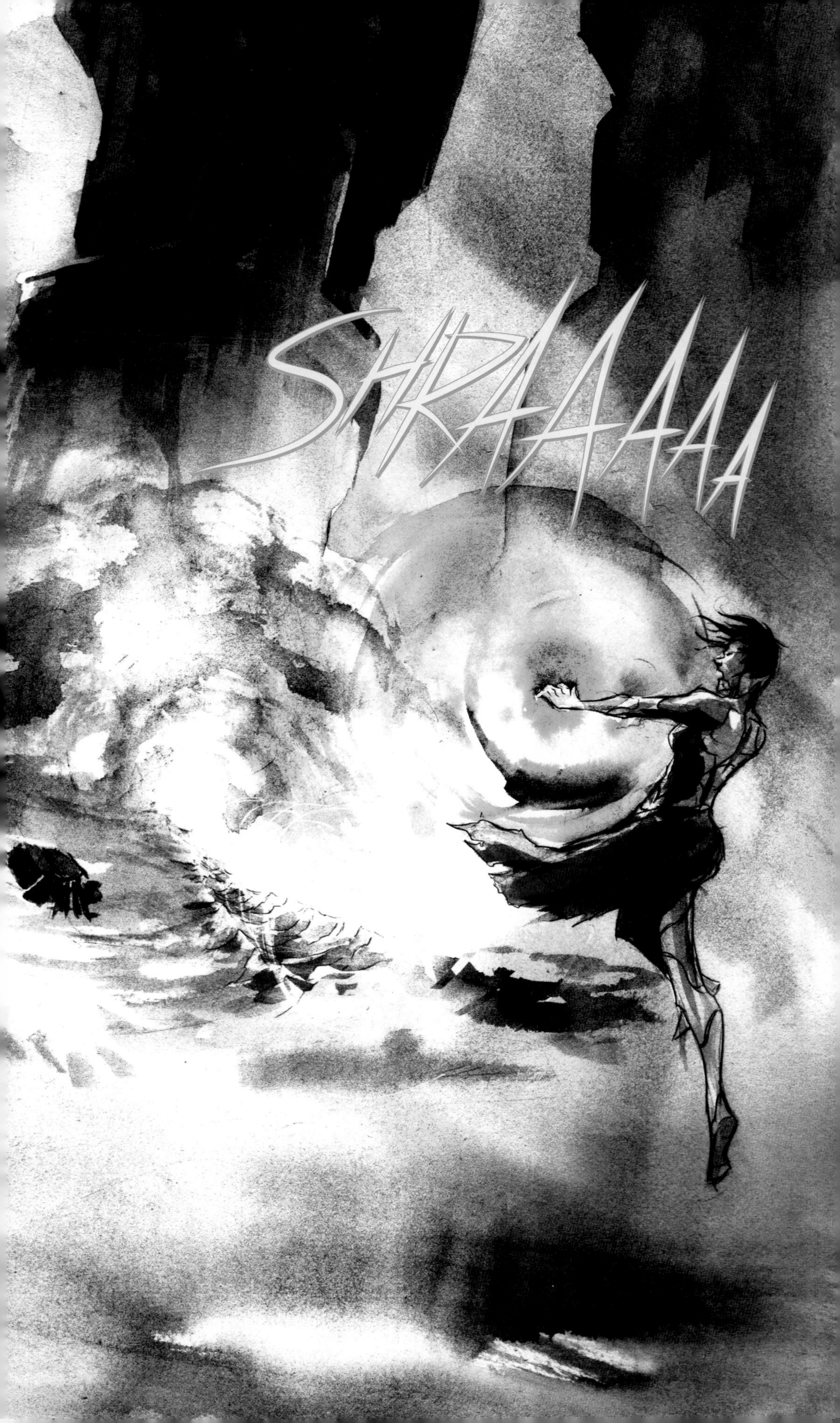
SHRAAAAAA

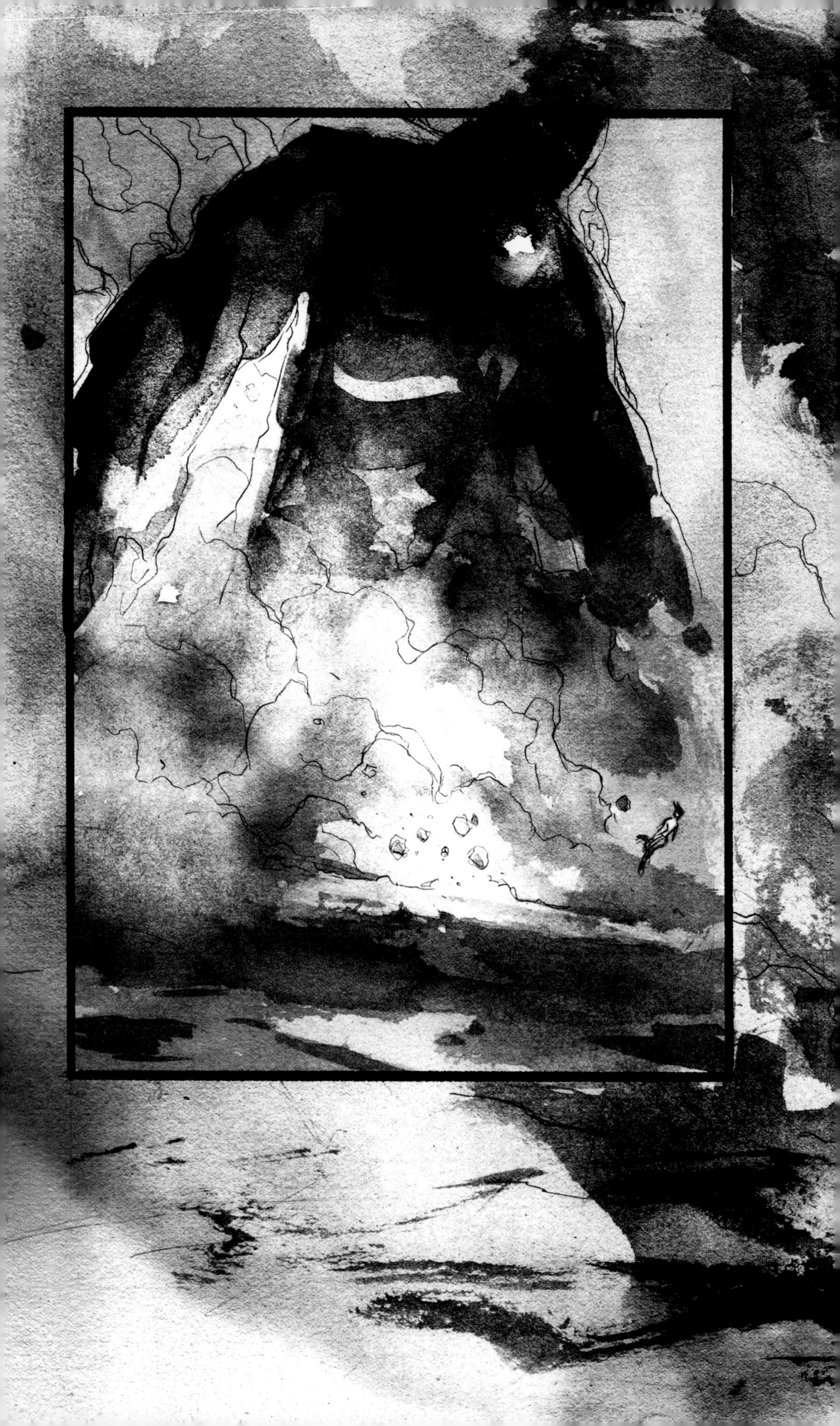

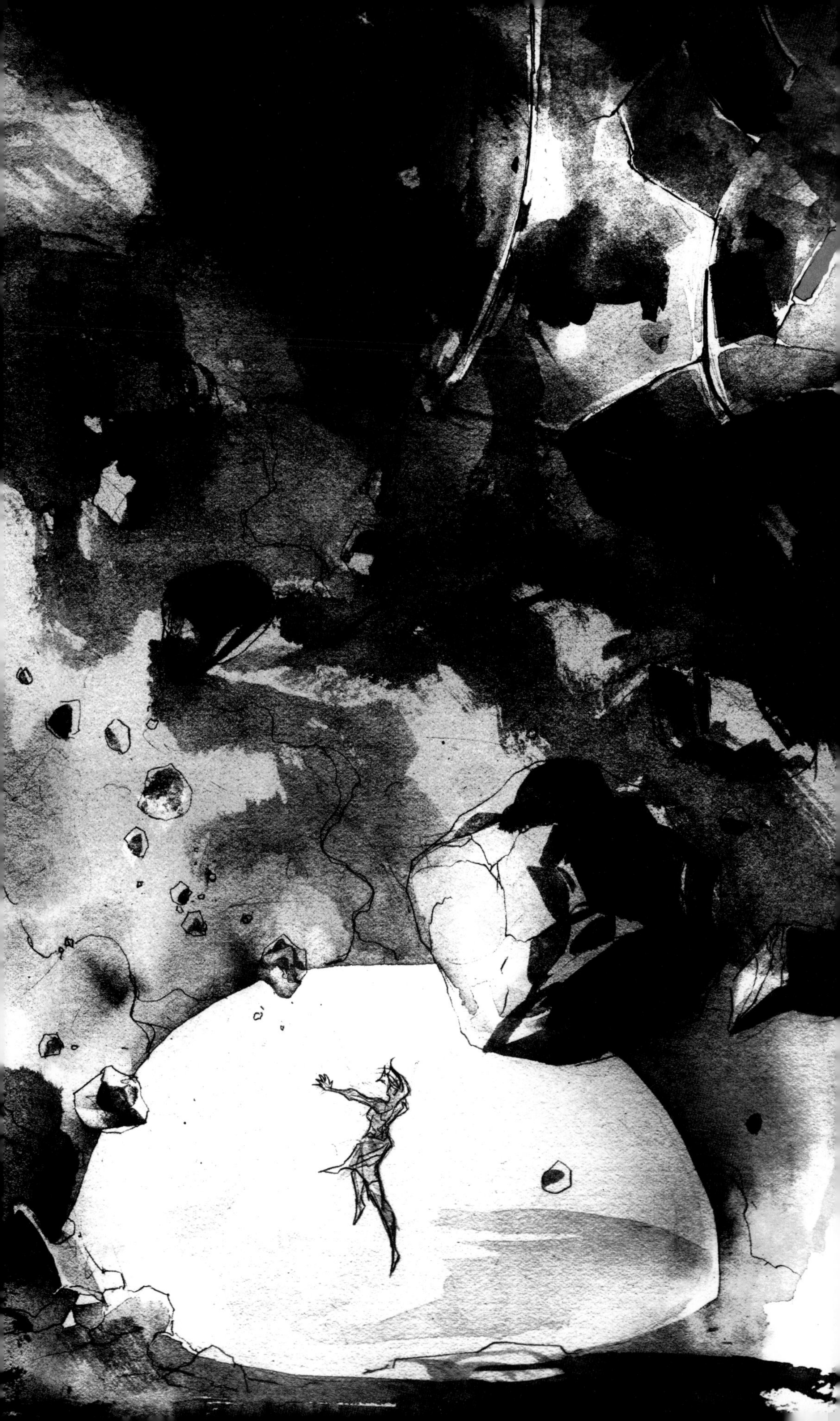

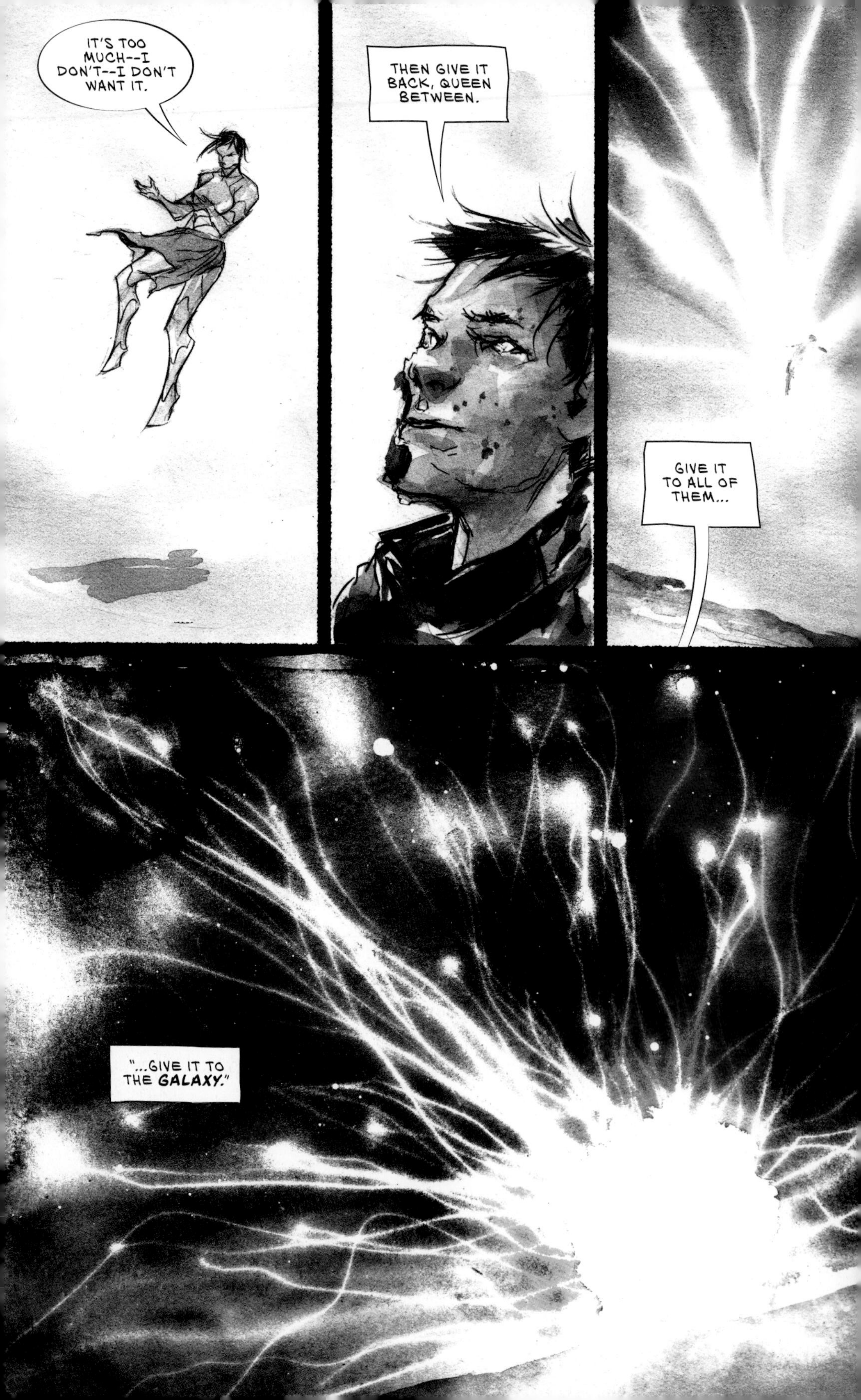
IT'S TOO MUCH--I DON'T--I DON'T WANT IT.
THEN GIVE IT BACK, QUEEN BETWEEN.
GIVE IT TO ALL OF THEM...
"...GIVE IT TO THE GALAXY."

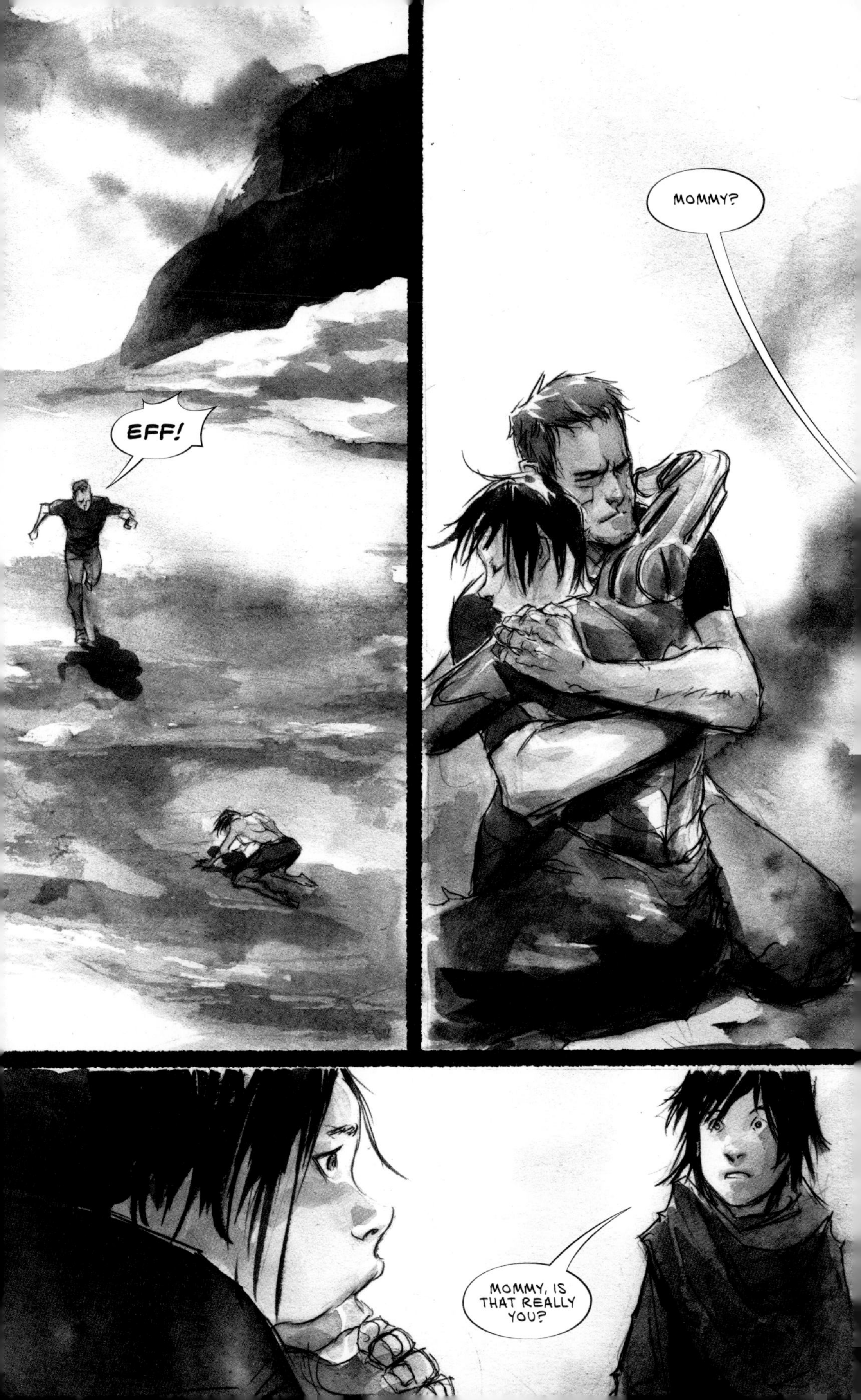
EFF!
MOMMY?
MOMMY, IS THAT REALLY YOU?

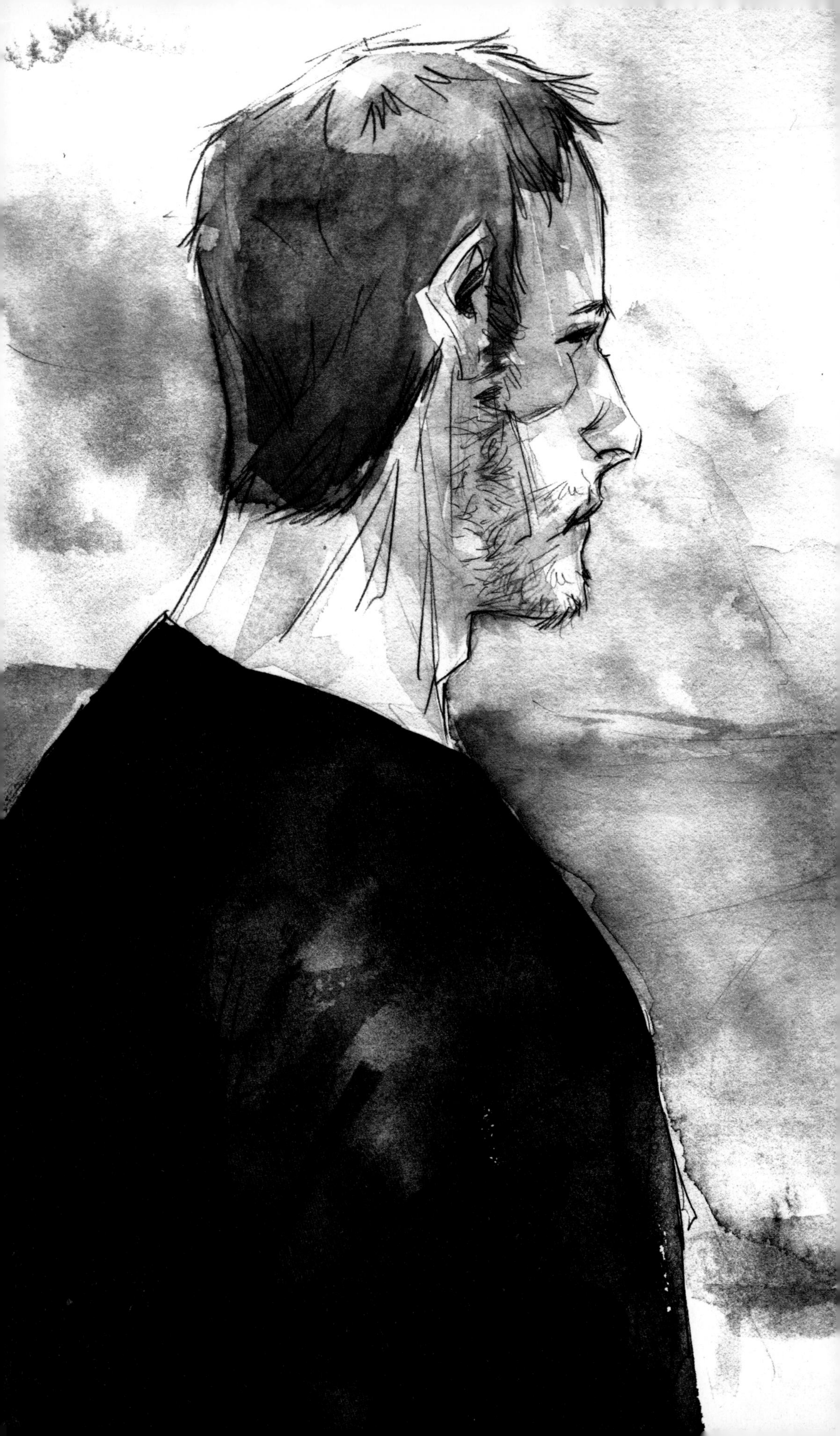

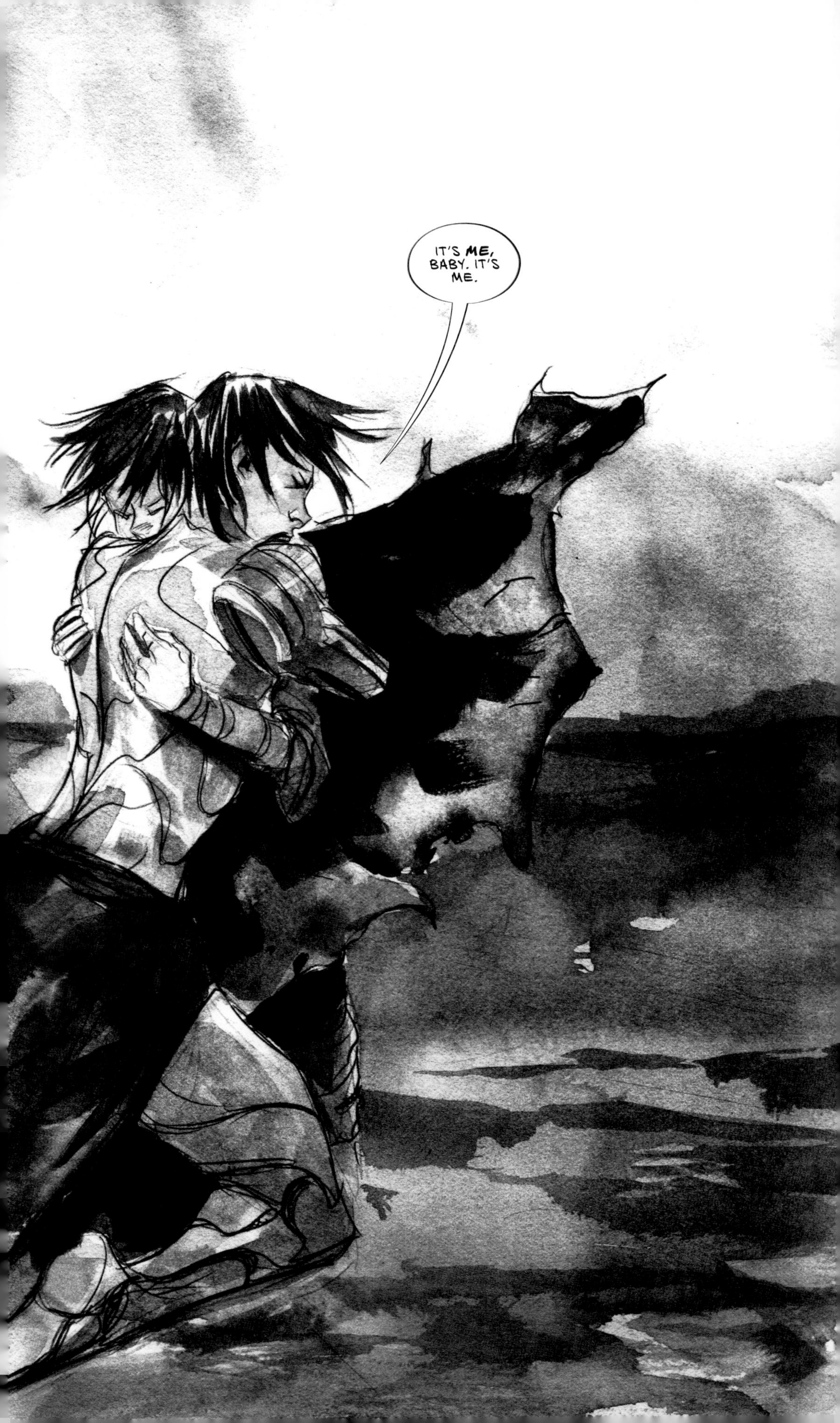
IT'S ME, BABY. IT'S ME.

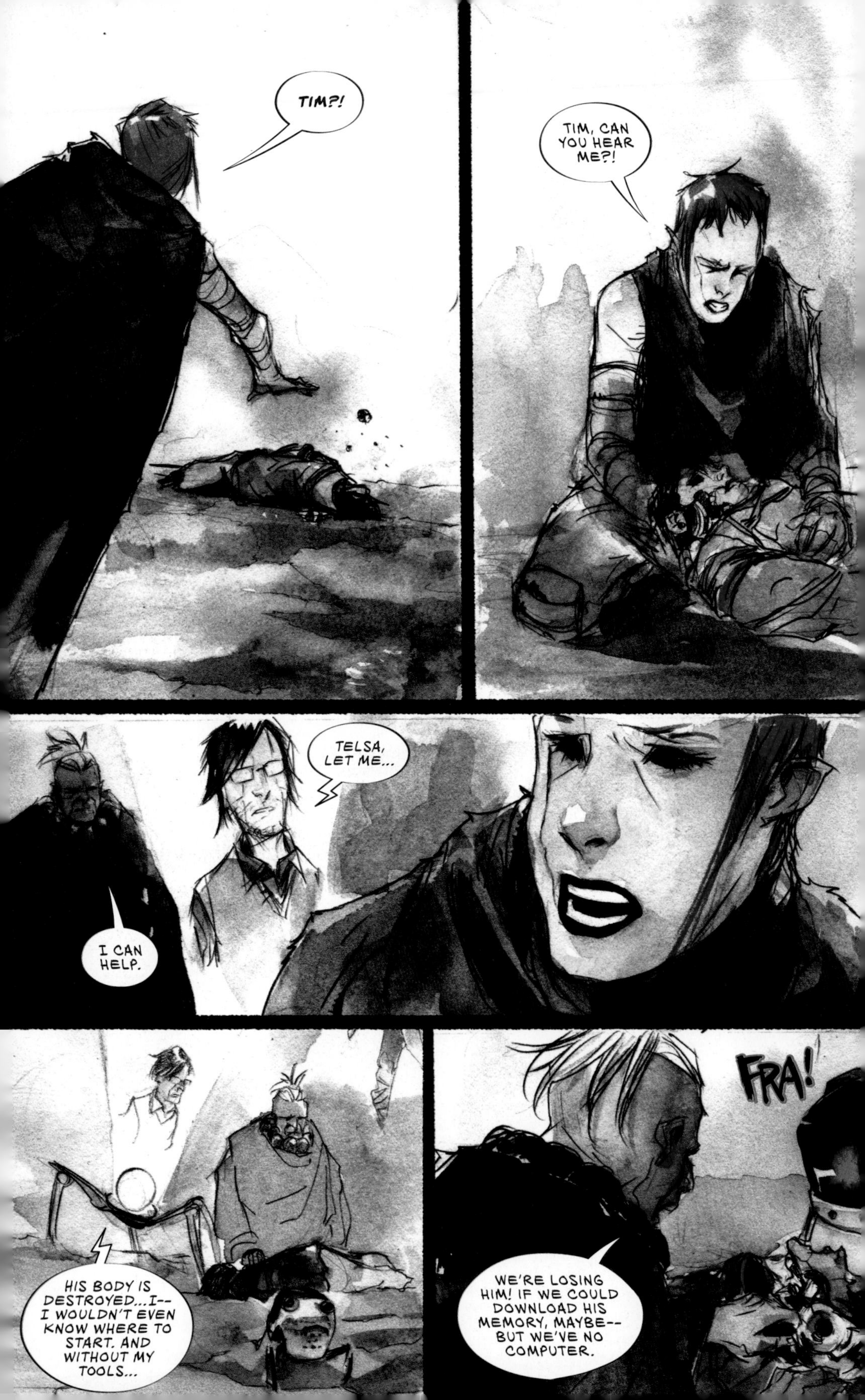
TIM?!
TIM, CAN YOU HEAR ME?!
TELSA, LET ME...
I CAN HELP.
HIS BODY IS DESTROYED... I-- I WOULDN'T EVEN KNOW WHERE TO START. AND WITHOUT MY TOOLS...
FRA!
WE'RE LOSING HIM! IF WE COULD DOWNLOAD HIS MEMORY, MAYBE-- BUT WE'VE NO COMPUTER.

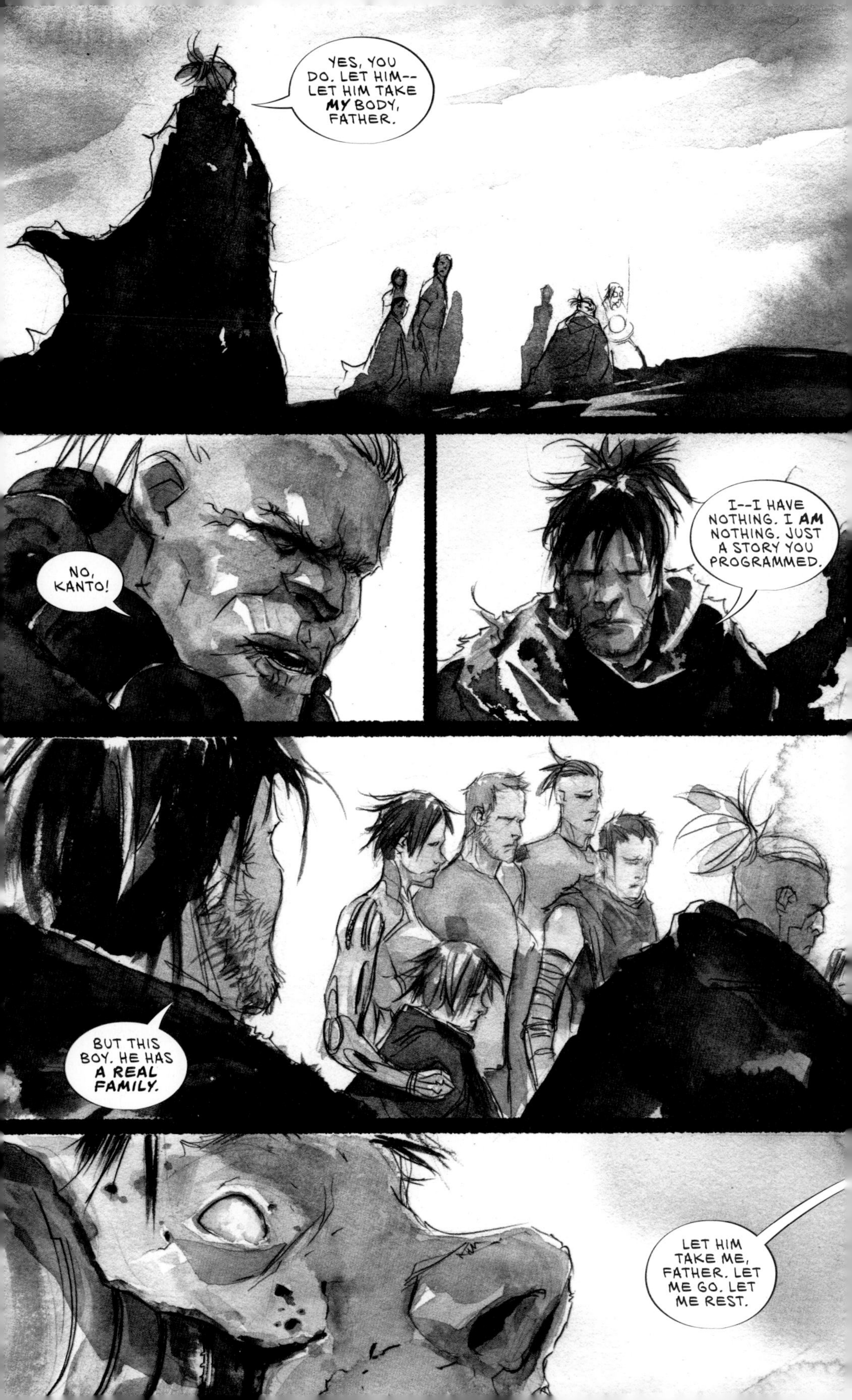
YES, YOU DO. LET HIM-- LET HIM TAKE **MY** BODY, FATHER.
NO, KANTO!
I--I HAVE NOTHING. I **AM** NOTHING. JUST A STORY YOU PROGRAMMED.
BUT THIS BOY. HE HAS **A REAL FAMILY.**
LET HIM TAKE ME, FATHER. LET ME GO. LET ME REST.

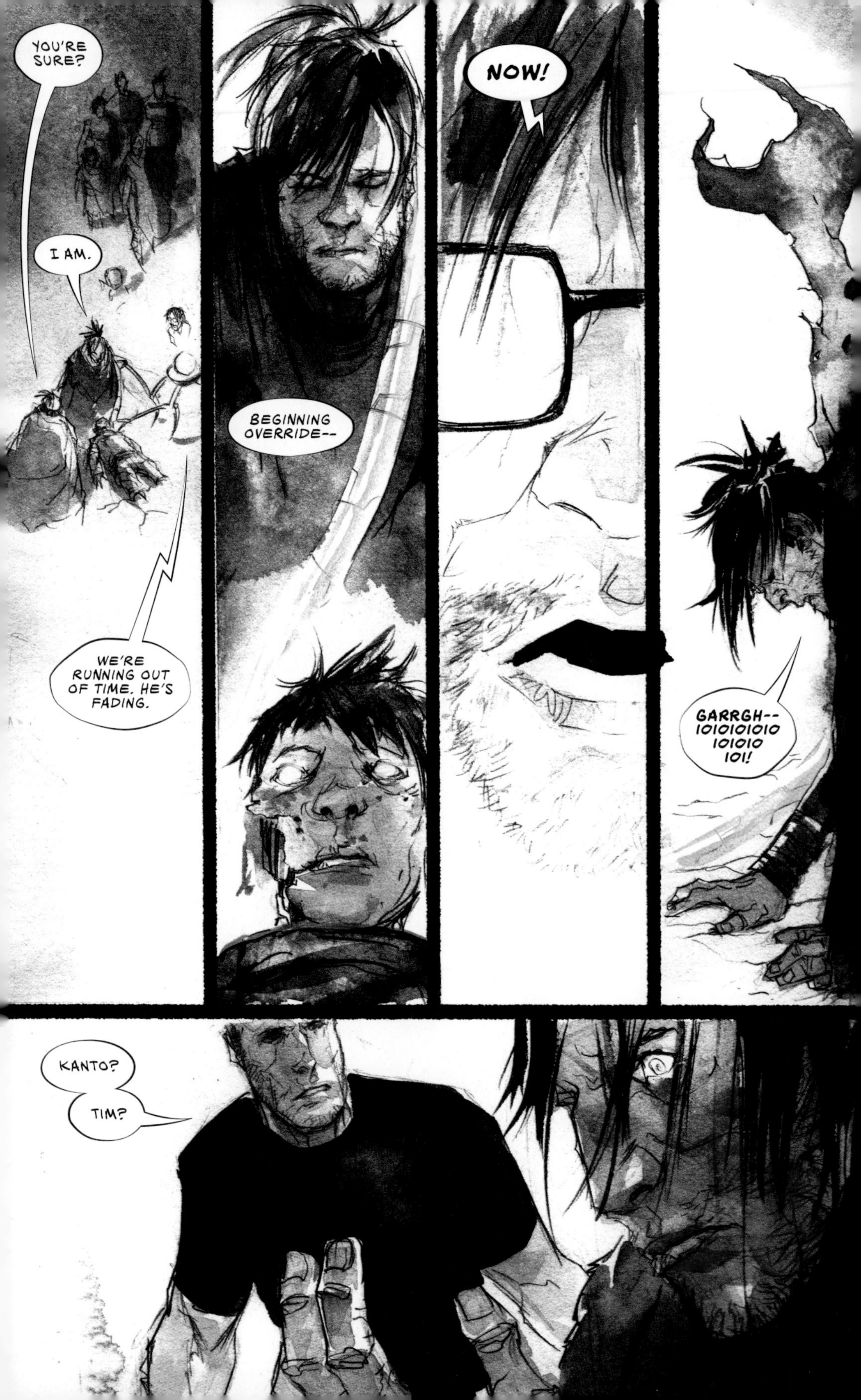
YOU'RE SURE?
I AM.
WE'RE RUNNING OUT OF TIME. HE'S FADING.
BEGINNING OVERRIDE--
NOW!
GARRGH--1010101010 101010 101!
KANTO?
TIM?

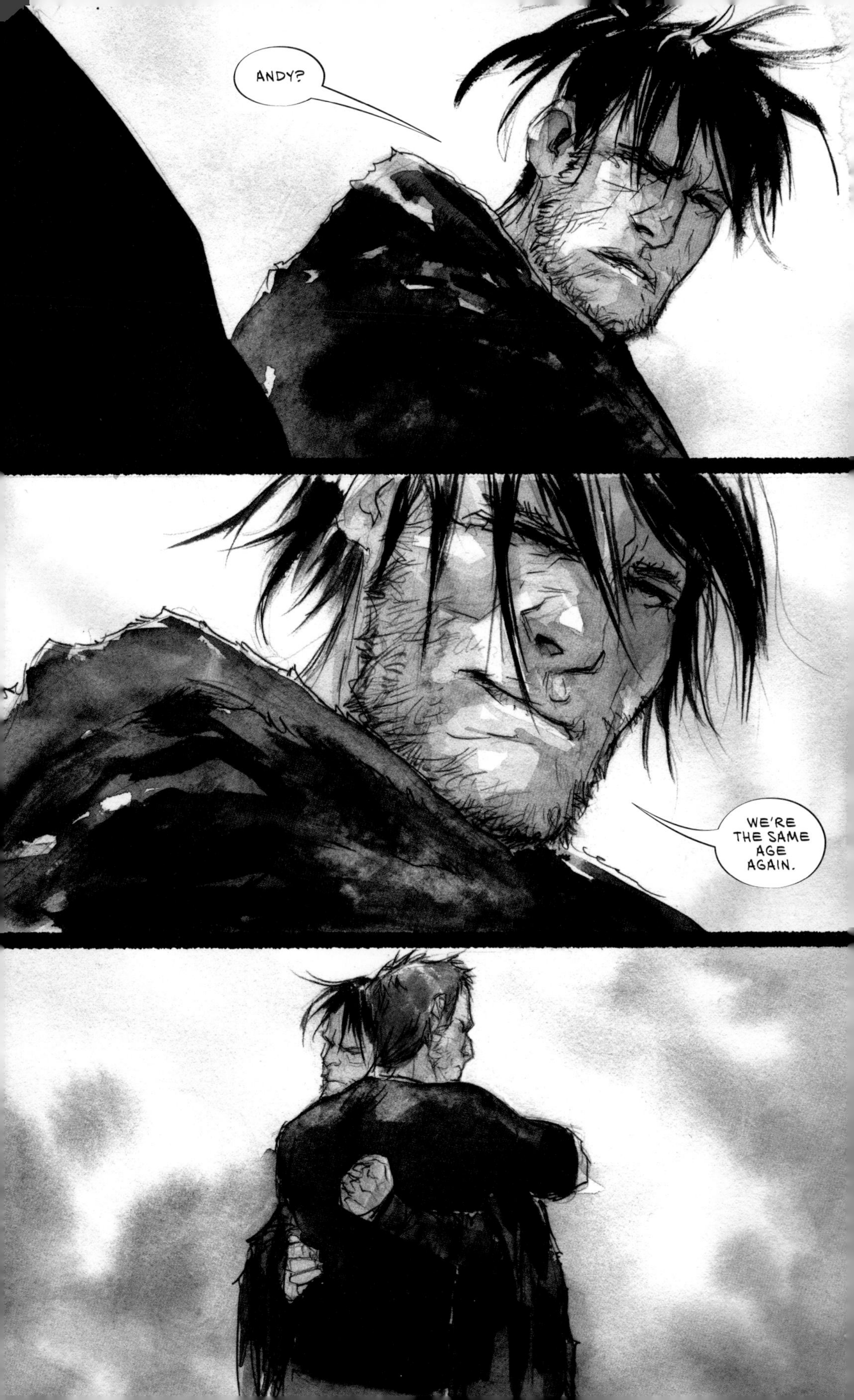
ANDY?
WE'RE THE SAME AGE AGAIN.

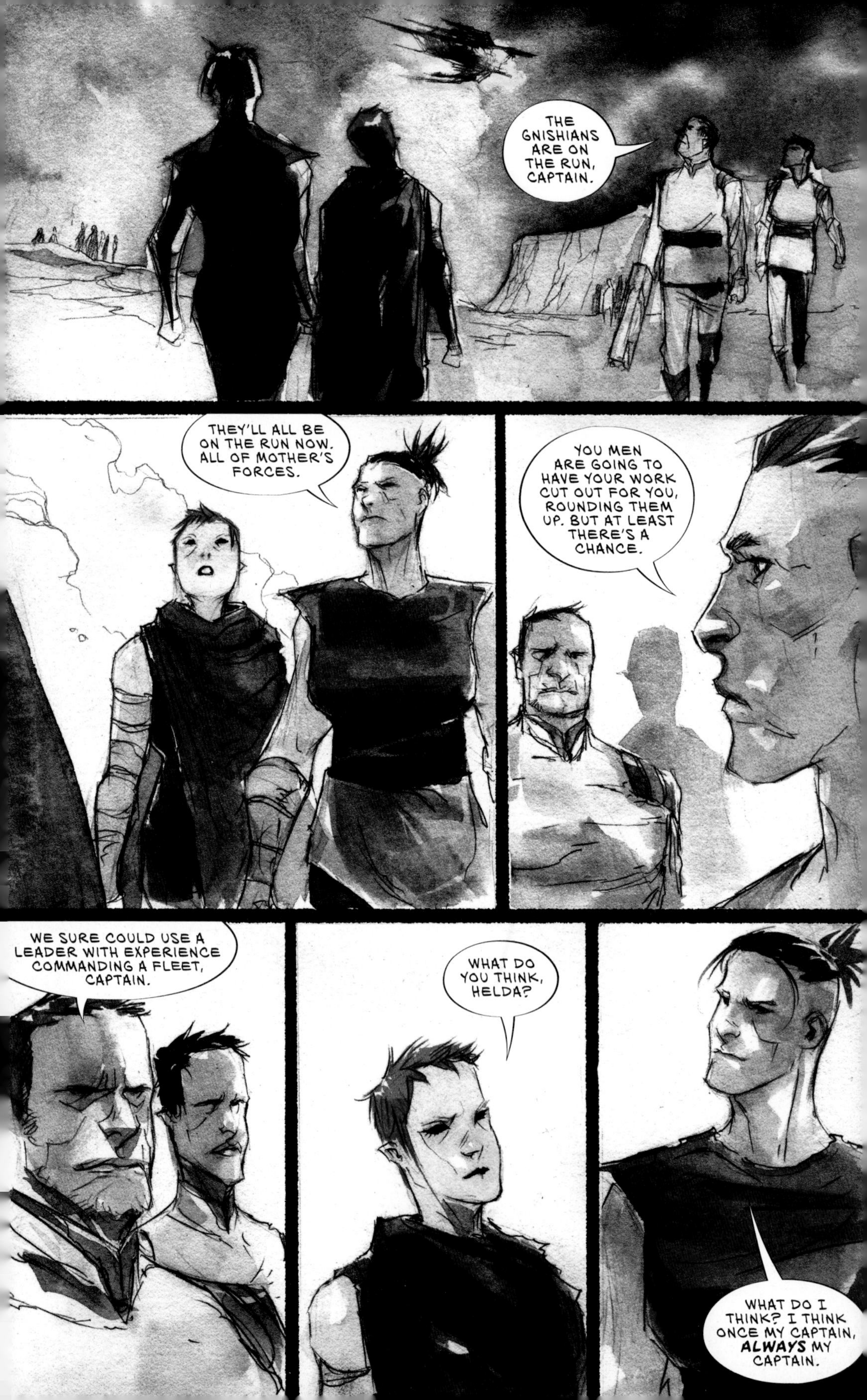
THE GNISHIANS ARE ON THE RUN, CAPTAIN.
THEY'LL ALL BE ON THE RUN NOW. ALL OF MOTHER'S FORCES.
YOU MEN ARE GOING TO HAVE YOUR WORK CUT OUT FOR YOU, ROUNDING THEM UP. BUT AT LEAST THERE'S A CHANCE.
WE SURE COULD USE A LEADER WITH EXPERIENCE COMMANDING A FLEET, CAPTAIN.
WHAT DO YOU THINK, HELDA?
WHAT DO I THINK? I THINK ONCE MY CAPTAIN, ALWAYS MY CAPTAIN.

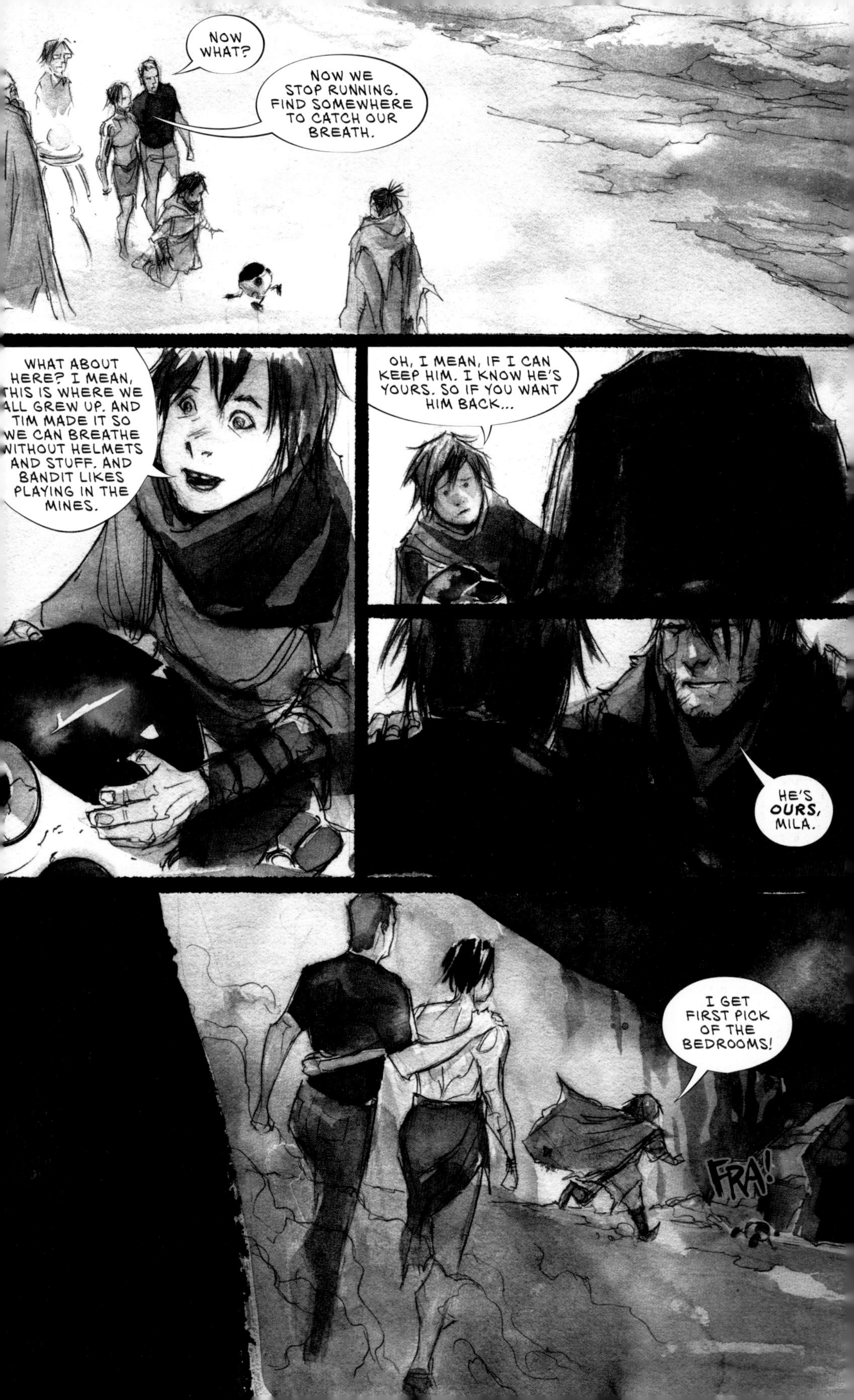
NOW WHAT?
NOW WE STOP RUNNING. FIND SOMEWHERE TO CATCH OUR BREATH.
WHAT ABOUT HERE? I MEAN, THIS IS WHERE WE ALL GREW UP. AND TIM MADE IT SO WE CAN BREATHE WITHOUT HELMETS AND STUFF. AND BANDIT LIKES PLAYING IN THE MINES.
OH, I MEAN, IF I CAN KEEP HIM. I KNOW HE'S YOURS. SO IF YOU WANT HIM BACK...
HE'S **OURS**, MILA.
I GET FIRST PICK OF THE BEDROOMS!
FRA!

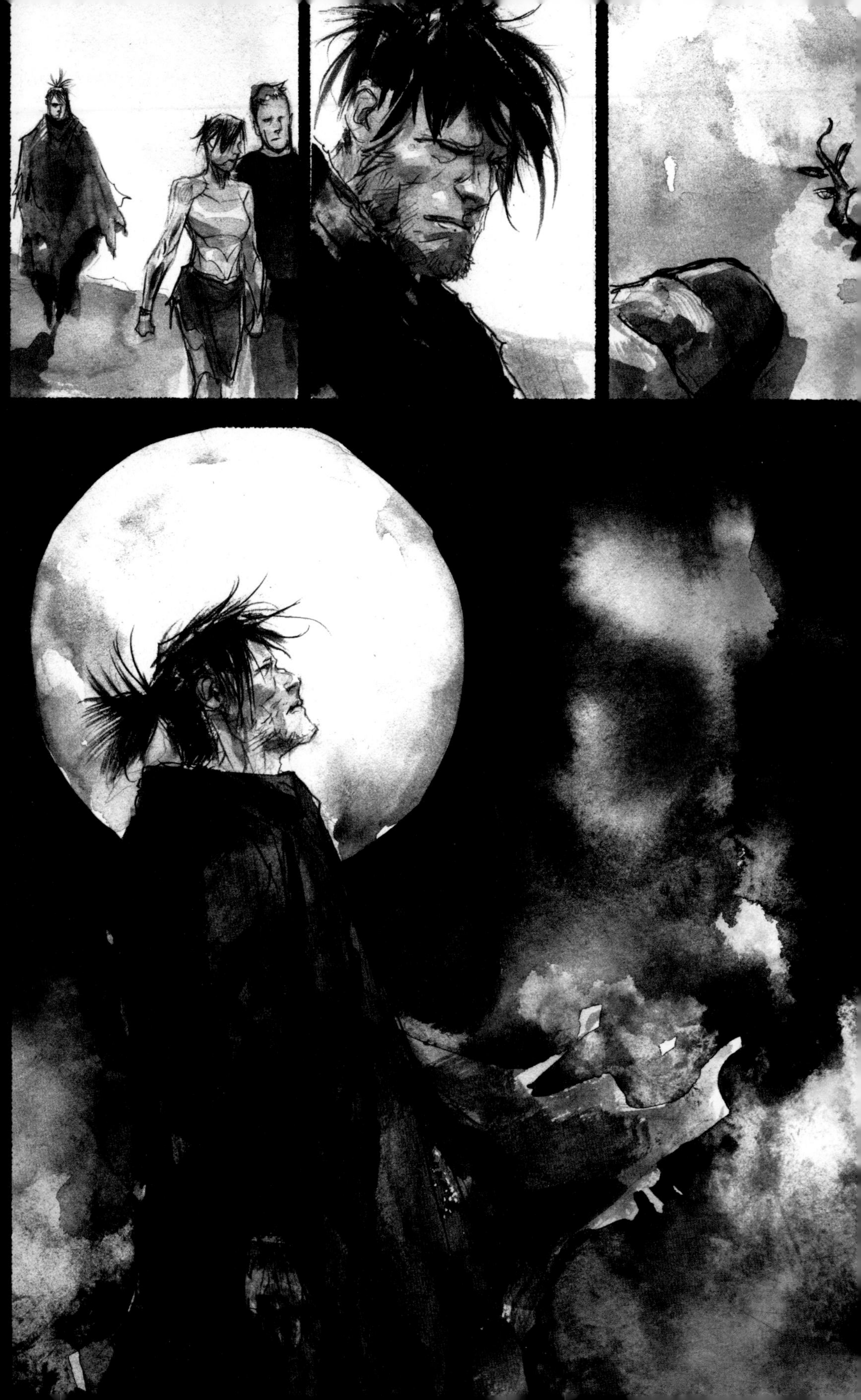

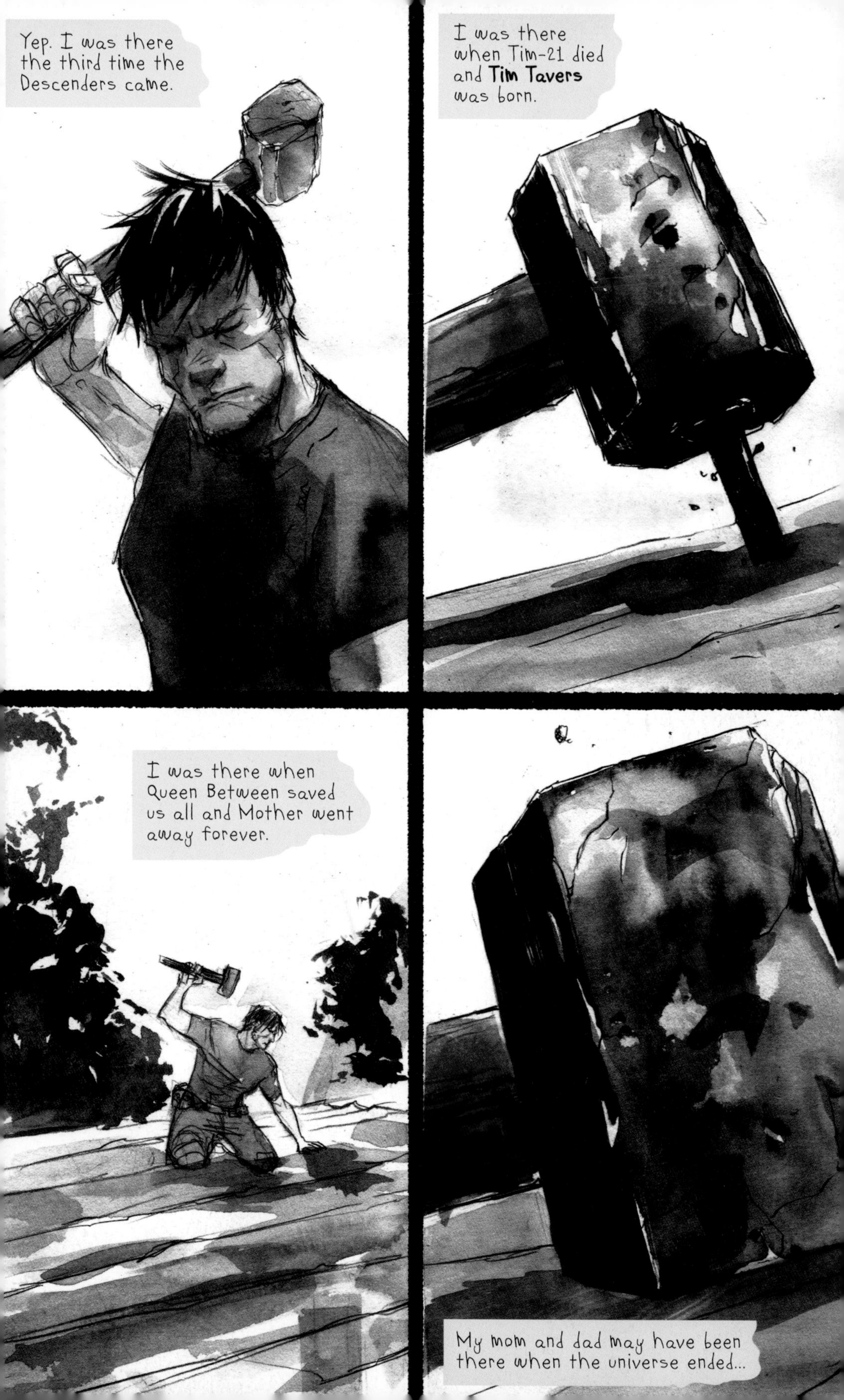
Yep. I was there the third time the Descenders came.
I was there when Tim-21 died and **Tim Tavers** was born.
I was there when Queen Between saved us all and Mother went away forever.
My mom and dad may have been there when the universe ended...

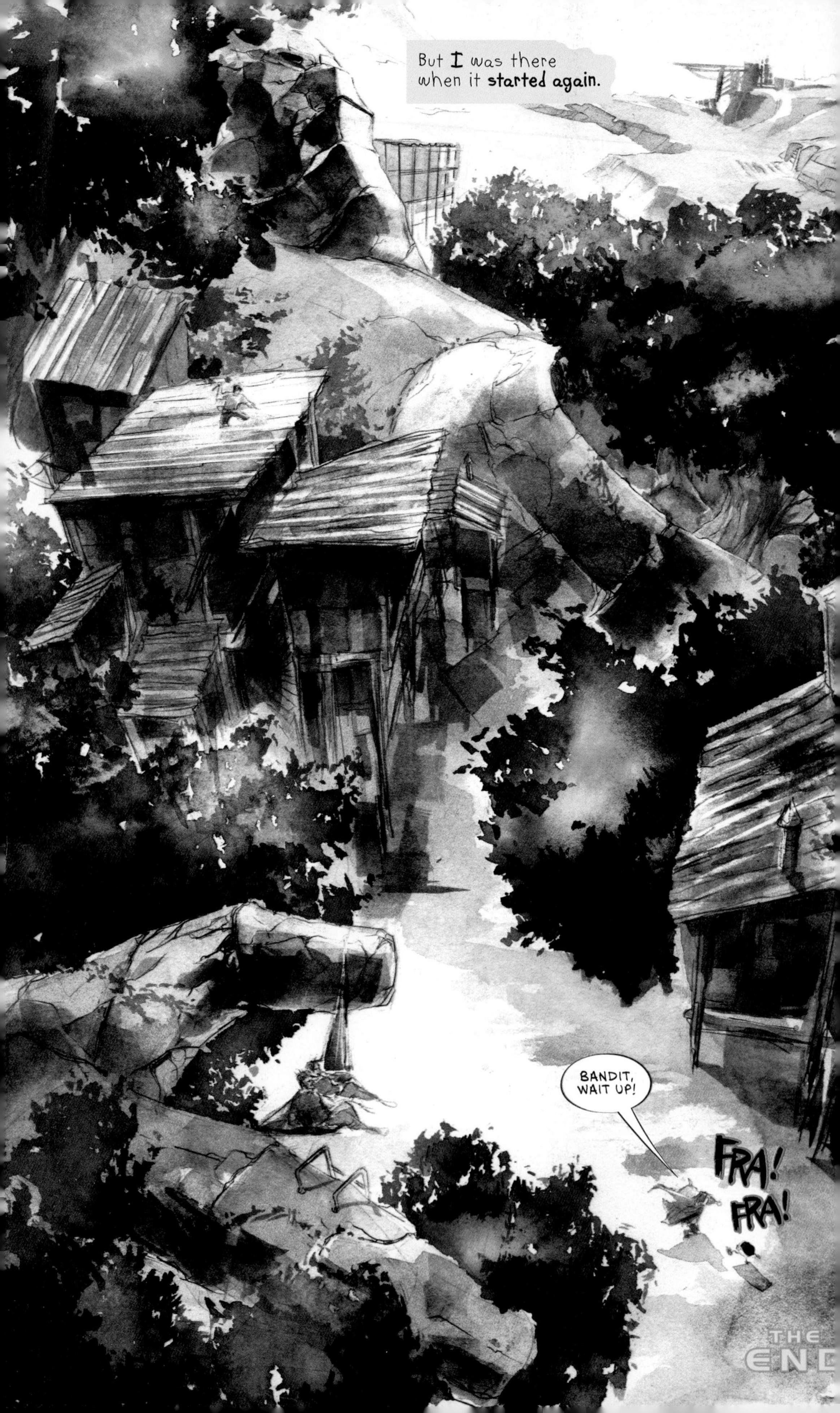

But I was there when it started again.
BANDIT, WAIT UP!
FRA! FRA!
THE END